"When we met this morning, I was very impolite." Mary twisted her fingers together.

"Forget it." Samuel cleared his throat.

"I let myself form an opinion of you without learning to know you first."

She smiled then and his heart wrenched at the soft curve of her lips.

"I wasn't very polite myself."

"You were fine. I mean, you didn't do anything—" Her face flushed a pretty pink. "I mean, you were friendly." Her face grew even redder. "Except for…when you winked… I mean, I'm sure you didn't mean to be forward." She bit her lip and turned away.

Samuel resisted the urge to step close to her, to cover her embarrassment with a hand on her arm. "I think I know what you mean."

She tilted her head toward the house in a quick nod. "I think it is *wonderful-gut* that you want to help with that poor farmer's work."

He felt a flush rise in his cheeks at her words of praise. "Thank you." If he could earn Mary Hochstetter's respect, maybe he could change everyone else's opinion, too.

Jan Drexler enjoys living in the Black Hills of South Dakota with her husband of more than thirty years and their four adult children. Intrigued by history and stories from an early age, she loves delving into the world of "what if?" with her characters. If she isn't at her computer giving life to imaginary people, she's probably hiking in the Hills or the Badlands, enjoying the spectacular scenery.

JAN DREXLER

An Amish Courtship

HARLEQUIN LOVE INSPIRED® HISTORICAL

Recycling programs
for this product may
not exist in your area.

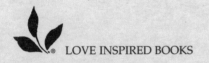

LOVE INSPIRED BOOKS

ISBN-13: 978-0-373-42536-5

An Amish Courtship

www.Harlequin.com

Printed in U.S.A.

Create in me a clean heart, O God, and renew
a right spirit within me. Cast me not away from
Thy presence; and take not Thy holy spirit from me.
Restore unto me the joy of Thy Salvation;
and uphold me with Thy free spirit.
—*Psalms* 51:10–12

To Mrs. Harrington,
the kind of teacher I would like to be someday.

Soli Deo Gloria

Chapter One

Shipshewana, Indiana
April 1937

"I'm so glad we aren't late," Aunt Sadie said as Mary turned the buggy into the farm lane.

Mary Hochstetter looked ahead, clutching the reins with damp hands. At least twenty buggies lined up along the barn like a flock of blackbirds on a telegraph wire and the lines of people moving toward the house were long.

So many strangers! But she must face them for Ida Mae's sake. She straightened her shoulders and glanced into the back seat to give her sister a reassuring smile. There was nothing frightening about attending the Sabbath meeting.

Ida Mae gave her a weak smile in return. "I'll be all right. After all, we already know the ladies we met at the quilting last week. The rest will soon become friends, too."

A boy stepped forward and grasped the horse's bridle. "I'll take care of Chester for you, Aunt Sadie."

"*Denki*, Stephen." Sadie climbed out of the buggy. Mary joined her, with Ida Mae right behind. "You're growing up so fast. I remember when your mother had to pull you out of mud puddles at Sunday meeting."

Stephen laughed, his voice slipping down to a deep bass and back up again. "That was a long time ago."

"Not to me, young man. The older I get, the faster time flies. You're a fine man, just like your father."

Sadie grasped Mary's arm to make sure she had her attention. "Here come the Lapp sisters, Judith and Esther, who you met at the quilting last week," she said. "That's their brother, Samuel, driving. They're our next-door neighbors." She leaned closer, dropping her voice. "And Mary, Samuel is a bachelor."

Mary shook her head. "I'm not looking for a husband."

"You never know what the Good Lord has planned."

Mary knew what the Good Lord had planned, and it was clear to her that marriage had no part of whatever He had in mind.

The Lapps' dusty buggy pulled up next to theirs and two young women jumped out. The man who was driving barely waited until they had stepped down before he started his horse forward to the buggy parking area. But just then Aunt Sadie's horse stepped sideways into his path.

Mutters and growls came from the buggy as it rocked under the weight of the man who jumped to the ground from the driver's seat, nearly landing on Sadie. He caught the older woman's arm to steady her.

"Sorry, Aunt Sadie." He waited until the older woman was stable again, then grasped his horse's bridle. "If someone hadn't left your buggy in the middle of the drive, I could have been out of the way by now."

"We just got here ourselves, Samuel," Aunt Sadie said. "There's no need to be in such a hurry." She turned to Mary with a satisfied smile. "I'm sure you and Mary will be able to straighten out the horses." She took Ida Mae's arm. "Let's go inside. I'll need your help."

Ida Mae gave Mary a helpless look.

"Go on in." Mary lifted her chin with confidence she didn't feel. "I'll be right there."

"It's going to take hours to get this mess straightened out." Samuel gestured toward the road where a buggy had just turned in, with another close behind it. "It's becoming a real log jam."

"Once I get Chester off to the side, things will clear up." Stephen took the horse's bridle and led him down the drive toward the barn, patting his brown neck.

As the buggy moved out of the way, Mary found herself face-to-face with Samuel Lapp. She felt her cheeks heat as he stared at her with dark blue eyes.

She leveled her gaze, focusing on the front of his coat. He was a solid wall in front of her, a man a couple years older than her own twenty-three years. His closeness sent her heart racing and she took a deep breath to steady her nerves. He wasn't Harvey Anderson. She bit her lip, forcing that thought out of her mind. Samuel was only an Amishman driving his sisters to Sunday meeting. There was nothing threatening about him.

Mary stepped to the side of the driveway so he could move past her.

"I think you can follow Stephen now."

He didn't budge.

"The way is clear."

Ignoring three more buggies that had driven into the barnyard, he still stared at her. Suddenly, his eyebrows shot up as if he had gotten a flash of insight. "You're that Mary Hochstetter that Sadie's been expecting."

"*Ja*, I am."

"From Ohio."

"*Ja.*"

He ran his hand down his short beard. "You're not what I imagined when Sadie said you were coming. I thought you'd be older, being her niece."

"Sadie is actually my mother's aunt." Mary glanced behind Samuel's buggy. Families walked toward the house, voices hushed as they separated into women's and men's lines. Stephen and two or three other boys had lined up the buggies in order and were unhitching the horses. The log jam had cleared.

She looked back at Samuel. "I should go in. Meeting is about to begin."

The corner of his mouth, visible above his short beard, quirked up.

"You're anxious to be rid of me?"

Now he was laughing at her, maybe even flirting with her. She drew herself up to her full height and looked him in the eyes, lowering her brow in the expression that always sent her younger brothers hurrying to do their chores.

He stepped forward to grasp his horse's bridle. "You're not only younger than I expected, but you're prettier, too."

Then he winked at her.

Mary stared at him, her fists clenched. What an infuriating man! Gruff and blustery until he found out who she was, as if any new woman he met would fall at his feet. As if she needed a man to run her life.

"Like I said, meeting is about to begin." She fought to keep her voice even.

"Go ahead," he said, gesturing toward the house. "I'll be in shortly."

But under her irritation, another feeling rose. That familiar twisting in her stomach that stole her breath. She swallowed, glancing around. The only other people in the barnyard were a few women on their way into the house. She would soon be alone in the yard with this man.

She shot another look in his direction, one that she reserved for her brothers' worst crimes, and hurried into the house.

She found a place on a bench next to Aunt Sadie and Ida Mae and took a deep breath, trying to forget that wink. No wonder he wasn't married. His beard only confirmed that he had given up looking for a wife. Only married men and old bachelors wore beards.

The worship began with a low, soft note sung by a man sitting on the front row. As the tune continued, she recognized the hymn from the *Ausbund* and joined in the singing with the rest of the community, settling into the familiar worship.

After the service ended, Mary followed Judith and Esther Lapp to the kitchen to help serve the meal.

"I can introduce you to the others," Esther said as she led the way through the lines of benches that the young men were already converting to tables for dinner.

"I'll never remember everyone's names."

Esther took her arm. "Don't worry. They don't expect you to. You'll learn them all eventually."

Mary joined in the work easily enough. The meal of

sandwiches, pickles and applesauce was similar to what the folks would be having in her home church in Holmes County. Mary opened jars and poured applesauce into serving dishes while the other young women whirled around her, taking the food to the tables as the young men set them up.

"Hello," said a girl as she took one of the dishes Mary had prepared. "You're one of Sadie's nieces, aren't you? I wish I could have gone to the quilting on Wednesday. I've been wanting to meet you ever since I heard you were coming."

Mary shook the jar she was holding to urge the last of the applesauce from the bottom. "I'm Mary. My sister is Ida Mae, over there helping with the rolls." She tilted her head toward the counter at the far end of the kitchen.

"I'm Sarah Hopplestadt. My mother said she met you at the quilting."

Hopplestadt? Mary sorted through the faces in her mind. "*Ja*, for sure. Isn't her name Effie?"

Sarah's face beamed. "It is!" She grabbed the filled serving dish and whirled away. "I'll be back with some empty dishes for you soon."

Mary watched her go as she reached for another jar. Sarah placed the applesauce on the table closest to the kitchen, in front of an older man. Across from him sat Samuel, red-faced with the tight collar fastened at his throat. He looked as uncomfortable as a cat in a room full of rocking chairs.

She shook her head at her own thoughts and glanced at him again. His brow was lowered and he kept his eyes on his plate, ignoring the other men around him. The confident man who had given her that exasperating wink was gone. He looked as out of place as she felt. She caught her lower lip between her teeth as she remembered how rude she had been before church. He might be a man, but he was also Aunt Sadie's neighbor. She quelled her shaking stomach. As much as she hated the thought of initiating a conversation with him, she needed to apologize.

As the men talked, their voices carried into the kitchen.

"Vernon Hershberger needs help with his plowing, I hear." The man sitting next to Samuel spoke, stopping the other conversations.

The man at the end of the table stroked his beard. "*Ja*, for sure. His leg is healing after his fall last month, but he still isn't able to get around very well."

A man on the other side of Samuel, one of the ministers who had preached that morning, gestured with his fork. "We can all help him get his fields plowed and planted. Is Saturday a good day for everyone?"

Beards waggled as the men around the table nodded, but Samuel still looked at his plate.

"What about you, Samuel?" the minister asked.

The man sitting at the end of the table shook his head. "He's a Lapp. He won't help."

Samuel's face grew even redder. He leaned on his elbows, his hands clenched together, not looking at the men around him.

"I'll help." His voice was as low as a growl.

One of the men laughed. "Just like his *daed*. Today he'll help, but we won't see him come Saturday."

Laughter rippled around the table, and Samuel stood, backing away from the bench. He glared at the laughing faces, then turned to the minister. "I said I'd be there, and I will."

The minister held his gaze for a long minute as the laughter died away. "I believe you. We'll look forward to it."

Samuel nodded, swept his glance around the table again and then went out of the house.

Mary startled as Sarah appeared at her elbow again.

"That Samuel Lapp. I don't see why the men even invite him to help with the work."

"Why not?"

Sarah shrugged. "He rarely shows up, and then when he does, he doesn't do anything but stand around. His father was the same way."

"Perhaps he has changed. He seemed sincere to me."

"Maybe." Sarah picked up two more dishes of applesauce. "But this is a Lapp we're talking about. Some people never change."

As the girl walked away, Mary looked up to see Esther watching her. Samuel's sister had heard every word of their conversation.

"Esther…" Mary stepped across the kitchen and took her arm. "I hope you weren't offended by what Sarah said."

Esther plucked at her apron. "*Ne.* It's true." She looked at Mary, her narrow chin set firm. "But what you said is true, too. Samuel isn't *Daed*, and he can change." She glanced at the kitchen door, where Samuel had disappeared. "I just hope more folks come to see that."

Samuel Lapp charged out of the Stutzmans' house, ignoring everyone he passed. He'd hitch up the mare, find his sisters and head for home. He was a fool to think this morning would be different than any other Sabbath morning that he had attended the meeting.

His steps slowed. When was the last time he had come to the Sabbath meeting? A month ago? Two months? When he reached the pasture gate, he leaned on the post. Several of the horses started walking toward him, but his mare stood next to the water trough, ignoring him and the other horses.

A bay gelding stopped a pace away from him and extended his nose slightly.

"I have no carrots for you." Samuel spoke softly. Whose horse was this one? He eyed the sleek neck and the muscled haunches. Someone who knew horses and took good care of them.

The words of the men around the dinner table washed over him again. Even two years after his father's death, the Lapp legacy followed him no matter what he did. No matter how much he wanted to change.

He bent his head down to meet his fist, quelling the sick feeling in his stomach. Why should he even try? Men like Martin Troyer would never let him forget whose son he was. Samuel squeezed his eyes closed, seeing Martin's pompous figure at the end of the table once more.

Then the minister's words echoed over Martin's mocking tone. Jonas Weaver had said he believed him. He expected him to show up to help with Vernon Hershberger's farm work. The minister's confidence made Samuel want to follow through with his promise.

But *Daed* had burned too many bridges with his habit of promising help that he never delivered, and he was guilty of the same thing.

His father had lived on the edge of being shunned and put under the *bann*. How many times had the deacons stopped by the farm to talk to *Daed*? To reprimand him?

And then he would promise to do better. He'd take the family to meeting for a month, maybe two. He'd promise to join in the community activities. He'd promise to stop the drinking...but then forget his promises.

Samuel rubbed his hands over his face. Could he face Martin again? Not when this slow burn continued in his stomach. The world was full of Martin Troyers who would never let him come out from under *Daed*'s shadow.

He leaned on the fence, watching the horses. They had lost interest in him and had gone back to cropping the grass.

When Bram had returned home after living in Chicago for twelve years, he had been able to avoid *Daed*'s legacy. His older brother had escaped the shame of the remarks and pitying looks and Samuel envied him.

The envy was worse than the shame.

When people spoke of Bram, respect echoed in their words. Respect Samuel had never heard when people spoke of their *daed*...or him.

As much as Samuel wanted to prove to the community that he wasn't the same man as his father, he had fallen short. Nothing he said made any difference. They treated him the same way they always had, as if a man could never change.

That girl with the brown eyes, Mary, was different, though. New in the community, she knew nothing about his past. Nothing to make her judge him. Perhaps if he could do something to earn her respect, the rest of the community would follow.

Samuel rubbed at his beard, remembering how Mary Hochstetter had stood up to him before church. If he could earn her respect, he wouldn't care about anyone else's opinion.

He picked at a loose sliver of wood on the fence post. It broke off and he stuck it in his mouth to use as a toothpick.

"Samuel?"

The woman's voice came from behind him. Unfamiliar. It wasn't Judith or Esther.

"Samuel Lapp? Is that you?"

He straightened and turned, facing this new challenge. But when he saw Mary Hochstetter standing next to the wheel of the last buggy in line, watching him, he felt his tense face relax into a smile.

"*Ja*, it's me."

She twisted her fingers together.

"When we met this morning, I was very impolite."

"Forget it." The words came out rough, and he cleared his throat.

She ran her hand along the wooden buggy wheel, brushing off a layer of dust. "I let myself form an opinion of you without learning to know you first. Sadie says I should be careful not to judge a book by its cover."

She smiled then, still watching the dust drift from the buggy wheel into the air. His heart wrenched at the soft curve of her lips.

"I wasn't very polite, myself."

"You were fine. I mean, you didn't do anything—" Her face flushed a pretty pink. "I mean, you were friendly." Her face grew even redder. "Except for…when you winked… I mean, I'm sure you didn't mean to be forward." She bit her lip and turned away.

Samuel resisted the urge to step close to her, to cover

her embarrassment with a hand on her arm. "I think I know what you mean."

"I heard what you said in there." She tilted her head toward the house in a quick nod. "I think it is *wonderful-gut* that you want to help with that poor farmer's work. In Ohio, the community always works together when one family is having trouble."

He felt a flush rise in his cheeks at her words of praise. "We do that here, too." He couldn't look at her face. If she had heard what he said, then she had also heard the derisive remarks from the other men.

"That's good."

Samuel dared to raise his eyes, but she was fingering the buggy wheel again. As another little cloud of dust drifted to the ground, she glanced at him and smiled. "I must go help wash the dishes."

Mary walked back toward the house, turning once when she reached the center of the yard to give him a final glance. Samuel raised his hand in answer and leaned against the fence post behind him. She opened the screen door and entered the covered porch, disappearing from his view.

Samuel scratched his beard, running his fingers through its short length. Sometime after Bram had come back last year he had stopped shaving. A clean chin had been a sign of his single status, but last fall he had stopped caring. Stopped thinking that what he looked like mattered to anyone.

But now, his insides warm from Mary's kind words, he suddenly cared what she thought about him and his farm. Maybe he could earn her respect. Maybe he could hope to move out from under *Daed*'s shadow and become a member of the community the way Bram was.

He tugged at his whiskers, watching the screen door that had given a slight bang as Mary had disappeared. He tugged at the whiskers again. Maybe he would shave in the morning.

"Who would think that two nice girls like Judith and Esther would have a brother like that?"

Ida Mae leaned her arms on the back of the front buggy seat and tilted her head forward between Mary and Aunt Sadie.

All three of them were tired after the long Sunday afternoon at the Stutzmans', but they had enjoyed a good time of fellowship. All of Mary's fears had been for nothing. This new community had welcomed them with open arms.

"Samuel has a burden, for sure." Aunt Sadie turned to Ida Mae. "Don't be too quick to dismiss him, though. There's more to him than he shows us."

"Judith and Esther are nice girls, didn't you think so, Mary? Judith is going to bring a knitting pattern over this evening. She is so friendly."

"*Ja*, they both are. Is it only the three of them in their family, Aunt Sadie?"

"Their parents have passed on." The older woman's expression softened as she looked back over the years. "There were six children. A nice family, it seemed, until…" She glanced at Mary and Ida Mae. "I don't want to gossip. They were a nice family. Bram is the oldest. He left the community during his *rumspringa*, but his mother never gave up hope. Even on her deathbed she had faith that Bram would come back home."

"Did he?" Ida Mae watched their aunt's face, interested in the story.

"*Ja*, he did. Not until after she had passed on, but he did come back. He married a widow from Eden Township and lives down there with their children. A good Amishman, even after all his troubles."

Ida Mae leaned closer. "What about the rest of the family?"

"Samuel inherited the farm when their father died a couple years ago. The oldest girl...her name...I can't remember it. Maybe Katie? Anyway, she married a man from Berlin, Ohio. We haven't seen her since then. The next girl is Annie. She married a Beachey from Eden Township, the oldest son of their deacon. I go to quilting with her every other Thursday, and she has a sweet little boy."

Sadie's voice trailed off, smiling as she watched the roadside pass by.

"And the rest?"

"You've met them. Esther and Judith. They keep house for Samuel and have since Annie got married." She brushed at some dust on her apron. "I've tried to help those girls once they were on their own after their older sisters left home. I don't know how much they remember about their mother, but they were quite young when she died."

"What kind of help?" Ida Mae asked.

"We made soap together last winter, but I've also been longing to help them with their sewing. You've seen how worn their clothes are. They haven't made new ones for a couple years, and I don't think Katie or Annie taught them to sew. If we had fabric, we could have a sewing frolic, just the five of us."

Mary glanced at the smile on Sadie's face. "I think

you would have a thing or two to teach us, too. We should invite them over."

"If they have time. They keep themselves at home most days. Our Wednesday quiltings are about the only time they get to be social with the rest of the women of the district."

"Maybe if we tell Samuel that we'll make new shirts and trousers for him, he'll like the idea."

"*Ja*, for sure." Aunt Sadie's chin rose and fell. "I'll talk to Samuel when he comes over tomorrow and make sure he encourages them to come."

Mary's stomach gave a little flutter at the thought of seeing Samuel again so soon. That flutter was very different than the clenching feeling she got when she thought of men like Harvey Anderson. She pushed it down anyway and cleared her throat.

"Why is Samuel coming over tomorrow?"

"He does my heavy chores for me." Sadie turned to her. "Didn't I tell you? He comes by to clean the chicken coop and cut the grass, and whatever else might need doing. He comes every Monday."

"Then Judith and Esther should come with him whenever he comes. We could have a sewing time every week," Ida Mae said. She was clearly excited about the idea.

They rode in silence for a while, and Mary watched the way ahead through Chester's upright ears. Now that she and Ida Mae were here, Samuel wouldn't need to bother doing Sadie's chores for her. She and her sister were more than capable of taking care of things without a man around.

As they passed the lane to the Lapps' farm, Mary

glanced toward the house and barn. The odor of a pigsty drifted through the air.

Aunt Sadie had spoken of the Lapps as if they were a normal Amish family, but Samuel wasn't a normal Amishman. He had been pleasant enough at church, but some of the folks had spoken of him as if there was something very wrong.

"Why don't some of the men like Samuel? The women seemed to like Judith and Esther."

"Sometimes Samuel is too much like his father." Sadie's voice was so soft that Mary barely caught her words. "He is a troubled man. He learned some bad habits from Ira, but there is hope for him."

Less than a half mile down the road from the Lapps' farm, Chester turned into the drive of Aunt Sadie's place without any signal from Mary. Mary pulled up at the narrow walk for Ida Mae and their aunt to go into the house, and then she drove the buggy the short distance to the small barn. As she unhitched the buggy and took care of Chester, her thoughts went back to the Lapp family.

It wasn't unusual for sisters to keep house for their brother after their mother passed on, but both Judith and Esther were pale and worn, like they worked too hard. Mary smiled to herself as she brushed Chester's coat. Here she was, judging people before she got to know them again. The sisters seemed like nice girls. And since they were Aunt Sadie's closest neighbors, they would be able to spend much time together.

Their brother, though…

Mary turned Chester out into his pasture and hung up the harness.

Samuel was a strange one. Mary had never met anyone quite like him. And what had Aunt Sadie meant when she said he was a troubled man?

Underneath the grouchy stares and gravelly voice, he was quite good-looking. And when she had apologized to him, he had been friendly. Even intriguing. And Aunt Sadie seemed to be very fond of him. He might be a puzzle worth figuring out.

Mary stopped her thoughts before they went any further. She wouldn't be the one to figure out the puzzle that was Samuel Lapp, so she should just forget about him. Forget about all men.

But she couldn't forget. It was too late. Her thoughts went on without her, down into that dark hole. Her skin crawled as if she could feel Harvey's sweaty palms through her dress, pressing close, and closer. She shuddered, willing the memory to disappear, but Harvey's hands groped and pulled. His breath smelled of stale tobacco and beer as he pushed his kisses on her.

Mary forced her eyes open, trembling all over. She concentrated her thoughts, trying to remember where she was—in Sadie's barn, hanging the buggy harness on its hooks.

Stroking the smooth leather of the harness, she focused on the buckle, the straps, the headpiece still damp from Chester's sweat. She kept her breathing even and controlled as she counted the tiny pinpoints of the stitching where the straps were fastened together until she reached one hundred.

Mary took a deep shaking breath. The memory had retreated to the back of her mind. She leaned her head against the warm wood of the barn wall. Someday those memories would stay buried. As long as she avoided men, she could forget the past.

But Samuel would be at the farm tomorrow, and she would see him again on other days. Mary pushed at the shadows that threatened at the edge of her mind. A brother. The shadow retreated. She would treat Samuel the same as she treated her brothers. He wasn't Harvey Anderson.

Chapter Two

Monday morning dawned with the promise of a hot, sticky day ahead. On the way back to the house with the basket of eggs, Mary stopped by the garden to look for some early peas to go with their noon dinner. Noticing some stray lettuce seedlings among the beans, she bent to pull them out, but then saw how many there were. It was as if Sadie had planted the beans and lettuce in the same row.

She left the lettuce where it was and picked a couple handfuls of peas from the vines in front of her for lunch. Continuing on to the house, she paused at the sink in the back porch to wash up. The others were in the kitchen fixing breakfast.

"I want to ask Judith about the knitting pattern she brought over yesterday evening if the girls come this week," Ida Mae was saying.

Mary set the peas on the counter. "What is the pattern?"

"It's for stockings that you knit from the toe up, rather than the top down. I've never seen one like it. I was trying to figure out how it works last night, but it's beyond me."

"Margaret used to make stockings like that," Aunt Sadie said. She sat at the table, paring potatoes. "Margaret Lapp, Judith and Esther's mother. I have a pair of stockings she made. I'll show them to you…" Her voice trailed off as she dropped her knife on the table and started to rise.

Mary put a hand on her shoulder. "You can show us after breakfast. There's no hurry."

Aunt Sadie sank back down into her chair. "*Ja.* No hurry." She sat with her hands in her lap, a frown creasing her brow.

"What's wrong?"

The older woman startled and looked at Mary. "What was I doing?"

"You were peeling potatoes."

Aunt Sadie looked at the paring knife and potatoes on the table, her face vague. Then her brow cleared. "*Ach, ja.* The potatoes."

Mary glanced at Ida Mae. This wasn't the first time they had needed to remind Aunt Sadie of what she had been doing. In the six days since they had arrived, small lapses in their aunt's memory had been frequent. Perhaps their older relative did need them to take care of her, even if she wasn't ready to admit it.

They finished fixing breakfast in silence, each of them caught up in their own thoughts. As Mary scrambled the eggs, Ida Mae fried the potatoes and onions, the aroma filling the little kitchen.

Mary hoped the move to Indiana would be the healing balm her sister needed. The death of Ida Mae's young, handsome beau in a farming accident six weeks ago had been a terrible thing, and even though Ida Mae had put on a brave face this morning, grief still shadowed her eyes.

At least Ida Mae's tragedy gave Mary an excuse whenever someone questioned her own pale face and shadowed eyes. No one needed to know the real reason for her own grief, even her closest sister.

Mary set the table, laying the spoons next to the plates, carefully lining them up next to the knives. One by one she set them down, her fingers lingering on the smooth handles. She missed, *ne*, she craved Ida Mae's cheerfulness. She relied on her sister to keep things going, to keep Mary's mind off the past.

Soon, though, Ida Mae would move on. She would meet a young man, get married, have a family of children and be happy again. The same dream that Mary had shared with her sister for so many years.

She blinked back tears as she straightened the fork she had just laid on the table. Ida Mae would see her hopes fulfilled, but not Mary. She laid another fork on the table. That dream belonged to an innocent girl with dreams of the future, and she had left that girl in Ohio.

The sun was already above the tops of the trees as Samuel walked to the barn. As he shoved the big sliding door open, he scanned the building's dusty interior, filled with equipment and clutter from days gone by. How would that Mary Hochstetter see *Daed*'s barn? Thinking about her coffee-brown eyes, so much like *Mamm*'s, pulled at something deep inside, something that reminded him of another time and another place.

A week, years ago, when he and his brother, Bram, had been sent to *Grossdawdi*'s farm in Eden Township.

He must have been four or five years old. *Grossmutti*'s kitchen had been a wonder of cinnamon and apples and as much food as he could eat. *Grossdawdi*'s brown eyes crinkled when he smiled, and he had smiled often. The barn had been a wonderful place to play, with hay piled in the lofty mow.

Samuel relaxed against the doorframe, remembering *Grossdawdi*'s patient hands teaching him how to rub oil into the gleaming leather harnesses. His hand cupping Samuel's head and pulling him close in the only hug he remembered.

He had never seen the old couple again, but he hadn't forgotten the peace that had reigned in their home. And one quiet glance of Mary's eyes had brought it all back.

Daed's barn had never been as orderly as *Grossdawdi*'s, even now when it was nearly empty. There hadn't been enough horses to fill the stalls since before *Daed* had passed on. Their driving mare spent her days in the meadow, too ornery for the girls to handle by themselves.

Samuel walked over to her stall and peered out the open side door to where the mare stood, one hip cocked and head down, drowsing in the afternoon sun as she swished flies with her tail.

Daed had left the barn a mess when he passed away two years ago. Broken harnesses still sat in a moldy pile in the corner and the unused stalls were knee deep in old straw. They had never been cleaned out when the work horses had been sold to pay off *Daed*'s debts. The cow was gone, too, and the bank barn's lower level was empty except for the mash cooker.

Every time he thought about trying to bring order to the chaos, Samuel felt like he was drowning in memories and past sins. Soon after *Daed*'s funeral, he had started clearing out the old, moldy harnesses and had found one of the bottles *Daed* kept stashed away. The smell brought back sickening scenes of *Daed* trying to hide the bottles from him with clumsy motions. When he found another stash among the straw in one of the empty box stalls, he had given up. Let the old barn keep its secrets.

Walking on to the horse's stall, he stopped at the stack of hay on the barn floor and pulled out a forkful. The mare poked her head into her stall, her feet planted firmly in the dried mud in the doorway between her pasture and the dim barn, watching Samuel. Her ears pricked forward as Samuel thumped the fork on the side of her manger to dump the hay off, but she didn't move. The horse was right to be suspicious. Samuel had never been overly kind to the beast. He had never been cruel, but had only followed *Daed*'s example.

Daed hadn't taken much time with the horses, using them until they were worn out and then buying new ones, and Samuel had always expected to do the same. He had never thought much about it until he saw the sleek horses in the pasture at meeting yesterday. His horse had looked sickly compared to them, and men judged a farmer's abilities by the condition of his stock. Anyone looking at his poor mare would know what the rest of his farm was like without even having to see it. They would know how he had been neglecting his legacy.

Samuel pulled the carrot he had brought from the root cellar out of his waistband. *Daed* had bought the mare cheap at a farm sale the year before he died. She had been strong enough, but with *Daed*'s lack of care, she had never become the sleek, healthy animal the other men at church kept.

He turned the carrot over in his hand. *Daed*'s horse,

Daed's problem. Except that *Daed* wasn't here anymore. Like everything else around the farm, the horse was his responsibility now whether he liked it or not.

"Hey there." Samuel kept his voice soft, and the mare's ears swiveled toward him. "Look what I have for you."

He broke the carrot in half and her head went up at the crisp snap. She stretched her neck toward him and took one step into the barn. He opened the gate and let himself into her stall.

"Come on, girl." He should give her a name, something *Daed* would never do. Searching his memory of other horse names, he decided on one. "Come on, Brownie."

Not much of a name. He stretched the carrot out toward her, wiggling it between his fingers. She took another step forward.

"You'll like this carrot." He tried another name. "Come on, Mabel."

She snorted.

"All right then. Tilly."

She swiveled her ears back and then forward again.

"Have a carrot, Tilly." The name fit. He took a step toward her. "Come on, Tilly-girl. You'll like it."

He held the carrot half on his outstretched hand and she picked it up, lipping it into her mouth. She stood, crunching the carrot as he grasped her halter. He gave her the other half.

She pulled wisps of hay from her manger as he brushed her lightly. She needed more than just grass to live on if he wanted her to become the kind of horse the other farmers kept. Sadie kept oats on hand and gave Chester a measured amount every day, rather than the hit-or-miss rations he gave Tilly. Sadie's horse thrived on her care.

So he would need to buy oats for the mare. Samuel held up the old brush, inspecting the matted and bent bristles. And he needed to buy a new brush. And a currycomb.

Taking care of this horse was going to cost money.

When Tilly finished her hay, he turned her out into the pasture again and grabbed the manure fork. He hauled forkfuls of soiled straw out to the pasture and started a pile. Somewhere in the past he remembered a manure pile in this spot. *Mamm* had used the soiled bedding on her garden after it had mellowed over the winter.

By the time he finished emptying the stall and spreading it with the last of the clean straw he had on hand, it was time for breakfast. The aroma of bacon frying pulled him to the house.

The girls didn't look up when he walked into the kitchen after washing up on the back porch.

"Good morning." Samuel broke the silence, and Esther stared at him in surprise. He didn't blame her. When had he ever greeted her in the morning?

Judith placed a bowl of scrambled eggs on the table with a smile. "Good morning, Samuel."

He started to reach for the platter of bacon, then remembered. He waited for Judith and Esther to take their seats, and then bowed his head for the silent prayer.

He had never prayed during this time, but had always let his mind wander while he waited for *Daed*'s signal to eat. But this morning, as the aroma of the bacon teased his hunger, he felt a nudge of guilt. Did his sisters pray during this moment of silence?

After the right amount of time had passed, Samuel

cleared his throat just as *Daed* had always done, and reached for the bacon.

"Some coffee, Samuel?" Esther stood at his elbow with the coffee pot.

Samuel nodded, his mouth full. She poured his coffee and then her own and Judith's. Her wrists, sticking out too far from the sleeves of her faded dress, were thin. The hollow places under her cheekbones were shadowed and gray.

Esther had been keeping house for him since Annie got married and before that had taken on her share of the work, just as Judith did now. Her brow was creased, as if she wore a perpetual frown at the young age of twenty-one. He had never noticed that before.

Not before he had met Mary. Tall and slim, Mary looked healthy and strong. Compared to her, Judith and Esther reminded him of last year's dry weeds along the fence.

Samuel shifted in his chair, the eggs tasting like dust in his mouth. The sight of the bacon on his plate turned his stomach. A sudden vision filled his memory. Sitting at this same table, watching *Daed* fill his plate with food, leaving just enough for the rest of the family to share between them. *Daed* eating the last piece of bacon every morning. And *Mamm* at the other end of the table, her face as thin and gray as Esther's, nibbling at a piece of toast.

Neither Judith nor Esther had taken any of the scrambled eggs but were eating toast with a bit of jam. Normally, Samuel would take two or three helpings of eggs and empty the platter of bacon. He pushed the bowl of eggs in their direction.

"I can't eat all of this. You take some."

Esther startled and looked at him, her eyes wide. "Did I fix too many eggs?"

He shook his head. "I'm just not as hungry this morning. You and Judith can eat them. Don't let them go to waste."

The girls glanced at each other, then Esther divided the last of the eggs between them. Judith dug in to hers eagerly.

"The bacon, too." Samuel pushed the platter in their direction. He had already eaten half of what Esther had prepared.

He drank his coffee, the bitter liquid hitting his stomach with a burn. The girls did without decent food and clothes…but whenever he had extra cash, he bought whatever he thought he needed. He stared at Esther's thin wrists. Just like *Daed* had done, he made his sisters make do with whatever was left over after he had taken what he wanted.

Samuel loosened his fingers carefully from his tight grip on the coffee cup. He had been so blind. No different from *Daed*.

"This afternoon I'll take you girls to town."

They exchanged looks.

"You don't need to do that," Esther said. "We don't need anything."

"I know you need groceries."

"We have no money."

"I'll take one of the hogs to sell at the butcher." Samuel drained his cup and rose from the table. "So make a list. I'm going over to Sadie's this morning, and then we'll head to town right after dinner."

Samuel took the path that led from the back of the barn through the fence row to Sadie's place. A well-worn path that he had traveled ever since he had been old enough to chore. *Daed* hadn't cared whether Sadie's chores were done or not, but *Grossdawdi* had drilled the habit of shouldering the responsibility into Bram and Samuel.

Grossdawdi Abe. Not the *grossdawdi* far away, *Mamm*'s parents, but *Daed*'s father. The old man had lived in the room off the kitchen for as long as Samuel could remember, until he became sick with fever fifteen years ago. *Grossdawdi* Abe had called Samuel and Bram into his room one afternoon when *Daed* was away.

"I want you boys to promise…" He had broken off, coughing, but then continued, "Promise me you'll look after Sadie Beiler. You boys are big enough to remember. Make sure her chores are done."

Then he had grasped Samuel's wrist and pulled him close.

"Promise me."

Samuel had nodded his promise. And he had kept his promise, even though Bram had forgotten. Every week, no matter what else happened, he was at Sadie's farm to do the chores he couldn't bring himself to do around *Daed*'s farm.

Choring on *Daed*'s farm brought too many memories to the surface, but when he worked on Sadie's farm, he could feel *Grossdawdi* Abe's approval. He did the chores for *Grossdawdi*, and for Sadie, and no one else.

Now that Sadie was elderly he made daily trips to her farm. Not to do the small chores that the old woman insisted on doing herself, but to make sure she was all right. Sadie was more frail and forgetful than she wanted to admit, so Samuel had taken it on himself to check the chickens after breakfast.

If the morning came when the eggs hadn't been gathered, he'd be there to make sure the elderly woman was all right. So far that morning hadn't come, but he still took the walk across the fields after breakfast each day. As far as he knew, Sadie had no clue that he made the daily visits.

On Mondays, though, she expected him to be there to clean the chicken coop and do some other heavy chores. She would meet him at the barn to visit for a few minutes before she went back to her work in the house and he went in to the barn. Those Monday morning talks were more than just idle chats with his neighbor. Sadie reminded him of better times, when *Mamm* was still alive. Before *Daed* became a slave to drink. Talking with her made him think that there were still peaceful and happy places in the world.

Today, as he rounded the corner of the woodlot, Sadie was nowhere to be seen. Mary was in the garden, attacking the weeds with a hoe.

"You don't need to do that, you know."

She jumped as he spoke, but relaxed when she recognized him.

"Good morning to you, too." She straightened and gave him a smile. "And why don't I need to weed the garden?"

"I do the heavy chores for Sadie. I always have."

"But Ida Mae and I are here now, so we can take care of things."

Samuel stared at her. He had to admit that there had been times when he had wished for someone else to take on the responsibility of watching out for Sadie, but now that Mary was offering, he didn't want to let it go. He clenched his hand, as if he could keep a wisp of smoke from slipping through it.

"At least I can clean out the chickens' pen."

She shook her head as she continued hoeing. "I've already finished that. Chester's stall, too."

Samuel looked around the orderly farmyard. "You've cut the grass?"

"Ida Mae did."

"Then I'll fix the hole in Chester's stall. Sadie told me about it yesterday and I said I'd get to it today."

Mary got to the end of the row and looked at him.

"You fixed the stall, too?"

"*Ja*, for sure." Her brown eyes twinkled in the morning sunlight. "My sister and I were taught to do all of the chores around the farm. *Daed*'s thinking was that everyone in the family needed to know how to do chores, from cooking breakfast to mucking stalls. So, we learned."

"And you've left me with nothing to do." Samuel felt the growl in his voice.

"There is something we do want you to do." Mary's face lit up. "We hoped you could bring Judith and Esther over for a sewing frolic. Just the five of us. Aunt Sadie knows so much that she can teach us, and we all need new dresses for summer." She twisted the hoe handle. "I'm sure the girls could make a new shirt or two for you, too."

Samuel scratched at his chin. The skin was itchy and irritated after being shaved this morning.

"I'll make you a deal."

Her eyes narrowed. "What kind of deal?"

"I'll bring my sisters over tomorrow morning, like you said, if you let me do some of the work around here.

There are some fence rails that need replacing, along with a few other things, so I'll have plenty to do."

She pressed her lips together, as if relinquishing the fence mending was the last thing she wanted to do.

"All right," she said. "You can mend the fence. But bring your sisters, and any fabric they might have. Even an old dress we can make over into something new."

Esther's faded and ragged sleeve edge flashed through his mind. He would make sure his sisters each chose a dress length of fabric while they were in town this afternoon. Maybe he would sell two hogs. Then he thought of the shadowed look on Esther's face. She would appreciate the time she spent with Sadie just as much as he did.

He nodded. "We have an agreement."

Samuel stuck out his hand to seal the deal the way he would with another farmer and Mary hesitated, then slipped her slender one into his, her grip firm.

"Agreed."

Tuesday morning Mary came back to the house after the morning barn chores to find Sadie and Ida Mae already sitting at the breakfast table waiting for her.

"I didn't think I was that late," Mary said, slipping into her chair at the small table.

"You aren't." Sadie folded her hands in preparation for their silent prayer. "We have company coming this morning, so we got breakfast started early."

Mary bent her head over her own folded hands, struggling to force her thoughts away from Sadie's comment. After a brief, silent prayer of thanks, she raised her head. Sadie sat with her fork poised, waiting for her to finish.

"I had nearly forgotten that the Lapps would be here

today." Mary cut a slice of sausage with the side of her fork.

"I'm glad Samuel is bringing the girls," Sadie said. "I always enjoy their company."

Ida Mae served herself some scrambled eggs from the bowl in the center of the round table. "Samuel looks different when he smiles. He was so gruff when we first met him, but then when he smiled, I nearly didn't recognize him."

Sadie sipped her coffee again. "He looks much like his grandfather did, years ago. Quite good-looking."

"You knew his grandfather?" Ida Mae picked up the ketchup bottle. "That must have been a long time ago."

"I was only sixteen when he asked to walk me home from Saturday night singing."

Ida Mae stared at Sadie. "Did he court you?"

Sadie pointed at Ida Mae's eggs. "You're putting on too much ketchup."

Ida Mae put the bottle down. Her eggs were covered with the sauce.

Mary passed her plate to her sister. "Here, spoon some onto my eggs, then it won't go to waste."

Sadie took another sip of her coffee, staring out the window as if she were watching her memories through it.

"He was my only suitor. We courted for two years."

"What was he like?" Mary asked.

"Tall, with dark hair, just like Samuel. But careless. My *daed* didn't like him very much."

Mary took a bite of her eggs, trying to imagine Aunt Sadie's father. He had been Mary and Ida Mae's great-grandfather, and their mother had always described him as kind and loving.

Ida Mae finished her breakfast and leaned forward, folding her arms on the table. "What happened?"

Sadie sighed. "Abe—that was his name—liked to play practical jokes. One day he came to pick me up in his spring wagon, and he had whitewashed his horse." Sadie smiled, shaking her head. "That scamp. We had a good laugh over his white horse, until *Daed* saw it."

Mary picked up her coffee cup. "Then what happened?"

"*Daed* said the waste of the paint and mistreating the poor horse was the last straw." Sadie's eyes sparkled as tears welled up and she lifted the hem of her apron to wipe her cheek. "He told Abe not to bother coming around again. I would see him at Sabbath meeting, of course, but he never spoke to me again. He found a girl from the Clinton district a year later and married her."

"So he just forgot about you?"

Sadie smiled at Ida Mae. "*Ach, ne.* You see, when *Daed* left the farm to my younger brother, your uncle Sol, I didn't want to live there anymore. It was one thing to be an unwed daughter in my parents' home, but with Sol and his wife having one baby after another, I was more in the way than I was a help. Elsie didn't want an old maiden aunt telling her how to raise her children."

"You couldn't have been that old," Ida Mae said.

"That was thirty-five years ago. I was fifty and had nowhere to go."

"So what did you do?"

"Somehow Abe knew of my predicament. He gave me these ten acres and the church built this house and barn." Sadie sighed. "Even after all those years, with his family grown and grandchildren coming along, Abe thought of me."

They sat in silence, and Mary thought about Sadie's story. How much was Samuel like his grandfather?

Sadie stood and started gathering the plates from the table. "The Lapps will be here soon. I have some scraps of material we can use to make a quilt top. We may as well start the sewing lessons sooner than later."

Before the mantel clock in the front room struck eight, Samuel's buggy drove into the yard.

"Go out and tell him to put his horse in the pasture with Chester," Sadie said, pushing Mary toward the door. "And tell him we'll have dinner ready at noon, and he and the girls should stay."

Mary got to the buggy just at Samuel was tying the horse to the hitching post. "Aunt Sadie says to put your mare in the pasture."

"I didn't think the job would take very long. The horse can stand."

"We'll have dinner ready for you and the girls. Aunt Sadie says we're to have a good visit."

Esther climbed down from the buggy, followed by Judith. Each of them carried a bundle of fabric. "I'm glad we're going to spend the day. We need Aunt Sadie's help with our dresses."

As the girls went into the house, Mary couldn't contain her smile. "I'm so glad they found material to bring. I wasn't sure they would have any."

"We went into town yesterday afternoon." Samuel fiddled with the reins in his hands as if he wasn't sure what to do. He shifted his gaze toward the door, where the girls had disappeared. "I appreciate the offer of dinner. The girls will enjoy the visit, and I have plenty of work to do here."

Mary stepped back as he climbed down from the

buggy. He was freshly shaven again today, and even with his worn work clothes, he was a fine-looking man. If Sadie's Abe had been anything like his grandson, she could understand why Sadie had fallen for him.

"I can show you where the repairs need to be done and where to put the horse."

He led the horse out from between the buggy shafts. "I know my way around. I've been helping Aunt Sadie since I was a boy." He gave her a brotherly grin as he walked away. "I'll see you at dinnertime."

Mary watched as he disappeared into the barn. Sadie's story of his grandfather had made him more intriguing than ever.

When she went inside the house, she followed the voices until she found Aunt Sadie and the others in the sewing room. Judith and Esther had spread lengths of light-colored muslin on the cutting table.

"Samuel surprised us with the trip to town," Judith was saying, stroking her piece of pale yellow fabric.

Esther fingered her own light green piece. "For some reason, he said we needed new dresses." She looked at Sadie. "He has never noticed what we've worn before, but yesterday in town he kept piling things on the shopkeeper's counter. Fabric, flour and sugar, butter. He even bought a new crock, since our old one broke last winter."

Sadie fingered the edge of the fabric. "That must have cost a lot of money."

Judith nodded. "I think it did. But he had taken two of the hogs to the butcher shop and sold them. He kept saying he should have done it months ago."

Sadie looked out the window toward the barn, and Mary followed her gaze. Samuel had just opened the gate to the pasture and was letting the mare in with Chester. He glanced toward the house, and then went back into the barn. He looked like a man who was eager to start working.

"I wonder what has gotten into him," Sadie said softly, and moved her gaze from Samuel to Mary.

Mary caught her look and felt her face turning red. Sadie couldn't think that Samuel was trying to impress her. Romance seemed to be as far from his mind as it was from hers.

Chapter Three

Samuel straightened and thumbed his hat back on his head. Chester had punched a hole in the side of the stall, all right. After pulling off the scrap wood Mary had used to patch the hole and tearing away the splintered remains of the broken plank, he could see the extent of the damage. Mary might have thought her patch was adequate, but this needed more than a temporary fix. The entire board should be replaced.

He climbed the ladder to the haymow, nearly empty after the long winter. Sadie had some hay left, but someone would have to fill the mow again before the summer was too far gone.

Someone? Samuel rubbed at his bare chin. That someone should be him. Other years, the deacons had made sure the mow was filled, but he could do it this year.

On the other side of the haymow a stack of planks rose from the dusty floor. They had been left from when the barn was built years ago. *Grossdawdi* had said something about building a chicken coop out of them someday, but Sadie had converted an empty stall for her few chickens, cutting a door through the outside wall for them to use, and the coop had never been built.

Samuel picked up the top plank and stood it upright, thumping it on the wooden haymow floor to shake the dust off. From here he could see Sadie's little house through the loft door. The windows were open to the spring air, and voices drifted up to him. He could distinguish Mary's low voice, bubbling with laughter. He couldn't keep a smile away at that thought.

Judith's voice rose above the others, cheerful and eager. If he had known a length of fabric would make her this happy, he would have taken the girls to town long ago. Why didn't he? He thumped the board one last time. Because *Daed* wouldn't have. He didn't remember *Daed* ever taking *Mamm* to town. None of them went anywhere except for *Daed*. He kept everyone at home, where no one would see *Mamm*'s bruised face.

He gripped the board as if he could split it in two. He had been following *Daed*'s example like a wheelbarrow following the rut he had left behind. As if he had no power over his own actions. He hadn't treated Judith and Esther any differently than *Daed* had, and there was no reason for it.

How had Bram gotten free of *Daed*'s shadow? Or had he? Did his pretty wife live in fear of Bram's temper?

Samuel leaned his head against the board, closing his eyes against the ache in his head. No woman would ever live in fear of him. He couldn't be sure of controlling his temper, but if he stayed single and kept to himself, he could avoid *Daed*'s legacy in at least one area of his life.

He lifted the board and took it to the main floor of the barn.

Replacing the plank didn't take much time. He spent

another hour giving Chester's stall a thorough cleaning, leveling the dirt floor and scrubbing the walls. The chickens' area, divided from the rest of the barn by a fence of wood slats and chicken wire, was already clean with fresh straw spread over the floor. Mary and Ida Mae were giving Sadie the help she had needed.

Movement in the vegetable garden caught his attention. Mary was there, picking lettuce. Samuel stood in the shadows just inside the door, watching the young woman in the garden. She bent, stooped and then straightened as she worked with a grace that drew him.

A few steps brought him close. Her back was turned to him as she leaned down to reach some lettuce that was tangled in the young bean plants.

"I've finished repairing the stall."

Mary jumped, whirling to face him. Her face was pale, and her hand clutched at the front of her apron.

"Are you all right?" Samuel took a step closer to her, but stopped when she moved away. "I didn't mean to scare you."

"Ne." She shook her head. "I mean, I'm all right. I just wasn't expecting anyone to be there. You surprised me."

Her hands trembled, and she clasped them together.

"Are you sure you're all right?"

She nodded and smiled, but the smile was stiff. "I'm picking some vegetables for dinner. Esther and Judith are having such fun with their new dresses. Aunt Sadie is teaching us all sorts of sewing tricks that I've never known before."

She chattered on as she turned to the peas. Her voice became more natural, and her trembling hands stilled as she worked. When she got to the end of the row, he lifted the basket of vegetables and carried them to the back porch.

After dinner, he would work on the pasture fence. A few loose boards near the gate needed to be tightened, and a few more around the perimeter needed to be replaced. When he finished with that, they would return home...

"Do you think they would want to come?"

Mary's question brought his attention back to her one-sided conversation. He was too used to ignoring his sisters' chatter.

"Where?"

"To the quilting in Eden Township on Thursday."

Samuel set the basket on the porch step. "Why would they want to go to another quilting?"

Mary's hands became fists that perched at her waist. "You weren't listening to me, were you?"

One look at her pursed lips, and he was done. Caught. He'd never be able to get anything by her.

"I missed the part about the quilting." He stared at her brown eyes. A trick he had learned from *Daed*. Put up a bluster. Make them think you are right, no matter what happens.

She met his stare, her eyes narrowing. He shifted his gaze to the peas, lifting one as if to inspect it for brown spots.

"You missed everything." She sighed and brushed some dirt off her apron. "On Thursday, the Eden Township group is meeting at your sister Annie's house. Aunt Sadie is planning to go, and we wondered if Judith and Esther would like to come along."

Annie. A pain he didn't know he held washed through him at the thought of her curly red hair. She had left...

how long ago? Almost two years? It had been soon after *Daed* passed away. He hadn't spoken to her since, and he never even thought of taking the girls to visit her. Why had he ignored her after she left to marry the deacon's son?

Because *Daed* would have been angry when she went behind his back, and he had followed in *Daed*'s footsteps without even thinking.

"Ja." He made the decision quickly, before he could think of all the reasons not to go to Eden Township. All the reasons to avoid mending the family ties. "And I'll drive you all in our buggy."

"You don't need to do that. We can take Chester."

"I'm going to drive. I have something to do down there, too."

Samuel lifted the basket and followed Mary into the kitchen. He needed to mend more than just the pasture fence. *Daed* had never apologized for anything he did, no matter how deep the wounds ran. But he wasn't *Daed*, and he wasn't going to act like him anymore.

He paused as Judith's and Esther's happy voices drifted into the kitchen from the back room. It was past time to apologize to Annie and her husband, and he had two days to prepare himself to face Bram.

"I can't wait until Thursday," Judith said.

The dress pieces had been cut out of the new fabric before dinner, and now, while Samuel mended the pasture fence and Aunt Sadie napped in her room, the girls sat together in the sewing room, each with pinned pieces to sew together.

"How long has it been since you've seen Annie?" Ida Mae asked.

"She left home two years ago." Esther snipped the end of her thread as she finished the shoulder of her dress, then tied a new knot to begin sewing the side seam. "She had met Matthew Beachey when he came to one of our singings, and they courted secretly for months."

"It wasn't a secret to us," Judith said.

Esther smiled, her sewing forgotten in her lap. "She was so happy with Matthew. When she came home from one of their buggy rides, we'd be waiting up for her. She'd tell us all about what they had done and where they had gone. Most often, he took her to his family's house after dinner to play games with his brothers and sisters in the evening, or he'd take her for a ride around Emma Lake. It sounded so romantic."

"Why was it such a secret?" Mary drew her thread through the seam. She had chosen the more difficult task of inserting the sleeves into the bodice of Judith's dress.

"She was afraid that if *Daed* had known she was seeing someone, he would have put a stop to it, the way he had tried to do with Katie." Esther's voice dropped, remembering. "Katie ran away with her beau to get married in Ohio, but Annie didn't want to run away. She didn't want to be separated from us."

Mary shifted in her chair. "But the bishop wouldn't allow them to marry without your *daed*'s permission, would he?"

"I don't know how Annie did it, but Bishop Yoder in Eden Township came here to talk to *Daed*, along with Matthew and Deacon Beachey. They wanted *Daed* to give his permission for the marriage."

Judith looked up from her sewing. "*Ach*, remember how angry he was?"

"He was so angry that Matthew left without Annie."

"I remember how she cried," Judith said. "She was afraid she would have to run away like Katie did."

"But Matthew came back when he heard *Daed* had died. It was after the funeral, but not too much time had passed." Esther sighed. "Samuel acted just like *Daed*, until Annie told him she was going to marry Matthew with his permission or without it."

"He stomped off to the barn then, didn't he?"

"But he gave her his permission first." Esther picked up her sewing again. "We haven't seen Annie since that day. We didn't go to the wedding, and we never go to visit the Eden Township folks."

"But she lives so close," Mary said. "I can understand that you wouldn't see Katie, living in Ohio the way she does, but Annie is only a few miles down the road."

"Even so," Esther said, "we've never gone for a visit, and she hasn't come here." Esther stopped to thread her needle. "I hope we get to see Bram on Thursday. He's our other brother, and also lives in Eden Township."

"I do, too," said Judith. "I was only five years old when he left home, and I hardly remember him."

Mary sewed basting stitches in the right sleeve and then gathered them before she pinned the sleeve to the bodice. She had never met a family like the Lapps, where the scattered family members didn't try to see one another, even when they lived in the same area. But if Samuel had been as angry as the girls said when Annie left…

Rethreading her needle, Mary tried to imagine Samuel being angry. She had seen him embarrassed, and a bit grumpy, but angry? She imagined his eyes darkening, his mouth twisting, his hand reaching toward her… Her vision suddenly blurred, swirling so that she couldn't see the needle's eye. She took a deep breath and started counting.

There was nothing to fear from Samuel. He was a neighbor. Judith and Esther's brother. She would never be foolish enough to be alone with him in a secluded place. She would never let herself be at the mercy of any man again.

She started over. *One, two, three, four...* She fixed her eyes on the wooden planks of the floor in front of her toes. *Ten, eleven, twelve...* Her breathing slowed and she relaxed. *Twenty-five, twenty-six...*

Safe. She was safe in Aunt Sadie's home. Safe with the girls and Ida Mae, without any men around to intrude.

Except Samuel, and he would soon learn that they didn't need him to do Sadie's chores any longer. Then she would only have to see him on church Sundays.

Esther's voice penetrated the hum in Mary's ears.

"What?"

"Did you enjoy church on Sunday?" Esther asked, looking at both Mary and Ida Mae.

"We did," Mary said. She forced herself to smile. "There were a lot of new people to meet, but other than that it was very much like church at home."

Judith giggled. "I saw someone taking notice of Ida Mae during dinner."

Mary exchanged glances with her sister, but Ida Mae shrugged, her eyebrows lifted.

"What do you mean? I didn't see anyone noticing me in particular."

The girl grinned, looking at their faces. "I can't be the only one who saw him. He couldn't take his eyes off you."

"Whoever it was," Mary said, "he was probably only looking at us because we're new."

Judith shook her head. "He was only looking at Ida Mae. I don't think he saw anyone else all day."

Esther leaned forward. "You have to tell us who it was."

Judith only grinned until Esther nudged her knee with her foot.

"It was Thomas Weaver."

"The minister's son?" Esther sat back in her chair. "Every girl around has been trying to catch his attention."

Ida Mae turned to Mary. Her face was mottled pink. "I…I'm going to check on Sadie. I'll be right back."

After she left the room, Esther said, "I hope we didn't say anything to upset her."

"It isn't anything to worry about. Ida Mae just isn't interested in getting to know any boys right now." She shifted the bodice in her lap and changed the subject. "There were so many other young people at church on Sunday. I'm looking forward to getting to know the girls. Do you attend the singings?"

"Samuel won't take us, and he won't let us drive ourselves. I think he's afraid we'll end up the same way as Annie and Katie."

"But he lets you go to the quilting on Wednesdays."

Judith nodded. "That's because there aren't any boys there."

Esther stifled a giggle. "Can you imagine a boy at a quilting frolic?"

They all laughed at that.

Ida Mae came back into the room. "Sadie is sound asleep."

"I'm so glad," Mary said. "If she doesn't take a rest she gets overtired in the evenings and forgets things too easily."

"Everyone is glad you came to live with her," said Esther. "She shouldn't live alone anymore, not at her age. Too many things can happen."

"Like when she didn't come to church one Sunday last winter." Judith's face had grown pale. "The deacons went to check on her after the worship service was over. It turns out she had made a wrong turn on the way to meeting. They got here to her house just as she returned. She had gone all the way to Middlebury, but when she knew she had gone the wrong way, she let Chester bring her home."

"It's a good thing she has a smart horse," Esther said.

Mary and Ida Mae looked at each other. Mary saw the same alarm she felt reflected in her sister's eyes.

"That could have ended in disaster."

"But it didn't." Esther tied a knot in her thread. "The Good Lord was watching out for her that day."

What would they do if something like that happened again? Mary rubbed her tired fingers. She and Ida Mae would have to watch Aunt Sadie very closely.

Samuel was at work early on Thursday, preparing for the trip to Eden Township. Tilly stood with a hind leg cocked, head down, her side to the morning sun as Samuel brushed her. The new bristles lifted the dust off her coat with little puffs that glinted in the sunlight. The mare's skin twitched in response. She was enjoying the pampering.

Samuel had curried and brushed her more in the last two days than he ever had before. He had even taken care of her hooves, trimming and polishing them until they shone. He stood back and inspected his brushing job. Her muscles could still use some filling out, but that would come with time. Meanwhile, her coat was beginning to take on the shine of a healthy animal. He didn't need to be ashamed of her when he faced Bram.

He left Tilly still basking in the sun as he went into the barn and put the brush and currycomb on their shelf with care. One thing he remembered from *Grossdawdi*'s barn was how clean and orderly everything had been. Each step he took in that direction was progress.

The old buggy stood in the middle of the barn floor, still clean from yesterday's washing. The wheels were worn, and should be replaced. The seats needed to be recovered, but the old blankets he had thrown over them would have to do for now. Even with as many years as the buggy had been around, though, the black lacquered oilcloth cover gleamed in the subdued light of the barn. Everything was ready for today's trip.

Samuel took off his new hat and ran his fingers through his hair. Everything was ready except him. The thought of seeing Annie again filled his stomach with something like a bundle of puppies, but Bram…

He whooshed out a breath at the thought of his last encounter with Bram at the barn raising last summer. He had been stupid, making idle threats that didn't mean anything, but Bram had responded like no Amishman ever did. He had drawn him close, like a brother would, but his grip had been hard on Samuel's shoulder, and his words dripped of danger. Samuel swallowed at the memory. He had never encountered anything like the tone in Bram's voice. The years his brother had spent working for gangsters in Chicago had hardened him.

Bram could be a dangerous man, but his life had changed since that hot day last summer. He had joined the church, married a pretty widow and was now a father to her three children. Was he any less threatening, though?

Samuel ran his hand through his hair again, making it stand up in spikes. He didn't have long to wait to find out. He planned to take the girls and Sadie to Annie's, where he would apologize to her and her husband. The puppies churned. That would be difficult enough. But then, once he learned where Bram lived, he would go to his farm and…what? Confront him? Try to make amends? Repair the broken places between them? It all depended on Bram's reaction.

He took a cloth and wiped a few stray specks of dust from the buggy, then led Tilly into the barn to harness her. Every clomp of her hooves on the wooden floor was one step closer to facing Bram. He tied Tilly to a post and stroked her neck.

"Well, Tilly-girl, it's going to be a day to remember."

Taking the harness from the hooks on the wall, he swung it onto the mare's back. She stepped away, but then stood quietly as he murmured to her. "So, Tilly, so. You know we're going for a drive, don't you?" Her ears swung back and then forward at the unfamiliar tone in his voice. He reached under her to grab a strap, and as he fastened the harness onto her, he kept talking. "We're going down to Eden Township today." He patted her rump as he walked around to her other side. "You'll like the drive. New places to see." Once the harness was on, he led her to the buggy and backed her into place between the shafts.

After she was hitched up, he led her out of the barn

to the hitching rail next to the house. Esther was waiting for him on the steps, bouncing on her toes and grinning. He had to smile at her.

"You look like you're ready to go."

"For sure I am!" She ran down the walk toward the buggy. "I haven't seen Annie since she got married." She stopped when she reached him and looked into his face, suddenly sober. "You don't think she has forgotten us, do you?"

The litter of puppies in Samuel's stomach clambered over each other as Esther's words sunk in. He had been so concerned with his own meeting with Annie that he hadn't considered how Esther and Judith must be feeling. They were her sisters, separated from her through no fault of their own.

"I'm sorry." The words came out garbled, strangled by his swelling throat. As Judith joined them, he put a hand on each of his sister's shoulders and tried again. "I'm sorry that I haven't taken you to see Annie before."

Judith and Esther glanced at each other.

"We understand," Esther said. "You were angry—"

Samuel cut off her excuses. "But I shouldn't have been. I shouldn't have acted like I did when she wanted to marry that young man."

"Matthew."

Samuel squeezed Judith's shoulder in silent thanks for providing the name he couldn't remember. The name he had blocked. "Matthew." He nodded. "Matthew." The serious young man who had claimed their Annie. The puppies wouldn't settle down.

Judith shrugged his hand off her shoulder. "Can we go now? I can't wait to get there."

Samuel stroked Tilly's nose as the girls climbed into

the buggy, ignoring their surprise at the changes he had made. He didn't have to go with them. He could send them over to Sadie's to ride with her. He didn't have to face Annie and Matthew. He could stay home. There was plenty of work to keep him busy.

He swallowed. He didn't have to risk Bram's rejection.

Tilly nibbled at his shoulder. It was the first sign of affection she had ever shown him. He patted her cheek and smoothed the hair under her bridle.

"Well, Tilly-girl, I guess it's time to face the lions."

He climbed into the buggy and lifted the reins. The girls chattered to each other in the back seat, talking about Annie and her baby. He rubbed at his freshly shaved chin as they talked. He hadn't thought that Annie would have a child. His nephew, from what the girls were saying.

Turning Tilly onto the road, he urged her into the quick trot she liked as they headed toward Sadie's house. As they turned in, he saw Sadie and Ida Mae waiting for them at the edge of the drive. The churning in his stomach eased as Mary stepped out of the house and joined them just as he drew the buggy up. She gave him one of her quiet smiles as Ida Mae climbed into the back of the buggy. He stepped out to help Sadie into the front seat.

"Good morning, Samuel." She clung to his hand as she put one foot on the buggy step. "It's a fine day for a drive."

"*Ja*, for sure."

He waited for her to move to the center of the seat so that Mary would be able to sit next to her, but Sadie waved him away.

"I'd like to sit here, if you don't mind. Mary can sit in the center, between us."

Mary shot a look toward her aunt, then walked around the back of the buggy with Samuel.

"You know why Sadie wants me to sit in the middle, don't you?" Mary whispered the words.

"Why?"

Mary stopped, out of sight of the others. "I think she's trying to push us together."

Samuel stared. Her cheeks were pink, and one wisp of hair curled around the edge of her bonnet, sending his thoughts down a path that led to tucking that wisp behind her ear. He gripped his suspenders to keep his hands still. "You mean like a matchmaker?"

"Shh." Mary turned away from the buggy. "Don't let her hear you." She twisted her fingers together. "If she sees that she isn't successful, then she'll give up. We just have to ignore her attempts to match us up."

"That sounds good to me."

Mary continued around the buggy to climb into the front seat and Samuel followed her. His plans didn't include a wife, and he should be glad that Mary had rejected the idea of the two of them making a match. So why did he feel like he had just watched something precious float away?

Chapter Four

The narrow seat on the buggy provided no opportunity for Mary to put any distance between her elbow and Samuel's. She finally gave up, resigning herself to the occasional bumps in the road that jostled her against his warm, strong arm. His muscles were tense as he handled the reins, so maybe he didn't notice when they made contact.

Sadie kept the conversation going with news about the neighbors as they made their way south.

"There's the Miller farm," she said as they passed a lovely shaded farmyard. Flowers lined the edge of the garden and some children were busy picking strawberries from the field next to the house. "They're Mennonite, and good neighbors." She went on without a pause. "And up ahead is the Jefferson place. They're *Englischers* and their family has lived here as long as ours." Sadie laid her hand on Mary's arm as she turned toward her. "My *daed* never understood Thomas Jefferson. *Ach, ja,* that was his name. No relation to the famous president, though. The man was a go-getter, never leaving things be. Now his son, Phillip, has the farm. You won't believe the bee he has in his hat."

Sadie fell silent and Mary exchanged glances with Samuel.

He grinned. "You're talking about the road paving he wants the county to do?"

Sadie nodded and set off again. "That's right! Pavement in the country! What trotting along on that hard surface will do to our poor horses, I don't know." She huffed as she settled back in her seat. "He just wants a smooth road for his fancy automobile, and wants the county to pay for it."

Samuel chirruped to the horse. "He says it will keep the dust down." His words were mild, but Mary could see his Adam's apple bobbing as he tried to keep from laughing.

Sadie crossed her arms. "There's nothing wrong with a little dust."

Samuel kept his voice calm, not letting the laughter emerge. "You just don't like to see progress."

"Of course not. Progress without wisdom isn't good for anyone. People like Phillip Jefferson can't see past the end of their own noses, and he has no thought of what unintended consequences this road of his might bring." Sadie sat up, her attention on the next farm. "There's the Zook farm. Good Amish folks, and now we're in Eden Township."

"Is that Levi Zook? I met him at a barn raising last summer," Samuel said.

Sadie shook her head. "*Ne*, his cousin, Caleb. Levi lives a few miles east of here." She leaned forward. "Matthew Beachey's place is just past this crossroad. Up there on the right."

Mary felt Samuel's body stiffen at Sadie's words. What must it be like for him to see Annie again after so long?

The other girls had been visiting in the back seat, but when Sadie pointed out their destination, Esther and Judith leaned forward to get a look.

"What a pretty place," Judith said.

"Look at all of the flowers. Annie always said gladiolus was her favorite, and she has planted a whole row of them."

Esther's voice sounded strained and Mary turned around as well as she could.

"Are you all right, Esther?"

She nodded. "I'm just so happy to see Annie again." She pointed, her arm extending between Mary and Sadie. "Look, there she is! Samuel, stop the buggy so we can get out."

"You can wait until I turn in the drive." Samuel's voice held a growl. His face was tense as he drove the horse toward Annie, who was waiting for them next to the gravel lane.

When he drew the buggy to a stop, Judith and Esther jumped out and into Annie's arms. The three sisters held each other close, none of them saying a word, until Annie pushed away from the embrace to look at the girls.

"You've both changed so much!" Annie's happy smile made Mary want to smile back.

As the girls launched into the story of everything that had happened since they had last been together, Annie looked toward the buggy, then back at her sisters. Samuel remained in his seat, watching the girls, but making no move to get out.

Sadie reached across Mary to poke his arm. "Samuel, it's time for you to say hello to Annie."

Samuel swallowed, his Adam's apple bobbing. *"Ja."* He sighed and secured the reins, but he didn't make a move to get out of the buggy.

Mary laid her hand on his arm. There must be some way she could help. The poor man looked like he was about to meet his doom.

"She's waiting for you."

Samuel looked past Mary and Sadie. Annie had glanced his way again, and had pulled her lower lip in between her teeth.

"Go on," Mary said. She pushed at his arm. "It's time."

His eyes met hers then, pleading with them as one of her younger brothers would do, but he climbed down from the buggy. Mary followed him and helped Sadie to the ground as she watched him greet his sister.

"Hello, Annie."

He stood back, but his sister reached toward him and grasped his hand.

"I'm so glad you came." Her eyes sparkled with tears. "I've missed you. All of you."

Sadie pulled on Mary's arm, and she led the way into the house with Ida Mae following.

"We'll let the four of them get acquainted again without us interfering."

Other buggies had already arrived, and as Mary stepped onto the porch, she could hear the hum of voices from inside the house. She swallowed down the thickness in her throat at the thought of all the strangers on the other side of that door, but she didn't have time to be nervous as Sadie walked in. They laid their bonnets with the others on a bed in the room off the kitchen, then followed the sound of women visiting.

The front room was filled with a quilt on a frame, and ten or twelve women sat around it, needles in their hands and all talking at once. Sadie led Ida Mae to three empty chairs on the far side of the quilt, stopping to greet the women they passed on the way.

"Good morning, Elizabeth." She grasped an older woman's shoulder. "These are my nieces from Ohio, Mary and Ida Mae." She went on to the next woman, a younger image of the first one. "And Ellie, I'm so glad you're here. Meet my nieces."

Mary had hardly had a chance to greet Elizabeth when she met Ellie's blue eyes. "I'm so happy to meet you. I'm Ellie Lapp."

"Lapp? Are you related to Esther and Judith?"

"*Ja*, for sure." Ellie's smile was relaxed and welcoming. "Their brother Bram is my husband, but I've never met the girls." She stuck her needle in the quilt and half rose from her seat. "Did they come with you? Are they outside?"

"They're talking with Annie. Samuel is there, too."

Ellie sat back in her chair. "Samuel came?"

"He said he had some business here in Eden Township, so he drove us down here this morning."

A little boy, about two years old, crawled out from under the quilting frame and pulled on Ellie's skirt. "*Memmie*, I'm thirsty."

Ellie cupped his head in her hand, a worried frown on her face. "*Ja*, Danny. We'll go to the kitchen and get a drink." She smiled at Mary, her brows still knit. "I'm so glad to meet you, Mary, and I hope we'll be able to get to know each other better."

She took the little boy by the hand and led him into the kitchen as Mary made her way to the chair next to Sadie and Ida Mae. For the first time, she wondered what business Samuel had in Eden Township. Whatever it was, it had Ellie worried.

Samuel let Tilly choose her own pace as he set off down the road toward Bram's farm. Annie's welcome had bolstered his courage enough to ask for directions to their brother's home, but when he saw Bram's wife peering at them through Annie's kitchen window, doubts began to crowd in again.

Meeting Bram wouldn't be as easy as seeing Annie again. His sister had always been quick to forgive and easy to talk to. Bram had never been easy to deal with.

Samuel stopped at a crossroad. Annie had said he would turn right after he passed over the creek, and he could see the wandering line of trees and bushes that marked the creek's progress through the fields ahead. Only one more mile before he turned onto Bram's road. When he clucked to Tilly, she shook her head and started off at a brisk trot.

He and Bram had never enjoyed the kind of brotherly love he saw in other families. *Daed* had pushed at them, and Samuel could hear his voice now. *"Bram can do it. Why can't you?"*

And then Bram would look at him with his superior, big-brother look that would spike Samuel's temper.

Whether it was pitching hay down from the loft or hauling buckets of slop for the hogs, Bram had always done it better, faster, easier.

Even after Bram had abandoned the family, *Daed*

had kept goading at Samuel, pushing him to be the man Bram was.

But he wasn't Bram. He didn't leave. He had stayed and absorbed the brunt of *Daed*'s anger right until the end.

Samuel fingered the reins. Why hadn't he left? He could have followed Bram, but he shied away from the accusing voice in his head that said he had been too cowardly to strike out on his own. His eyes stung and he rubbed at them. He wasn't a coward. He was the good son. The one who had stayed home. But *Mamm* had still died.

Tilly trotted across the culvert over the stream and the next crossroad was in sight. A quarter mile west, Annie had said. His stomach churned with something. Anger? Resentment? Or was he only nervous?

Samuel pulled Tilly to a stop at the corner. He didn't have to turn. He could continue down this road, find a spot to rest until it was time to pick up the girls again and face Bram another day.

But he was done with putting things off. That's the way *Daed* would have handled this. He would have ignored Bram, pretended he didn't exist to punish him for taking off to Chicago all those years ago. If he was going to come out from his *daed*'s shadow, he needed to face Bram.

Make amends.

He turned the corner and headed west, keeping Tilly's pace to a slow trot, even though she shook her head in protest. Samuel kept the reins tight, holding her in. He wanted time.

The farm was on the left after he crossed another little creek. A *Dawdi Haus* nestled in the grass near the creek, with a flower garden in the front. The main house stood on a rise near it, and a white barn sat at the back of the lane. A field next to the lane was planted with corn, and the stalks stood nearly a foot high. A team of four matching Belgian horses grazed in the pasture beyond the barn.

Samuel pulled Tilly to a halt in the road. The horses in the pasture meant that Bram was at home, not out in the fields. He fought the urge to keep driving down the road and turned Tilly into the lane. Someone had seen him coming. An old man watched him from the porch of the *Dawdi Haus*, but Samuel followed the sound of metal hammering on metal that rang from the barn.

He halted Tilly near the barn door and climbed out of the buggy. The ringing continued. He tied the horse to the rail alongside the barn. No break in the rhythmic hammering from inside.

Looking around, Samuel spied the old man, who had walked up to the main house and stood on the front porch. He lifted his hand in a wave and Samuel returned the gesture. There was no alternative now except to face Bram. Wiping his hands on his trousers, he walked into the barn.

Just inside the door, he stopped to let his eyes adjust to the dim light. Bram was at the end of the main bay, working on a plow, his back to the door. A boy stood next to him. The seven-year-old held his hands over his ears to block out the noise, but leaned as close to Bram as he could, fascinated by the work.

Bram stopped hammering and bent down to inspect his work. "You see here, Johnny," he said as he pointed, "that was the piece that had come loose. But now it's fastened in good and tight and should work fine."

Samuel walked toward them and the boy saw him.

"*Daed*, someone's here."

Bram straightened and turned, a welcoming smile on his face until he saw who it was.

"Samuel." His voice held a note of surprise.

"Hello, Bram."

Bram pulled off his gloves and laid one hand on the boy's shoulder without taking his gaze away from Samuel. "Johnny, we're done here. Why don't you go see if your *grossdawdi* needs any help?"

Johnny ran out the back door of the barn and Bram stepped closer.

"I didn't expect to see you."

Samuel tried to smile. "Annie told me where you live."

"You've been to Annie's?"

"I brought Judith and Esther to her house for the quilting this morning, and I thought I'd stop and see how you were doing."

Bram stared at him. "If I remember right, when I stopped by the farm last year you told me that I didn't belong there, and you didn't want to see me again."

Samuel took a step back. *Ja*, for sure, he remembered that day. Bram had been all slicked up in a gabardine suit. An *Englischer* through and through.

"You didn't look like you wanted to stay."

Bram stepped closer. "You didn't even let me go to the house to see the girls."

Samuel looked him in the eyes. "You weren't our brother anymore. You were some fancy *Englischer*. How did I know what you wanted from us?"

His brother looked down. "You were probably right." He rubbed at the back of his neck. "I was hoping to hide out at home, but when you sent me on my way, I had to make other plans." He smiled then, looking at Samuel again. "I should probably thank you for that. If you hadn't forced me to move on to Annie and Matthew's, I would never have met Ellie."

"But the last time we spoke, at the barn raising, you threatened me."

"*Ja*, well, I did, didn't I? You must understand, there were some dangerous men around and I didn't want you to get mixed up with them. I was hoping to scare you off."

Samuel felt the corner of his mouth twitch. "More dangerous than you?"

Bram's mouth widened in a wry grin. "Dangerous enough. But that's in the past. My life is different now. Better. Much better."

Samuel nodded, looking around at the neat, clean barn. "Life has been good to you."

"God has been good to me." Bram grabbed Samuel's shoulder and squeezed it. "What about you? How are things going for you?"

Samuel scratched at his chin, missing the whiskers. "Not as good."

"When I stopped by last year, it looked like the farm was doing all right."

He shrugged. "As well as when *Daed* ran it. The hogs sell, and that brings in cash when we need it."

"I'm sorry I wasn't there when *Mamm* died. How did *Daed* take it?"

"You don't know how she died? Annie didn't tell you?"

Bram shot him a look. "What do you mean?"

"*Daed* was drunk. He and *Mamm* were arguing." Samuel shut his eyes, trying to block out the memory of the shouts, *Mamm*'s cries. "She fell down the stairs and died three days later."

"Annie never told me any of this." Bram ran his hand over his face. "What do you think happened?"

"You know what *Daed* was like when he lost his temper."

Bram nodded. "Especially when he was drunk." He paused and their eyes met. "Do you think that had anything to do with the accident?"

Samuel shook his head. "I don't know. Sometimes I wonder if it wasn't an accident. I've gone over it in my head again and again. All I know is if he hadn't been drinking, he wouldn't have been fighting with her. But he drank all the time back then."

They stood in silence as Samuel relived the memories again, and felt the release of having someone to share his suspicions with. Whether or not *Daed* had shoved *Mamm*, causing her fall, or if she lost her balance, he would never know. He had never told anyone about what he had witnessed that day.

Finally, Bram sighed. "I'm sorry, Samuel. I left home because I couldn't take *Daed* and his temper anymore, but I left you alone with him. I shouldn't have done that. We should have faced him together."

Samuel shrugged. "You know *Daed*. He kept us working against each other so that we wouldn't work against him." Samuel stared at the barn floor as he realized just how strong their father's influence had been. "We were never friends, were we?"

Bram shook his head. "*Daed* always picked at me, asking me why I couldn't be more like you. He always did like you the best, you know."

Samuel stared. "What do you mean? He always told me that I should be more like you."

Bram stared back at him, then his laugh came out as a short bark. "That old rascal."

"It isn't funny. I've spent my life hating you."

"Same here." One corner of Bram's mouth still held a grin. "*Ach*, then, what do we do about it now?"

Samuel's thoughts whirled. What did he want? Could he be friends with this man when so many painful memories crowded in?

He stuck his hands in his pockets. "I'm not sure we can ever be brothers."

Bram had bent his head down, and now looked at him from under the brim of his hat. "Could we be friends?"

Samuel shrugged. "I don't know."

"Let's start with a truce, and then go on from there."

Bram stuck his hand out and Samuel looked at it. Calloused, strong, tanned by the sun. The mirror image of his own as he slowly took the offered hand. Bram's grip was sure. Firm. Samuel tightened his fingers and Bram's grip grew firmer. Samuel felt a grin starting as he met Bram's eyes.

"Truce."

Mary sat at the kitchen table while Ida Mae helped Sadie get ready for bed. They had quickly discovered that Sadie became confused easily at night, and more than once had gone to bed with her dress still on, or neglecting a final trip to the outhouse, so the two of them took turns keeping Sadie focused on her bedtime routine until she was finally settled and asleep.

But only half of Mary's mind was on Sadie and Ida Mae. She drummed her fingers on the table, echoing the rolling thunder of an approaching storm. The rain would be welcome, if they got any. Last year's drought was one for the history books, *Daed* had said often enough. But the thunder was outdone by the rising bubble of guilt that pricked at her conscience.

After the quilting today, Annie had sent some jars of canned asparagus and a loaf of bread home with Sadie. Mary hadn't thought much about it until this evening. While she had been washing up after supper, she had realized that Sadie's cellar was full of canned goods, and the kitchen cupboards held sacks of flour. Even baking powder and cinnamon. All items that were hard to come by at home.

The entire community was supporting Sadie, not only here in Shipshewana but even folks in Eden Township. They made sure she had enough food in her cupboards and plenty of staples to keep her comfortable. Even Samuel helped with her chores.

Ida Mae came into the kitchen, stifling a yawn. "It's been a long day, and I'm going to go to bed."

"Sit down for a minute, first." Mary used her foot to push a chair out from the table. "We need to talk."

Her sister yawned again, but sat down. "What about?"

"You know people give food and other things to Sadie. And the Yoders across the road bring a gallon of milk every day."

"Of course they do. Our church at home does the same for older people and others who can't work for themselves."

Mary nodded. "And that is the right thing to do, except that we're here now. Have you noticed that the Yoders used to send a quart of milk for Sadie, but now it's a gallon? Everyone has sent more food for Sadie since we came. They aren't only making sure Sadie has enough, but they're sending extra for us."

Ida Mae lifted an eyebrow.

"We can and should work for ourselves, and support Sadie, too. We should be helping to support the community, not taking aid that another family might need more than we do."

Ida Mae shifted in her chair as another roll of thunder sounded in the distance. "Are you suggesting we start farming? Or raising hogs like Samuel does?" She shook her head. "I don't think we could do anything like that and care for Sadie, too."

"I'm not sure what we could do, but there must be something. We will need to raise money to pay the property taxes, for sure, so we need a cash income."

"Could we sell vegetables by the road? Or baked goods?"

"Perhaps. But no one has money to buy such things, and we aren't on a main road to catch the attention of travelers." Mary tapped one finger against her chin. "Maybe we could plant fruit trees like we have at home. Apples always sell well."

Ida Mae rubbed her eyes. "It would take at least three years for the trees to give enough apples to sell. We can't wait that long, can we?"

Mary shook her head. She ran her finger along the edge of the table, her heart pounding at the possibility that she dreaded. "I suppose one of us could hire out as farm help somewhere."

"I wouldn't want to work for *Englischers*, even if you found someone to hire us. You wouldn't, either. Besides, we need to be here at home so we can take care of Aunt Sadie."

"You're right." Mary leaned back in her chair, glad that Ida Mae had found the perfect excuse. She couldn't imagine working in an *Englischer*'s house, possibly facing an *Englisch* man every day. And she wouldn't even think about taking a job in town, like she had at home in Ohio. She tapped her chin again. "The chickens are producing pretty well."

"Don't remind me. They're giving us so many eggs that we'll be eating custard every day." Ida Mae rolled her eyes and Mary grinned. Her sister hated custard.

"Maybe we can sell the extra eggs, or trade them for something at the store in Shipshewana."

Ida Mae covered her mouth as another yawn took over. "That sounds like a good idea. They won't bring in much money, but every little bit helps."

Mary stood. "You need to get to bed, and so do I. If you can stay here with Sadie tomorrow, I'll take the trip to town and make inquiries."

Ida Mae pushed her chair away from the table. "If you can sell those eggs, I'll be thankful."

"I'll see what I can get for them. The storekeeper might only take them in trade instead of buying them."

"Well, make a list of things we need, just in case he does." Ida Mae glanced at the stove. "Have you banked the fire yet?"

"I forgot. But go on to bed and I'll take care of it."

Rain spattered against the window panes as Ida Mae went up the narrow stairway off the kitchen. Mary opened the fire box on the stove. Coals glowed in the ashes, nearly out. If Ida Mae hadn't reminded her to check, they would have awakened to a cold stove in the morning. She set a small log in the ashes and added kindling to build the fire up. Blowing gently on the coals, she watched as the dry bits of wood caught the heat, then as the pulsing glow turned to flame. The fire licked at the log until it, too, was burning.

Mary sat back on her heels as she waited for the fire to grow enough to keep the log smoldering all night. Watching the flames took her back to when she was a girl and helped *Mamm* build up the stove fire each morning. She had always loved feeding the fire and watching the flames take hold. The warmth of the fire fascinated her, and she still didn't understand where the heat came from. *Daed* said it was from the sunshine stored in the trees while they lived, but that didn't satisfy her curiosity. How did the trees do that? And why did the wood burn like it did?

She sighed and raked the coals close to the burning log. That was one mystery she would never solve. She shut the fire box door and closed the dampers. The log would smolder all night and leave a bed of live coals to start the morning's fire. As she passed the table on her way to the stairs, she turned down the lamp that hung from the ceiling until the flame went out.

Tomorrow she would take the extra eggs to town, but which store should she take them to? Rain pattered on the roof overhead as she felt her way up the dark stairs. And then the answer came to her. She would stop by the Lapps' farm on her way to town. Judith or Esther might know the best place for her to trade, and where she would get the best deal for the eggs. Hopefully the storekeeper would want to buy a few dozen every week, and their problems would be eased.

Mary shut her eyes against the thought of going to town and interacting with strangers. But she couldn't let things go on as they had been. She and Ida Mae would support themselves and Sadie, and help others with the surplus.

She leaned on the table as a low moan escaped. She would have to face the *Englisch* storekeepers in Shipshewana. Her knees grew weak at the thought. Where would she find the strength?

Chapter Five

The storms overnight had turned the hog pen into a morass of stinking mud. Samuel leaned on the top fence rail and plucked at a grass stem just out of the greedy sows' reach. The hogs milled around in the pen, rooting in the mud, stirring the mess into an ankle-deep slough. As he watched, one big sow dug under the feeding trough and lifted it until it rolled over, then grunted contentedly as she snagged bits of food that had been buried underneath it.

What would *Daed* do with this? Samuel rubbed at his forehead, trying to erase the memories that surfaced. *Daed* would send him into the mud to wrestle the trough upright and pour another bucket of slops in for the pigs, all while trying to keep from getting bitten or shoved down into the mud himself. Today, he would have to send himself into the pen.

No use putting it off. He climbed over the fence and waited for his boots to settle in the mud. Here by the fence it wasn't too bad. Samuel glanced at the sow that was trying to flip the feeding trough again. She was belly deep in the stuff. He headed toward the trough, one step at a time, the mud sucking at his boots. Fending off the rest of the sows that shoved at him, looking for the slops they knew he would soon give them, he grabbed the edge of the trough, set it upright and dragged it back to the fence.

Finally back on dry ground, he picked up a bucket to pour the slops into the mud-caked trough, but the sight of Chester pulling Sadie's buggy into the yard stopped him. Mary was driving, alone. He set the pail down and started toward the buggy. The only reason he could think of for Mary to drive over here by herself was that something had happened to Sadie. He quickened his pace to a trot.

He reached the hitching rail the same time Mary pulled Chester to a stop. Her smile of greeting faded as she stared at him.

Samuel panted, out of breath. "What's wrong? Is Sadie ill?"

She shook her head slowly, still staring. "I'm on my way to Shipshewana, and I thought the girls might like to go with me."

"So Sadie is all right?"

"For sure, she is. She and Ida Mae are spending the morning piecing a quilt top."

Samuel straightened his shoulders. He hated when his mind leaped ahead of him. "Then why are you staring at me?"

Mary blinked and moved her gaze to his face. "You're filthy."

"*Ja*, of course I am." He waved a dismissing hand, then caught sight of the mud. His hands, arms, shirt, trousers…every inch was covered in the muck from the hogs' pen. "The pigsty is deep in mud, and those sows had shoved their trough into the center of it all again."

"Do you fasten it to the fence?"

It was his turn to blink. "What?"

"The trough. Do you tie it to the fence so they can't move it?"

He had never thought of such a thing. *Daed* had never thought of such a thing…

"Here, I'll show you what I mean." Mary jumped out of the buggy and tied Chester to the rail before leading the way to the side of the pen where the buckets of slop were lined up.

Samuel had no choice but to follow. Surely she wouldn't get close to the hogs with a clean dress on. And shoes. She was wearing shoes to town.

Before his thoughts went any further, he followed her, catching up before she reached the fence.

"You want to be careful not to get muddy."

She looked at him, her eyes crinkling as she smiled. "Don't worry. I know my way around pigs." She pointed to the fence posts. "My *daed* uses pieces of barbed wire fencing and attaches the ends of the trough to the fence posts."

Samuel looked at the mud-covered wooden trough. "He must drill holes for the wire to go through?"

Mary nodded. "Four of them. One in each end and two in the sides near the corners. He strings the wire through them and then twists in onto the fence post. The barbs on the wire keep the hogs from fooling with it and getting it loose."

"That would do it, I suppose."

"And it would save you the trouble of climbing into the wallow with them."

He shot a sideways glance. *Ja,* for sure, she was laughing at him. He picked up the first bucket and poured the slops into the trough. The hogs squealed, fought and grunted as they buried their snouts in the mixture of cooked grain, garden refuse and sour milk.

"The girls said you sold a couple of the pigs last week."

Samuel nodded as he grabbed two more buckets of slops and went around the side of the barn to where the young pigs were kept in a separate sty. Mary followed him, picking her way between mud puddles. Smaller and thinner than the sows, these pigs ate as much as their mothers. By fall they would be filled out and ready to butcher.

He dumped some slops into their trough. "I took two of these to the butcher last week."

"Aren't they a bit underweight?"

Samuel glanced at her again. She knew her hogs. The butcher had said the same thing, but Samuel fed them the same food *Daed* had always done.

He turned to the final pen. "This is my boar." He heard the note of pride creep into his voice.

Mary leaned over the fence. "He's a big one."

"Over six hundred pounds, according to my calculations."

"Measuring his girth and length?"

"Ja." He shook the pail to get all the slops out of it and into the trough. This girl knew her hogs, for sure.

"It's time to sell him, isn't it? I mean, *Daed* would have sold him before he got too big to…do what boars need to do." Her face turned bright red.

"The sows are just as big, so there's no problem." And no money to buy a new boar. That was the real problem.

Samuel stacked the empty pails and led the way into the barn cellar. As he set them next to the mash cooker, Mary stepped to the cellar gate and looked out over the fields.

"Is all this land yours?"

"From the woodlot to the creek, and to Sadie's place on the other side. Fifty acres tillable."

"Why haven't you planted anything?"

He stared at her back. Maybe her *daed* had sent her to Indiana so he wouldn't have to listen to the constant questions.

"No plow. No work horses."

"You should consider it, anyway. Growing your own corn or barley to feed your hogs would save you money in the long run."

Samuel thought about her suggestion as she turned back to gaze toward the woodlot. He had purchased a neighbor's field of corn last fall, stunted from the drought and heat. Chopped and stored in the silo, the silage had fed the hogs through the winter. But now that source of feed was gone, and he was feeding them seed barley that had sprouted. The grain elevator in Shipshewana had sold it cheap, but it still cost something. What would he feed them when that ran out?

Shoving his hat back on his head, Samuel stepped up next to Mary and gazed out at the fields. Eighty acres stretched out, including the wood lot and the ten acres *Grossdawdi* had given to Sadie for her use. That left plenty to plant, but *Daed* had sold the plow and work horses years ago. Nothing had been planted in the fields as long as Samuel could remember. He had tried haying it once, but weeds had overtaken the land and there wasn't enough grass to make the work worthwhile.

It was a wasteland.

And he was spending the little cash he had to buy grain to feed his hogs. *Daed*'s way of doing things just didn't make sense sometimes.

Mary leaned on the top of the gate in Samuel's barn cellar. He stood next to her, looking out on the fallow acres of his farm. He was a confusing man.

On one hand, strong and solid. Comfortable. He was becoming a friend.

On the other hand, the way he kept his hogs was the most wasteful and lazy way she had ever seen. *Daed* kept his hogs in a field, not closed in some pen. And he let them graze in the pastures, moving them often so they wouldn't overgraze the grass.

"Where did you learn how to raise hogs?" She turned toward him as she asked the question.

Samuel shrugged, the caked mud on his shirt flaking off as it dried. "From *Daed*. I take care of them the way he taught me."

"At home, we pastured the hogs. They ate grass and other things in the fields, and being out in the sunshine helped them grow faster and better."

Samuel scowled. "They're doing fine. *Daed*'s ways have been working for years."

Mary bit her lower lip to keep the words in that she wanted to say. That Samuel was wrong, and perhaps his *daed* wasn't the best teacher. But that would only spoil their tenuous friendship, and it wasn't her place to tell a man how to manage his own farm.

He flicked at a glop of mud on his arm, then looked at her. "You never said why you're going to Shipshewana."

"We have some extra eggs, and I thought I'd see if any of the shopkeepers are interested in buying them."

"Eggs?"

"The hens are laying well, and we don't want them to go to waste."

"You can always can them. Save them for winter when the chickens don't produce so well."

Mary swallowed quickly as the thought of the quarts and quarts of canned eggs filling the cellar shelves made her stomach turn. "We already have too many pickled eggs. Folks have been very generous sharing canned goods with Sadie."

"I give our extra eggs to the hogs. They love them."

Mary glanced at the sacks of grain piled near the mash cooker. "You buy grain to feed the pigs?"

"When I can get it cheap."

"I still think you should raise your own grain." She bit her bottom lip before she said any more. He would think she was trying to tell him how to farm.

"I told you, I don't have the equipment to plant."

"I noticed the Yoders, across the road, have finished with their planting already. Ask if you can borrow their horses and plow."

Samuel rubbed at his chin. At least he wasn't getting angry at her suggestion.

"I suppose it wouldn't hurt to ask."

"If they aren't willing to help, there will be someone at church who will, for sure." She smiled, confident that he would take her advice. "You can ask tomorrow, when you help with the plowing."

"The plowing?"

"I heard you talking about it with the other men at

dinner last Sunday. You haven't forgotten, have you? You promised you would be there."

Samuel rubbed at a spot of mud on his shirt. How he could worry about that one spot when the rest of him was caked with the stuff was beyond her.

When he didn't answer, she took a step closer. "You did forget, didn't you?"

"I didn't forget. But they don't want me there. It will be best for me to stay home."

Mary shook her head. Did he even hear what he was saying?

"If you don't go, you'll only prove that the one man was right. Remember? He said you wouldn't show up. You need to prove to him that he's wrong."

"Martin Troyer. And I can't prove that he's wrong." He looked at her from under his lowered brow. "He was right. Everything he said was true. You heard what he said."

Mary studied the man standing beside her. He looked just like a six-year-old boy waiting to be punished for some infraction as he stood with his thumbs threaded through his suspenders and one foot kicking at the dirt.

"Just because you haven't helped in the past doesn't mean you can't help tomorrow." This was the perfect opportunity to start over, to prove that he could change.

"I tried to help at a barn raising last summer." He straightened, rolling his shoulders as if he bore a weight that was too heavy for him. "They didn't want me there. Didn't want my help."

"I heard you tell the minister that you'd be there. You gave your word."

Samuel sighed and rubbed the back of his neck. "My

daed's word never meant anything. He never kept his promises, and they don't expect me to, either."

"You," Mary said, pointing her finger at his chest, "are not your *daed*. He isn't here, but you are. You don't have to follow in his footsteps." Especially when those footsteps are leading to ruin, she wanted to add. But she pressed her lips together, holding the words in.

He leaned on the top rail of the gate and looked across the fields, but didn't answer her. She left him standing there and made her way out of the barn, past the hogs and toward the house.

Judith stood at the clothesline, hanging dishtowels. When she saw Mary, she stuck the last clothespin on the line and waved.

"I saw you talking with Samuel and hoped you'd come up to the house."

"For sure I will. The real reason I came was to see if you and Esther want to go to town with me." Mary kept her words casual, but her heart pounded. If neither of them wanted to ride with her, she would have to go into town alone.

"I'd love to go, but I'll have to ask Esther. I'm not sure what she has planned for today."

Judith ran up the wooden steps to the covered back porch while Mary followed. The porch held a washtub on a stand, with a wringer attached.

As Mary stepped into the kitchen, she felt like she had walked into a house from a bygone era. Sadie's kitchen was modern and clean, with linoleum floors and painted cabinets, but the Lapps' kitchen had not been changed in years. With no doors on the cabinets, the bare shelves were open to the room. A small table stood near the stove, barely large enough to seat more than four people.

The floor, clean and smooth, was bare wood, with remnants of brown paint showing around the edges.

Judith led Esther into the kitchen from the front room. "We would both like to come with you, if you don't mind."

Esther's smile was contagious. "It will be a fun lark, won't it? Going to town twice in one week!"

"And Mary won't hurry us along so that we can't look at the things in the store, will you?" Judith's grin was as wide as Esther's.

Mary felt the tension drop from her shoulders. "We'll have a lot of fun. I want to sell or trade some eggs, and I thought you might be able to help me find the best store to do that."

"*Ach*, for sure. We'll have to ask Samuel, but I'm sure he'll say we can go. His dinner is in the oven." Esther said. She untied her apron as she turned toward a narrow stairway. "We'll just change to clean aprons and we'll be ready."

As the sisters ran up the stairs, Mary peered out the window over the sink. The hogs' pen and the barn filled the view. The barn needed paint as much as the kitchen floor did. The entire farm spoke of long years of neglect. Of poverty. Sadie had told them about Samuel's *grossdawdi*, but not of his *daed*. Whatever kind of man he had been, Samuel seemed to be caught in the same habits he learned as a boy.

As Mary drove off with the girls, Samuel checked the angle of the sun. Not even midmorning yet.

Before he could talk himself out of it, he cleaned up on the back porch and changed into clean trousers. Scrubbing as much of the muck from the pigsty off his hands as he could, he rehearsed what he would say to Dale Yoder.

"Good morning, Dale."

He shook his head. He had never had much to say to his neighbor. These Yoders were Mennonite, and other than a wave when they passed on the road, he couldn't remember talking to the man in years.

"Fine day today, *ja*?"

At least the Yoders were Old Order Mennonite. They spoke *Deitsch* as plainly as he did, so they wouldn't have to worry about *Englisch* words coming between them. And he had known Dale since they were both boys in school. They weren't strangers.

He wiped his face with a towel, shoved his shirttail in and hauled his suspenders over his shoulders. *Daed* had never asked anyone for help. Never.

Samuel looked across the road toward the red hip-roofed barn. Mary was right. The fields had been plowed and planted. He hitched his trousers up and set his feet toward the road, wiping the sweat off his upper lip. His steps faltered as he reached the entrance to the Yoders' lane, and he stopped. Pulling off his hat, he ran his fingers through his hair.

"What's the worst he can do? Tell me to get lost?"

A boy riding a bike came down the lane toward him, gave him a wave and turned onto the road. Samuel hitched up his trousers again. If an eight-year-old could wave to him, he could talk to his neighbor.

He found Dale in the barn, cleaning the haymow.

"Good morning!" He shouted toward the high barn roof, hoping his neighbor would hear.

Dale looked over the edge of the mow. "Samuel Lapp? *Ach*, is there anything wrong?"

Samuel shook his head and stepped back from the ladder as Dale climbed down. "*Ne*, nothing wrong." He took a deep breath. "I need to plant some corn…"

The other man brushed some chaff off his trousers. "I don't remember the last time you folks planted anything."

"*Ja*, well, times are hard."

Dale looked at him, his eyes narrowed. "How have you been getting on since your *daed*'s accident? I've meant to come over but—"

Samuel held up a hand. "Don't worry about it. I didn't expect you to stop by after the way *Daed* treated you the last time."

He had forgotten until just now, but it all came back. Dale and his wife coming to *Mamm*'s funeral, and *Daed* throwing them off the farm in front of everyone.

"I'm sorry about that. *Daed* wasn't feeling well that day."

Daed had been drunk. But that wasn't the polite excuse for the way he had acted.

Dale led the way to a bucket of water placed under the shade of a sycamore tree in the yard. He took the cover off and offered a dipper of water to Samuel.

"So, you're going to plant some corn?"

Samuel smiled as the water slid down his throat. It had been flavored with ginger and tasted crisp and refreshing.

"I hope to. Someone suggested that if I grew my own grain the farm would be more profitable."

Dale nodded and finished off his dipper of water. "You're buying grain to feed your hogs?"

Samuel relaxed, leaning against the tree. Dale was just as easy to talk to now as he had been when they were boys. "When I can."

"Too bad the hogs can't forage on their own like the cattle do."

"Is that what you're raising these days?"

Dale gestured toward the eighty-acre pasture behind the barn where a good herd of steers grazed in the knee-deep grass. "The price of beef is high, and they're cheap to feed. I buy about twenty weaned calves at the Shipshewana auction each year, feed them on pasture for a few years and then sell them. I run about sixty head of the cattle on this pasture, buying and selling a third of the herd every year. It brings in a profit, and I don't have to fool with mixing slops for them like you do for hogs."

Samuel rubbed at his chin. Dale had a point.

"So then, you're planting corn?"

Samuel rubbed his chin again. "What do you feed the cattle during the winter?"

"Hay and silage. We're going to be mowing the back pasture next month and start loading the haymow."

"And you raise your own corn for the silage?" Samuel nodded toward the plowed fields between the house and the road.

"For sure. Raising our own feed for the cattle is necessary. Otherwise I wouldn't make any money doing it."

Samuel looked toward the cattle again and took a deep breath. Clean, sweet, fresh air filled his lungs. Dale had given him a lot to think about. If he grew his own grain, and pastured the hogs like Mary had suggested, would it make a difference? Could she have been right?

The thought strengthened his courage. He hitched his trousers up. "I came over to see if I could borrow your plow and team, if you're done with your planting."

Dale rubbed at the smooth bark of the sycamore tree. "I heard that your *daed* sold his equipment."

Samuel nodded, feeling his face redden. "He needed cash." For the next bottle. *Daed* had sold anything he could to buy the next bottle.

Dale's eyes narrowed again. "I've heard that you're just like him. Is it true?"

Samuel shoved down the sudden anger that had risen at Dale's words, but his jaw clenched.

"You mean, do I drink like he did? Just say it, Dale, and have done with it. You're wondering if I'm going to sell your team and drink away the cash."

Dale dipped into the ginger water again and held the dripping scoop as he looked at Samuel for a long minute. He drained the dipper and dropped it back in the bucket.

"I don't blame you for getting riled." His voice was mild. "But I had to ask. There are rumors, and I don't want to believe them. Now that I see you and talk to you, I can see that you aren't a slave to the drink the way he was."

"Rumors?"

Dale shrugged. "You know how people talk." He glanced at Samuel again. "I'll let you borrow my plow and team on one condition."

"Anything."

"I want to handle my own team, so I'll do the plowing and planting for you. In exchange, you give me ten percent of the crop."

Samuel chewed on his lip. Dale's suspicion rankled, but he had the upper hand and he knew it.

"Agreed. I'll buy the seed today."

"And I'll plow the field tomorrow. I'll be over first thing."

Samuel was supposed to help with Vernon Hershberger's plowing tomorrow. This could be the excuse he needed to avoid facing Martin Troyer and the others in the morning…but Mary was right. He had given his word.

"I'm busy tomorrow. Can we do it on Monday?"

Dale peered at him. "You're busy on a Saturday?"

"I'm helping a man from church with his plowing."

"You?" Dale grinned. "Maybe you're less like your *daed* than you look." He nodded. "Monday it is, then."

Mary guided Chester down the main street of Shipshewana, past the train depot and across the railroad tracks. On the corner of Middlebury Street and State Road 5 was a grocery store and Mary pulled into a spot along the hitching rail.

Even though Chester was standing quietly, she still grasped the reins as if she was driving. The store looked just like the one at home in Ohio. She glanced at Esther, sitting next to her. "Is this where you usually buy your groceries?"

"Samuel took us to a different store when we were here on Monday." Esther took the reins from Mary and secured them. "But we can try here."

Judith jumped to the ground on the other side of the buggy.

"I'll carry the eggs," she said as she reached for the basket in the back, "and you do the talking."

Mary's mouth was dry, but she felt better with Judith and Esther along. How could she have faced these *Englischers* without them?

She nodded and climbed down from the buggy seat. "Let's go in."

Mary led the way into the store with Esther and Judith following. A few men stood next to a display of tobacco, but didn't look up as they walked by. Mary headed straight to the counter at the back of the store where a woman waited for them.

"Good morning," she said. She eyed the basket Judith set on the counter. "I don't think I've seen you folks in here before."

Mary lifted her chin and smiled. She reached for the basket and pulled the towel off, revealing the eggs that she and Ida Mae had carefully washed that morning.

"I was wondering if you buy—"

"Nope. Never. The mister says we don't barter, and we don't buy except from our suppliers."

Mary felt her jaw drop at the woman's rudeness. She tried again. "But they're fresh, just gathered this morning."

The woman's head shook. "No it is, and no it will be." She smiled, but it didn't reach her eyes. "I'll be glad to sell you anything you need, though."

Mary's knees shook, but she straightened her shoulders. "No, thank you. I'm only interested in selling the eggs or trading."

The men's conversation had stopped and she heard footsteps heading their way.

"Anything wrong, Millie?"

The woman frowned over Mary's shoulder. "I told them we don't take barter."

Esther leaned forward. "Can you tell us if there's a store in town that would buy them?"

Millie started shaking her head, but the man behind Mary cleared his throat. She turned toward him as Judith picked up the eggs.

"You might try at the elevator. I heard they was buying eggs."

Mary kept her eyes focused on his shirt buttons and took a deep breath. "Thank you. We'll try there."

She followed Judith and Esther out the door, her knees shaking so much that she was afraid of falling with each step. She pressed her lips together as she felt the pounding in her head turn to a roaring. Not here. She couldn't faint here. She reached for Chester's tie as the girls climbed into the buggy and focused on the prickly hairs of the horse's chin. She counted silently, taking deep breaths. She had spoken to an *Englisch* man and nothing bad had happened. She would never need to talk to him again.

Fumbling with the tie rope, Mary climbed into the buggy and took the reins. By the time she sat down, her breathing had returned to normal and she could smile at Esther.

"Do you know where the grain elevator is?"

"Samuel went there on Monday. It's on the other side of the railroad station."

Mary clicked her tongue and Chester turned the buggy into the street again. A sudden thought made her stomach clench.

"The elevator," she said, trying to keep her voice from shaking, "is it owned by *Englischers*?"

"Mennonites." Esther pointed out the turn ahead. "They're a nice family, according to what Samuel said."

Mennonites. Mary pulled her lower lip in between her teeth. Perhaps dealing with Mennonites wouldn't be as bad as the *Englisch* men in the store.

She guided Chester to the hitching rail outside the grain elevator's office, next to a team of Belgians hitched to a farm wagon, and Judith jumped out of the buggy.

"I hope they take your eggs here, Mary." She looked

up at the tall storage towers that dwarfed the office building. "It doesn't look like the sort of place that you could trade them for anything, though."

"It won't hurt to ask," Esther said, climbing down next to her sister. "This is the only grain elevator in town, so it must be the one the man meant. And it is a feed store, also."

Mary finished tying Chester to the rail, clasped her hands together to stop their shaking, and led the way to the store. Dust was the first thing that greeted her. As she opened the door on its squeaking hinges, motes swirled in the sunshine that fell into the room ahead of the girls.

"*Ja*, well, I think you'll find we have the best prices around." A plain-dressed man stood behind the counter, speaking to an Amish farmer in a mixture of *Deitsch* and English. "On top of that, if you go to Elkhart to buy your seed, you'll have to factor in the cost of the trip." He glanced toward the door and smiled at the three of them. "I'll be right with you folks, if you don't mind waiting."

Mary smiled back, and she turned to look at the sacks of grain piled along the walls. Near each stack was a pail with a sample of what grain the sacks held. Next to the door was a display of Extension Office bulletins. Mary had just read the titles of the first two when the bell above the door rang, signaling the farmer's exit.

"What can I do for you?" the man asked. He was middle-aged, and wore his beard without a mustache, just like the married Amish men did.

Judith set the basket of eggs on his counter. "Do you buy eggs?"

He moved the cover aside and picked two of the eggs out of the basket and held them to the light that filtered in through the window. "We do, if they're top quality."

He returned those eggs to the basket and picked up two more. "These look fresh."

Mary stepped forward. "*Ja*, they are. Gathered just this morning."

The man peered in the basket, and then at Mary. "Do you have any more?"

Mary swallowed down the quick flutter in her throat. "These are all we have today. Does this mean you want to buy them?"

"I'll buy all the eggs you can bring me." He reached under the counter for an egg tray and started transferring the eggs from the basket into it. "I have buyers from Detroit who stop in every Tuesday, and buyers from Fort Wayne on Fridays. They buy as many eggs as I can supply for them. They sell them to groceries in the big cities."

Mary's head spun. If she and Ida Mae could deliver two dozen eggs a week…

"Could you bring twelve dozen a week?"

She stared at him. "Twelve dozen?"

"Fifteen dozen would be better. I can't get enough eggs to make the buyers happy." He grinned as Mary's mouth fell open and reached for a brochure from the display of Extension Office literature. "Take this home and look through it. It explains how to raise chickens for egg production on a large scale. A lot of the local farm wives have started providing eggs and butter for the city markets to help their family's income."

Mary looked at the drawing of a chicken on the front as the flutter turned into a bubble. She did some quick calculations in her head. To get twelve dozen eggs a week, they would need at least twenty hens. Twenty-four would be better. Or even thirty. She and Ida Mae would need to build a larger henhouse, and buy feed for the chickens. It would be a lot of work, but would it be worth it?

She cleared her throat. "How much do you pay?"

"Ten cents a dozen, if they're as good quality as these."

Ten cents. Fifteen dozen a week would bring in one dollar and fifty cents. Six dollars a month. Mary flipped through the brochure until she reached a picture of a large henhouse. *Dimensions for seventy-five hens*, said the caption. The bubble expanded. She could do this, with Ida Mae's help. Visions of a clean, airy new henhouse and yard filled with contented chickens swirled through her mind.

"And if I could bring you forty dozen?"

The man leaned his hands on the counter, his brow knitted as he looked her over. Wondering if she could deliver on her word, she figured.

"Now you're talking about going into business. That would be a mighty bit of work. You're sure your father won't mind?"

Mary smiled. Four dollars a week would be enough to pay all the household expenses and leave some cash to save. "Don't worry. We will enjoy the work."

He leaned forward. "You'll need a larger chicken coop, right? And fencing, feed, waterers? And more chickens?"

Mary nodded as the bubble deflated. She hadn't thought of the expense of going into this business. She would need boards and wire fencing for the new henhouse, and chicken feed. How much would it all cost?

"I'll loan you the money to supply what you need to get started. I'll front six dollars so you can buy the lumber, fencing and anything else you need. You should be able to pick up chickens at the livestock auction on Tuesdays, so you can build your flock up that way." He pointed a finger at the brochure in her hand. "But before you do anything, read up on what raising chickens on this scale demands. It isn't easy work."

"Why would you loan me the money?" Mary fingered the brochure, ready to hand it back to him. Her dream was slipping away as she considered the enormity of the project.

He waited until she looked up at him. "I have a daughter your age, and her family is struggling to make ends meet. She enjoys helping her husband by bringing in the income from her chickens, and she has worked hard enough to make it pay off. I'm sure you can do the same thing." He smiled again. "Besides, we both win on this deal. You sell your eggs, and I keep the big city buyers coming back."

He opened the drawer below his cash register and took out two dimes. "Here's your payment for the eggs you brought in today. Take the brochure home and discuss it with your family. Then the next time you come into town, you can tell me what you decide."

Mary rubbed the dimes together between her fingers as Judith picked up her empty basket and they headed for the door. Twenty cents, cash money. And this was just the beginning.

The girls were climbing into the buggy before Mary remembered. She ran back to the door and opened it.

"*Denki*, Mister… Mister…"

"Holdeman. Enosh Holdeman."

The bubble was back as she grinned at him. "*Denki*, Mister Holdeman. I will let you know what we decide."

Chapter Six

Saturday morning dawned cool and clear. A perfect day for spring field chores. Samuel frowned at the bright sunshine as Tilly trotted down the gravel road. Rain would have given him a good excuse to stay home.

Ahead, the Hershberger farmyard was crowded with horses. Some men had driven buggies, but a few had driven their plows, hitched to teams of Belgians or Clydesdales. Samuel chewed at his bottom lip as he glanced at the faces. Every one of those men had known *Daed*. Every one of them expected nothing more from his son. But Mary's words came back to him, and he rubbed the spot on his chest where her finger had pointed when she said them.

Mary was right. He wasn't *Daed*, and he didn't have to keep following in his footsteps. He turned Tilly in the drive and pulled to a stop alongside the other buggies. He considered unhitching her and tying her to the rope someone had strung along the shady side of the barn, but that meant he was committed to helping. Instead, he loosened her harness and left her standing in the shade of a tree.

He took a step toward the six men who had gathered in a group near the equipment, and then as he hesitated, he felt Mary's words prodding at him, as if she was poking that finger in his back. Taking a deep breath, he walked the rest of the way.

Martin Troyer was the first to spot him.

"Look who showed up."

As some other men stared at him, Samuel's steps faltered. Distrust clouded their features.

Jonas Weaver came toward him with a hand held out. "Good to see you, Samuel. We're just getting ready to divide the work, and we can use someone to drive Vernon's team."

Samuel glanced at the Percherons Jonas indicated. The giant horses stood quietly, but Samuel hadn't driven a team of work horses in more years than he could count. He glanced at the group of men. Martin Troyer and another man faced him with folded arms and lowered brows.

"I don't think driving a team is the right job for me." Samuel kept his voice quiet, but his words carried beyond Preacher Jonas.

"*Ja*, for sure." Martin Troyer stepped closer. "No job is the right one for you, is it?" He took the other men into his sweeping glance as he let out a short laugh. "Just like his *daed*. If he shows up, we still don't get any work out of him."

"Martin, that isn't fair." Preacher Jonas stepped between Samuel and the other men.

"You know it is. We know how these Lapps are. Lazy as the hogs that roll in that stinking wallow they keep them in."

Samuel's head pounded as he stepped toward Martin with his fists clenched. "I said I'd help. Tell me what you want me to do."

Martin laughed, and Samuel noticed smiles on the rest of the faces. "Give up, Lapp. You're cut from the same cloth as your *daed*. Make a big noise about how you are part of the community, and make promises to help, but then when the time comes—" Martin shrugged "—you're nowhere to be found."

"I'm here now." Samuel heard the growl in his own voice. *Daed*'s voice.

"Here, but are you sober?" Martin stepped closer and sniffed. "Can't tell. All I can smell is hog."

"I don't drink."

A quiet chuckle was Martin's response. He didn't believe a word Samuel said, so what was the use of trying?

Jonas's quiet voice cut through Samuel's growing headache. "We can't judge Samuel based on his father's actions." Jonas held up a hand as Martin started to protest. "Nor can we refuse to let Samuel help when he is willing."

Jonas turned to Samuel. "Why don't you think driving a team is the job for you?"

Samuel's hands clenched and unclenched. What did Preacher Jonas want? To make a fool of him?

"Forget it. Just forget it." He turned on his heel and headed back to his horse, anxious to be hidden by the line of buggies.

He fumbled with Tilly's harness as he heard footsteps approaching. The voices of the men drifted toward him as they arranged which team would lead the line of plows through the field. The footsteps stopped at the back corner of his buggy, but he ignored the intruder as he tightened the harness.

"What are you doing, Samuel?"

Preacher Jonas stood with his hands clasped behind his back, waiting for his answer.

"I'm going home. I'm not wanted here. You can see that as plainly as I can."

"Are you serious about wanting to help?"

Samuel rubbed the edge of the harness with his finger. Why was he here? He felt Mary's prodding finger in his chest. He was here to prove that he didn't walk in his father's footsteps, but he had thrown a tantrum worthy of the Lapp name. He leaned his forehead on Tilly's flank. Would he ever escape *Daed*'s legacy?

Jonas stepped closer and laid a hand on Samuel's shoulder. "You aren't your father, Samuel. You don't have to act like him."

Samuel turned his head to face the preacher. "But I am like him. Don't you see? Whatever I try, I end up acting just like he would." He swallowed down the tightness in his throat. "It's no use, is it?"

"There's a verse in the Good Book that speaks to this. I'm sure you know it."

Samuel's gut clenched. "*Ja*, I know the one. Somewhere it says that the iniquities of the fathers are visited upon the sons to the third and fourth generations."

"But that isn't the end of the story." Jonas squeezed Samuel's shoulder, then stepped over to lean against the tree a few feet away. "When a father acts as yours did, he sets a poor example for his family. Then the children can suffer. But there is another verse in Deuteronomy that tells us that each one of us faces the punishment for our own sins."

"So *Daed* was right? He always said a person couldn't

trust the Good Book because of all the contradictions in it."

Jonas shook his head. "There are no contradictions. Your troubles now might be because of your father's weaknesses, but that doesn't mean that you will face eternal punishment for them. You are your own man, and responsible for your own choices." He let these words sink in. "You can change the course of your life, and your family's life, by making the decisions your father couldn't. Your brother made that choice."

Bram again. The farmyard was quiet. The men and teams had gone out to the field.

Jonas straightened. "I need to join the others in the field. Vernon's team is waiting. You're sure you don't want to drive them?"

Samuel pushed the words out. "I can't."

"Think about what I said. With God's help, you can come out of the hole you've gotten yourself into. You can become a full member of the community, rather than a stray hanging around the edges."

Samuel eyed the preacher. His expression was as mild as ever, but his eyes burned with enthusiasm, as if he had just finished preaching a sermon.

"I'll consider it. I just don't know if it will do any good. The men won't give me a chance."

"Don't use that as an excuse." Jonas started back toward the barn and the waiting team. "There will always be Martin Troyers in your life. It's up to you to prove them wrong."

Samuel ran a finger between the harness and Tilly's warm side. Preacher Jonas was right, and if he was ever going to change Martin Troyer's opinion, it had to start today.

"Wait," he called to Jonas. "I'll drive the team, if they're well trained."

The preacher paused. "Why did you refuse before?"

Samuel glanced at the Percherons. "*Daed* sold our horses before he died, and I haven't driven a team since then. I'm afraid I'm out of practice."

Jonas grinned. "It's as easy as falling off a log with a team like this one. I'll help you refresh your memory, and then you'll be all set."

Samuel took the reins as Jonas handed them over and climbed into the seat of the plow. The thick leather straps molded to his hands and he gathered up the slack. One of the horses looked at him, as if he knew a stranger held the reins, but then, at Jonas's signal, Samuel called, "Hi-yup, there!" and the horses started toward the field.

Jonas jumped onto the step next to the seat and stood there as Samuel guided the team into the line of plows and engaged the blades. Martin Troyer kept his face straight ahead, but a couple of the other men gave him a friendly wave as he joined them.

"I don't think you need my help at all," Jonas said.

Samuel grinned. "Like you said, it's as easy as falling off a log."

Mary guided Chester through the crowded streets of Shipshewana. Tuesday morning meant the weekly auction, and folks from all over northern Indiana had flocked to town to either buy or sell goods. At the corner of State Road 5, she waited until the traffic cleared, then clucked Chester into a swift trot across the busy road.

Ida Mae leaned forward from the back seat. "Are you sure Mr. Holdeman will buy eggs again? You were just here on Friday."

"He said he would buy as many as I could bring him."

Sadie had been quiet during the trip to town, but as Mary turned into the Holdemans' parking lot she said, "I thought we were going to church." She turned toward Mary, her face pinched with worry.

Mary laid her hand over her aunt's. "You must have misunderstood me. I said we were going to town."

Sadie looked toward the feed store. "Why are we here? We don't buy things here."

Ida Mae and Mary exchanged glances. This seemed to be one of Aunt Sadie's bad days.

"It's all right." Mary picked up the egg basket and climbed out of the buggy. "You stay here with Ida Mae while I go in to sell the eggs."

Walking into the elevator's office, Mary smiled at the sound of the bell over the door. The ringing had jangled her nerves on Friday, but today the bell sounded like an old friend. Mr. Holdeman came out of a back room, wiping his hands on a rag.

"Well, good morning. I thought you might be back today." He gestured toward her basket as she set it on the counter. "I'm glad you brought more eggs. The buyer from Detroit will be here this afternoon."

Mary smiled at his welcome. "I only have one dozen today, if that's all right." Much to her dismay, Ida Mae had opened one of the many jars of pickled eggs for their lunch yesterday instead of cooking eggs for breakfast. But between that and skimping on the eggs they used during other meals, they had ended up with a full dozen.

"Like I said before, I can take as many as you bring me." He started transferring the eggs from her basket to a tray. "Have you given any more thought to my offer of helping to expand your business?"

"We have. My sister and I will work on the project together."

He nodded. "I thought you would, so I've talked to Hal Stutzman over at the lumberyard. All you need to do is stop by there, and he'll see that you get the lumber you need."

"I don't know what to say…"

"Don't say anything." He opened the cash drawer for her dime and handed it to her. "Just bring more eggs."

Mary had already climbed back in the buggy before she remembered that she had no way to take the lumber home. She told Ida Mae about Mr. Holdeman's offer.

"Then we'll just have to borrow Samuel's wagon and come back tomorrow."

"We won't need to," Sadie said as Chester turned the corner by the auction barn. "Samuel's here already."

Samuel had just pulled his springwagon into the driveway ahead of them, and the girls were with him. Pig snouts stuck out through the board sides.

Ida Mae leaned out of their buggy. "Judith! Esther!"

When the girls saw them, they spoke to Samuel and he halted the wagon while they jumped off and ran back to the buggy.

"It's a surprise to see you here," Esther said as she climbed into the back seat with Ida Mae.

"It's a surprise for us, too." Mary turned Chester into the field where lines of buggies and horses were tied along a hitching rail. "Did I see pigs in the back of Samuel's wagon?"

"He's taking them to the auction to sell so that he can buy seed corn."

Mary glanced at Sadie. She looked around with interest, as if she might see someone she knew. She seemed to have accepted that they were in Shipshewana this morning, rather than church. She turned in her seat to listen to the girls' conversation, and her face had lost the vague expression from earlier.

"What are you girls doing here today?" Judith asked.

"We're looking for some chickens to add to our flock," Ida Mae said as Mary pulled Chester to a stop along the hitching rail next to a bay horse.

"Then you decided to go into the egg business!" Esther grasped Mary's shoulder and gave it a squeeze. "That's exciting."

Sadie's face clouded again. "What business?"

"We talked about this yesterday, remember? Ida Mae and I are going to build a chicken coop and buy more chickens so that we can sell the eggs to Mr. Holdeman."

Her aunt smiled. "*Ach, ja.* I remember."

They went into the auction barn together, but Mary stopped just inside the entrance. The place was filled with people and noise, everything from cows bawling to horses neighing. All she could see were men in their summer straw hats and women in dark dresses. Old friends greeted one another with glad cries, while others walked along the aisles, peering at the animals for sale in the rows of pens.

Mary kept her hand in Sadie's elbow. "How will we ever find the chickens?" She had to shout, even though the other girls were gathered around her.

A man waved to get her attention. "Chickens are along the north side, over there."

She made her way through the crowds with Sadie, while Ida Mae followed with the girls. Nearly thirty cages of chickens were stacked in a corner, next to pens filled with hogs. Each cage held three or four chickens.

She happened to look toward the pigpens as Samuel guided a pair of his sows through a gate and closed it behind them. He wiped his face with a handkerchief before he looked around and saw them. A smile appeared as his eyes met Mary's and he made his way over to them.

"You're looking to buy some chickens?"

"*Ja*, for sure," Ida Mae said. "Mary and I are going into the egg business."

He had leaned over to look into a cage of Rhode Island Reds, but at Ida Mae's words, he shot a glance at Mary. "The egg business?"

As she nodded, he gave Esther a couple coins. "The hogs and chickens won't be up for a while yet. Why don't you take Sadie somewhere a little quieter and get some lemonade for everyone?"

Esther gave him a quick hug. "*Denki*, Samuel. We will."

Samuel grasped Mary's elbow as the others left. "Not you. We need to talk."

"What about?"

He ushered her out of the aisle until they stood alongside the pen holding his sows. "What is this about going into business?"

"Just what Ida Mae said. We're going to add to our flock. Mr. Holdeman at the grain elevator said he will buy as many eggs as we can bring him."

Samuel crossed his arms and rubbed at his chin with one hand. He looked much better today than he had the last time she saw him. His clothes were clean, and he wore the new trousers Esther had made.

"You can't put many more hens into the chicken coop in Sadie's barn."

"I know. That's why we're building a new henhouse."

His eyebrows rose. "A new henhouse? How many chickens are you thinking about?"

"I think seventy-five will be enough."

"Seventy-five?" He leaned against the hog's fence. "I don't think you know what you're getting into."

Mary pressed her lips together and counted to ten before she spoke. The barn echoed as the auctioneer started warming up for the horse auction. As the noise rose, she stepped closer to Samuel so she wouldn't have to shout. She looked up into his face, waiting for the panic that being this close to a man should bring, but there was only irritation with Samuel's assumptions that she wouldn't be able to follow through on her plans.

"I know exactly what I'm getting into."

"A lot of work and bother."

"*Ja*, a lot of work. But Ida Mae and I can do it."

He looked toward the auction arena, and then back at her. "Why? Are you bored? You don't have enough to do, taking care of Sadie?"

"I'm not bored. It's a way to earn a living. This is a good opportunity."

"You don't need to earn a living. There are plenty of single men around who are looking for a wife." He ran his thumbs up and down his suspenders. "Any one of them would be glad to marry you."

Mary's stomach seethed. "As if I'm some brood mare or sow, depending on some man for everything so that I can have a comfortable life?"

Samuel leaned toward her with amusement in his eyes. He was laughing at her!

"The man takes care of the woman and their children. That's how it is, and how it should be. You need to get married, not start a business."

Mary folded her arms around her middle. "That may be how it is for some women, but not for me." She bit her lip to hold back the sudden tears that threatened. The dream of a loving husband who would care for her and their family was gone. Long gone. She wasn't fit to be any man's wife.

Samuel tried to laugh at the set line of Mary's lips. She was as stubborn as Sadie, for sure.

"All right, all right. You don't have to get married." Samuel smiled as Mary's brows lowered. She reminded him of a setting hen, herself, with her mind focused on one idea. "But you don't have to worry about supporting yourselves. The church and our family have always taken care of Sadie. It doesn't make much difference if you girls are there or not."

"It does make a difference. Folks can't afford to give us as much as they have been. And there are other families in need." Her expression shifted. "Ida Mae and I are willing and able to work, but we need to stay on the farm to do it. Mr. Holdeman said that many of the farmers' wives are earning money this way."

"Holdeman." Samuel watched two men as they looked his sows over, but they moved on without asking any questions. "Holdeman is a fair businessman, and good to work with." He turned to Mary again. "I guess if you're determined to do this, I could help."

She allowed a smile then. "I hoped you would say that. We need to pick up some items at the lumberyard, but we don't have a wagon."

Her hands were clasped in front of her, and Samuel had the sudden urge to take them in his own. But his were calloused and worn. Dirty from handling the horse and the sows. Not worthy to touch her soft, slim fingers. He drew his fingers into a loose fist, hiding them.

"I'll be happy to help. We can swing by the lumber-yard after the sale is over." He was gratified to see her nod her thanks. "Do you want to see if the others have found some lemonade?"

Mary glanced toward the cages of chickens. "I'd rather look at the chickens. I've never bought anything at an auction before. How do I know I'll get the ones I want?"

He followed her to a cage of Plymouth Rock hens. The black-and-white bars on their wings set them apart from the cages of White Leghorns next to them. "First, don't get your heart set on any particular lot."

"Lot?"

"Each cage is sold either singly or in a group. Either way, that's called a lot."

"So I don't choose one? I just wait to see which one I win?"

Samuel shook his head. She didn't have any experience, and yet she thought she could go into business?

"It isn't as easy as that. You need to choose the ones you want to bid on, but be willing to let them go if the price is too high. How much did you plan to spend?"

"I have two dollars. Will that be enough?"

"The way the prices went the last time I was here, you should be able to get a dozen hens or so. Which breed are you thinking of?"

"I like these Plymouth Rocks. They're the same breed Sadie already has. But the Extension Office bulletin said that the White Leghorns are better layers."

"Extension Office bulletin? What's that?"

"Mr. Holdeman had a display of them in his store at the grain elevator. There were bulletins on nearly anything you can think of when it comes to farming. Ida Mae and I read the one on egg production. It was very informative."

"So if the White Leghorns are better layers, why would anyone want to buy the Plymouth Rocks?"

She turned toward him. "Because the Plymouth Rocks are also good for meat. It depends on why you're raising them." Her eyes narrowed. "I thought a man would know that."

He shrugged as he felt his face heat. "*Mamm* and the girls always took care of the chickens. I've never had much to do with them."

"So perhaps going into the egg business isn't such a strange idea after all." She perched her fists at her waist.

Samuel grinned. "I already said I would help you, didn't I?"

She smiled back. "You did, but I wasn't sure if you still thought I would be better off letting someone else take care of me."

Samuel felt his grin widen. Mary was smart, and could keep up with his teasing. She turned back to the chickens and examined a cage holding a rooster. Why had he said that stuff about her needing to get married? If she married someone, he would never be able to talk with her like this. As long as she was single, he was free to spend as much time with her as he wished.

"I think I'll bid on these." Mary indicated the ten white hens. "Do you think I need the rooster, too? Sadie doesn't have one."

"Only if you want to raise chicks. The hens will lay just as many eggs whether there's a rooster around or not."

She smoothed her apron as she considered his words.

"I guess if women can get along fine without men, then hens can, too."

She turned and walked toward another group of cages. Samuel followed her. Bantering with her was one thing, but this was going too far.

He grasped her elbow and turned her toward him. "What do you mean, women can get along—" He stopped when he saw the laughter in her eyes.

"I was only teasing you. I have to admit, men are convenient when there are heavy chores to do."

Folding his arms across his chest, Samuel planted his feet. "Haven't you known any men who were useful for more than chores?"

The light went out of her eyes as if he had blown out a flame. She sucked her lower lip in between her teeth. When she spoke, her voice shook like a willow in a storm. "Only my *daed*." She walked toward a large cage filled with six Leghorns.

Samuel swallowed. The look in her eyes...his mother had had that look.

He followed her again. In this corner of the sale barn, the noise was a dull roar. Everyone was focused on the horse sale, and no one paid any attention to the two of them.

"Mary, tell me. Has someone hurt you?"

She didn't look at him, but cleared her throat. "What makes you think that? Who would hurt me?"

She ended her speech with a little laugh, but he didn't believe her. *Mamm* had acted the same way, in the mornings at breakfast, even though Samuel had heard *Daed*'s voice through the floor berating her the night before. The averted gaze, the shaking voice. The denial that anything was amiss.

Something had happened to Mary. But if she wouldn't tell him the truth, wouldn't confide in him, he was as helpless as he had been as a boy. There was no way he could protect her.

Chapter Seven

After Samuel had unloaded the lumber and cages of the White Leghorn hens into the barn, where they would be protected, and taken Esther and Judith home, Ida Mae and Mary fixed a light supper of canned bean soup and some lettuce from the garden.

Sadie sat at the kitchen table, watching them work. "You didn't need to buy those hens."

Mary sighed. Some days Sadie required all the patience she could muster. "We've talked about this. Ida Mae and I need those hens to lay the eggs we're going to sell to Mr. Holdeman."

Her aunt muttered something as she picked an invisible piece of lint off the sleeve of her dress.

Ida Mae set the table with bowls and plates. "What did you say?"

"I said those white hens are evil. The speckled ones we have are good chickens."

Ida Mae sat next to Sadie and took her hand. "They aren't evil. Don't you think they're pretty with their white feathers?"

Sadie gestured toward Mary. "What is she doing here?

We don't need someone cooking for us. You're the only cook we need, Martha."

Ida Mae looked at Mary, and then back at Sadie. "Who is Martha?"

Sadie laughed. "Don't be silly. You're my favorite sister, you know that." She leaned toward Ida Mae. "Don't tell anyone else, but your cakes are the best around. Be careful, or that fellow from Holmes County will steal you away from us." Her finger, slender and slightly crooked, shook in Ida Mae's face.

Mary gripped the edge of the counter. "She thinks you're our *grossmutti*, Martha."

Ida Mae left Sadie at the table and stirred the pot of soup. "What are we going to do?" Her voice was a whisper, but Sadie heard her.

"Do? We're going to eat supper, that's what we're going to do. Send that other girl away and call the boys in from the barn." Sadie stood on shaky legs and walked to the silverware drawer. "I'll finish setting the table. You know the boys will be hungry when they come in."

Mary drew close to Ida Mae. "Let's just play along with her. We'll have supper, and then she'll be ready for bed. She'll be better in the morning."

Ida Mae nodded at Mary's suggestion, but she still wore a worried frown.

"The boys aren't eating here tonight. It's just us girls." She steered Sadie away from the drawer and back to her seat. "Mary is going to eat with us."

Sadie nodded and sat at the table, her expression vague once more.

She stared at the tablecloth while Mary dipped soup out for each of them and Ida Mae put the bowl of wilted lettuce on the table. The spicy vinegar smell of the dressing soothed Mary's nerves, and Sadie was quiet all through the meal. Perhaps the trip to Shipshewana had been too much for her aunt, but today had been a difficult day for her all around. When Sadie had eaten about half of her soup, she set her spoon down and folded her hands in her lap.

Mary nudged her sister under the table with her foot. "Why don't you go ahead and help Sadie get to bed while I do dishes? I want to get the chickens settled in before it gets dark, too."

"I think I'm going to go to bed right after Sadie," Ida Mae said as she rose and helped their aunt to her feet. "It's been a long day."

"It was fun to go to the sale again," Sadie said. She took Ida Mae's arm and her eyes were bright once more. "I don't think we've gone to the sale since we were girls, have we, Martha?"

"Sadie, you can call me Martha as long as it makes you smile." Ida Mae leaned down and kissed the top of the older woman's *kapp* as they headed toward the stairs.

Mary cleaned up the dishes in a few minutes, then went out to the barn. The sun was nearly gone, but the sky still held its light. She lit the lantern next to the barn door as she entered and peered into the stall that had been converted to a chicken coop. Sadie's hens clucked at the light, and peered out through their wire fence at the cages holding the new white chickens. Both groups started clucking at the disturbance Mary made in the quiet barn.

According to the extension bulletin, she would have to introduce the new chickens to the older ones gradually, or they would fight. Samuel had suggested lining the empty stall next to the chicken coop with chicken wire so the hens could see each other, but couldn't reach through to peck at the strangers. They had picked up some of the fencing at the lumberyard, and Mary rolled it out and started on the task.

As she worked, she thought of her soft bed and clean sheets. Ida Mae was right. It had been a long day. *Mamm* had taught her to take some time each evening to think of the worst part of each day, and ask the Good Lord for help with it. And then to think of the best part, and give thanks for it. As she hammered the staples into the wood to keep the wire fencing in place, she went over the day's events.

The worst part was easy. It was the crowds of people. Ever since… She stopped and reset the hammer. Ever since the attack, she had hated crowds. Especially crowds of strangers. It had been worse at home, before she and Ida Mae had moved here. There, she imagined she saw… She reached for more staples and braced the fencing again. Harvey. She whacked the staple with the hammer and positioned the next one. Harvey Anderson could be around any corner. The staple sank into the wood. If only she could make Harvey disappear as easily. Whack, whack, whack. Three staples in a row, and it was time to turn the corner.

The best part. What was the best part of the day? She hammered in a staple to hold the top edge of the fencing.

Buying the new chickens? Twelve new chickens to start building up their flock. That was a good part of the day. But was it the best?

She finished fastening the fence along the top rail of the stall, and then started the bottom row.

Samuel. The look in his eyes as he stared at her hands.

As if… She straightened her back and stretched. As if he wanted to hold them.

Mary shook her head and hammered in five staples in a row. Her thoughts had no business dwelling on Samuel and what he might want to do. He was Judith and Esther's brother, that was all. A helpful friend. A man she could feel comfortable with.

The hammer slowed and she sat back on her heels. But this change in him… Lately he had been kind rather than gruff. And he had asked if someone had hurt her. How could he have known? She hadn't told anyone her secret. No one knew. And yet Samuel had asked.

She couldn't tell him. Not that shameful secret. She couldn't tell anyone.

Her eyes pricked as she fought to hold back the tears. Harvey Anderson had taken everything from her. Her future. Her dreams. She wasn't fit to be a wife to any man.

She swallowed the knot that was growing in her throat and dropped the hammer onto the dirt floor of the stall. She had tried to convince herself that she could spend her life as Sadie had, unmarried but still a blessing to her community…but would that ever replace the life that had been stolen from her?

Samuel left the wagon in the center of the barn floor, still loaded with the sacks of seed corn he had bought at Holdeman's Feed Store. The two sows had brought in enough to buy the corn he needed, but just barely. He still didn't understand why they hadn't sold for more. They were in their prime, and had a few years left to produce litters of piglets.

He rubbed down Tilly and let her into her stall. The door to her pasture was open, and she walked out to the grass and rolled before settling down to graze. Samuel leaned on the stall gate watching her. Her coat gleamed in the rosy light from the setting sun and the chestnut color contrasted with the deep green of the grass. He rubbed his nose, letting the scene soak into his mind. Beauty. He had never thought of his farm being beautiful before. Work. Hard work. Care. Worry. Dirt. But not beauty.

By the time he reached the house, Esther and Judith had supper ready. After the usual moment of silence, Samuel reached for the biscuits.

"We had so much fun in Shipshewana today," Esther said. She set a glass of water at his place and poured one for Judith. "I hope we can go to the sale again sometime."

"I'd like to have more time to shop. Did you see the glassware in the window of the department store?" Judith said.

She took the biscuits as Samuel crumbled one on his plate and reached for the bowl of gravy.

He looked at her, the gravy spoon in midair. "You're not thinking of buying new dishes?"

"*Ach, ne.* That would cost too much money. But I do like to look at them. They are so pretty."

Pretty. He looked around at the bare kitchen cupboards and gray, sooty ceiling over the stove. No one could call this kitchen pretty. Not like Sadie's kitchen, with the white cabinet doors to keep the dishes clean and the scrubbed floor.

"Perhaps you'll receive some dishes like that for a wedding present." Esther's voice held a smile.

Samuel looked from Esther to Judith. "Who is getting married?"

Judith looked down at her plate and Esther's smile

disappeared. "No one, Samuel. I was only saying when the time comes for Judith—"

"That time will never come." Judith cut a bite of her biscuit covered with gravy with the side of her fork. She shrugged. "No fellows will come here to court one of us."

Samuel looked at them again, the steaming food on his plate forgotten. "Why not? Katie and Annie both found husbands."

He didn't remind them of how hard it had been for both of their older sisters to go against *Daed*'s—and his—wishes. They had disobeyed, sneaking out to attend Youth Singings in neighboring districts, meeting boys.

Judith pressed her lips together, making him wonder if she had ever thought of sneaking away to a Singing.

"But their beaus never came to the house." Esther pushed at her food with her fork. "No one wants to come here."

"There's no reason why a boy shouldn't stop by." An unsettled feeling rumbled in Samuel's stomach. "I mean, if he's the right type of boy."

He stuck his fork into a biscuit. As far as he was concerned, no boy would be the right type for one of his sisters.

Esther and Judith exchanged glances. "It's the hogs."

Samuel had just taken a bite and he let Esther's words sink in as he chewed.

"What about the hogs?"

Judith wrinkled her nose. "They smell."

He let out a short laugh. "Of course they smell. They're hogs."

Esther leaned forward. "But they don't smell good. They smell terrible. The neighbors complain about it."

"Not to me they don't."

His sister bit her lip, as if she was afraid to go on.

"Why don't I hear the complaints?"

Judith squirmed in her seat. "They know what a short temper you have."

He felt his face heating and he gritted his teeth to keep his voice even. "I don't have a short temper."

The girls glanced at each other, but didn't say anything.

"Who said I have a short temper?" The words came out as a bark, but Samuel didn't care. He hit the table with his fist to make them look at him. "Who said it?"

Judith's face mottled pink as she ran from the table and up the stairs. Esther dared to glance at him.

"Sometimes…" Her voice was quiet and her face was as pink as Judith's. "Sometimes you act just like *Daed*."

Samuel stared at his hand, clenched and ready to strike the table again. He swallowed and loosened his fist. *Ach, ja.* Just like *Daed*. Why did he even try to deny the rage that boiled inside him?

"Esther…" His voice failed. He cleared his throat. "Tell Judith I'm sorry. Go find her and tell her to finish her supper."

She sat in her chair on the opposite side of the table, holding her elbows, staring at her plate…the table…anywhere but at him. Looking just like *Mamm*.

"You're right." She raised her eyes at his voice. "Sometimes I'm too much like *Daed*, and I hate it."

He left the table and went into the front room. Lighting the lantern on the table, he walked over to *Daed*'s desk along the wall. It was an ancient piece, with a lid that closed. He unlocked it with the key that was left in the lock and opened the lid, pulling out the supports as he lowered it to make the desk surface. He hadn't opened this desk since *Daed* died. Hadn't wanted to face him or anything he had left behind.

Bringing a chair over, he sat down and reached for a small black book. A diary. Opening it, he saw *Daed*'s scribbled handwriting.

Worked in the woods today. Got paid ten cents.

Samuel looked for the date. January first, nineteen thirty-five. The year *Daed* had died.

The next two days were blank. Then the fourth day: *Worked in the woods. Ten cents. Went to town.*

Samuel flipped forward to May. The month before Daed died.

Sold ten pigs. Paid off note at Harmon's.

Samuel shifted in his chair. Harmon's was the store in Elkhart that sold liquor.

Sick today. No work.

The next week was blank. Then: *S asked about selling the hogs. Wants to try cattle. Told him to...*

Samuel closed the book and buried his face in his hands, elbows on the desk top. He had forgotten that day. *Daed* had gotten angry when the subject of cattle was mentioned. Took after him with a hay fork and Samuel hadn't come home until after he was sure *Daed* was in bed.

He opened a drawer. It was filled with *Daed*'s diaries. Small leather-bound books, each with the year's date on it. He flipped through the one dated nineteen thirty-one. The year *Mamm* had died. He stopped when he got to October twelfth.

Margaret died today. Funeral tomorrow.

Nothing more. The next page was blank. The following one said: *Old sow farrowed out of season.*

The following pages held sporadic notes about the

farm or work he had done, but *Daed* had written nothing more about his wife of twenty-five years.

Samuel got the old tin waste basket from its place by Esther's…*Mamm*'s…rocking chair and dumped the diaries into it. He went through the papers in the cubbyholes. Bills of sale. A mortgage on the farm. Lists of debts. Samuel put the bills that had been paid off into the trash. The mortgage paper went back into the slot it had come from.

When the waste basket was full, he took it out to the burning barrel next to the boar's pen by the barn. Taking a match from his hat brim, he struck it on the side of the barrel and held the match to the first piece of paper. A receipt from Harmon's. The fire licked at the edge, then as it caught, Samuel dropped it into the barrel. He added the papers, one at a time. When they were burning, he opened the first diary and tore out the pages. He dropped them into the flames, then threw in the cover. When the diaries were all in the barrel, he turned the waste can over and shook it so that every last scrap went into the flames.

The flames lit the darkness around him.

Scrap wood was next, from the pile he kept next to the barrel. He fed the fire slowly, watching the flames eat up the papers and leather-bound diaries. Watching *Daed* disappear.

Mary turned the buggy onto the road and gripped the reins firmly as Chester set off toward town. If only her knees would stop shaking. This was her first time to go to town alone since the attack. But she was only going to Shipshewana, she reminded herself. No need to be nervous.

It had been a week since she and Ida Mae had purchased the new hens, and she had four dozen eggs in her basket. The chickens were beginning to settle into the new chicken coop Dale Yoder had built for them, using the lumber from Enosh Holdeman, and Mary was determined to pay off her debt as soon as possible.

Ida Mae had asked why she didn't get Samuel to build the new chicken coop and Mary still didn't have an answer. She glanced toward the Lapp farm as Chester trotted by, but there were no answers there, either.

It wasn't that Samuel wouldn't have done the work for them, but... Mary loosened her hold on the reins as Chester's pace became steady. But what? Was it because of the expression on Samuel's face every time she saw him during the past week? It had to be only her imagination that Samuel had guessed her secret.

Perhaps she had asked Dale because then she wouldn't have to defend her actions to Samuel.

Either way, the new henhouse looked just like the picture in the extension brochure. A roomy building with nest boxes and a large outdoor pen for the hens to scratch and peck all day long. The White Leghorns and Sadie's Plymouth Rocks had finally learned to accept each other, and the hens lived in as much harmony as sixteen chickens could.

As Mary drew closer to town, she suddenly remembered that Tuesdays were the day for the auction. Dozens of buggies filled the roads, and she had to let Chester pick his way through the crowds to the far side of town and the grain elevator and feed store. She tied Chester to the rail outside the feed store and reached for the basket of eggs.

Facing the door, she smoothed her apron and checked

her bonnet. She would do her business with Mr. Holdeman and then return home. Nothing could be more simple.

She frowned at her shaking hand as she reached for the doorknob, and walked into the store. The bell chimed and she took a deep breath.

Mr. Holdeman came out of the back room. "Hello, Mary. Good to see you again. How are those new chickens?"

"They are doing well and beginning to lay eggs." She set the basket on the counter and took off the towel.

"Then you must be making them feel at home."

Mr. Holdeman reached for a tray and transferred the eggs, counting as he went.

"Four dozen even." He opened the cash drawer. "And here are your forty cents." He laid the money on the counter.

Mary shook her head. "I want to use the money to start paying off my loan."

"Are you sure?"

As Mary nodded her head, the sound of peeping came from the back room. Mr. Holdeman thumbed over his shoulder.

"We just got in some baby chicks, and I have a dozen that aren't spoken for yet."

The peeping continued and Mary looked past the grinning man to a cardboard box on a table. Little beaks poked through the holes.

"Besides, if you use all your income to pay back the loan, you won't be able to continue growing your business until it's paid off."

He got the box and set it on the counter next to Mary's

dimes. He opened the lid and Mary couldn't help herself. She reached into the pile of chicks.

"They're so little." She picked up one of the fuzzy black-and-yellow balls. Plymouth Rock chicks.

"Just a day old. All they need is warmth, food and water. In six months, they'll be laying for you. An extra dozen eggs a day for a nickel's investment now."

"Five cents?" Mary ran a finger along the fuzzy back.

"Five cents for the chicks. Another nickel for the starter feed I sell. Enough to keep them going until they can be put in with the older chickens." He picked up another one of the chicks. "Don't forget, they need to be kept warm, so keep them in a box by your stove for the first couple weeks."

She couldn't help smiling at the tiny things. Returning the chick to the box, she said, "All right. Take the thirty cents to start paying the debt, and the last dime for these wee things."

"You carry the box of chicks and I'll get your bag of starter feed."

He followed her out to the buggy and put a heavy bag in the back seat. Mary frowned at Mr. Holdeman. It had to weigh at least fifty pounds the way he had hefted it.

"Are you sure that big sack of feed is only five cents?"

"Well, you caught me on that." He held up a hand as she started to protest. "Take it as a gift from me. You and your sister remind me of my own daughters. Think of it as an investment in your business."

"*Denki*, then. And I'll be back on Friday with more eggs."

He waved as she turned Chester toward the street again. The chicks peeped louder as the buggy lurched onto the road and Mary felt a giggle tickling her throat.

She smiled at the frantic peeping that settled down as soon as Chester was on the pavement of the city street.

As she stopped at the corner of State Road 5, a familiar wagon on the opposite side of the intersection turned to the right, heading toward the sale barn.

"Hello!" Samuel waved as his horse made the turn. "What are you doing here?"

Mary wasn't about to shout across the intersection to answer him—the other drivers were already laughing at Samuel—so she turned Chester to follow Samuel's wagon down the road and into the driveway leading to the auction. She pulled up to the hitching rail next to the other buggies like she had last week, then headed toward the livestock area behind the barn where Samuel had disappeared.

As soon as she started through the line of wagons waiting to turn into the lot behind the sale barn, she was sorry. The men were all farmers, and none of them spoke to her, but she could feel them staring as she strained to see Samuel's wagon among the others.

She was ready to turn back to her buggy when she saw him standing on the seat of his wagon, looking through the crowds. She waved to get his attention, and he jumped to the ground and started toward her. When he reached her side and took her elbow, she nearly grasped his hand, she was so relieved to see him. He led her back to his wagon and helped her onto the high seat.

"Wait here while I unload the hogs."

She smiled her answer and settled herself, looking around. A few other women sat with their wagons like she was doing, while their husbands or brothers unloaded the stock they were hoping to sell at today's auction. The noise made calling from one wagon to another impossible, so she nodded to the ones who waved to her, and waited.

Samuel had a wagon full of hogs. In a crate by himself was his boar. The rest of the wagon bed was packed with the animals standing head to flank, pressed against each other so they wouldn't fall during the trip. Mary counted them as Samuel backed the wagon to a chute leading into the larger pens outside the barn. Twenty-three pigs. His entire stock, including the sows.

She grabbed his sleeve as the wagon halted. "Are you selling all of your hogs?"

His smile was grim. "That's right. No more hogs for me."

"Then what will you do?"

"I'm buying weaned steer calves." He gestured to another wagon that was unloading into a pen across the way. "Like those. Half grown, ready for pasture."

He went around the wagon and opened the back gate. As he guided the hogs down the chute and into the pen, Mary noticed the difference in his features. With every hog that clambered down the chute, Samuel looked a little bit happier. A little more relaxed. When the wagon was unloaded, including the crate with the boar, Samuel drove out of the livestock yard and back to the field where she had left the buggy.

As he pulled the horse to a halt, he turned to her. "You still haven't answered my question. What are you doing in town today? Buying more chickens?"

"I came to sell eggs to Mr. Holdeman, and I did end up buying some chicks."

"You're really going into this egg business, aren't you?" He jumped down from the wagon and gave her his hand to steady her climb down. "I saw the new chicken coop the other day."

"Ida Mae and I are enjoying the work. The new chicken coop just makes things easier."

He leaned against the wagon, more relaxed than she had ever seen him. She smiled at how much he reminded her of her brothers. But he was more than a brother, he was a friend. A good friend.

"I guess we're both starting new projects." The corner of his mouth twitched. "Since we're both here, and I have some time before the hog sale starts—" he ran his thumb up and down his suspender "—I don't suppose you'd like to have lunch with me at the café."

At the thought of lunch, her stomach rumbled, turning the twitch into a full grin. "I think I had better take you up on the offer before I faint from hunger."

He offered her his arm and she took it. A friendly gesture demanding nothing in return.

She smiled up at him as they walked across the grass toward the café, her hand safe in the crook of his elbow. She hadn't been this relaxed with a man in months. If only every day could be like this.

Chapter Eight

No-church Sundays were the best days of the month. Samuel leaned on the gate enclosing the twenty-acre pasture holding the young steers. A day with no work, no trip to a church meeting, no demands.

He leaned down to pluck a grass stem and chewed on the sweet end. The young steers had settled into their new home easily enough. After he bought them at the auction, Samuel had spent last week strengthening the existing fence and using the old hog fencing to divide the pasture from the corn field. Dale had planted the seed corn on Wednesday, and now all he had to do was wait for rain.

The pasture had everything the cattle needed except water. He had a well near the barn, but had to pump the trough full three times a day. He could use a larger watering trough, but until he sold the cattle there was no cash to pay for it. So, he pumped. He threw the grass stem away and plucked another. Maybe he should try fixing the old windmill.

"Samuel! Dinner is ready."

Esther's call was faint, drifting from the house to the

YOUR PARTICIPATION IS REQUESTED!

Dear Reader,

Since you are a lover of our books – we would like to get to know you!

Inside you will find a short Reader's Survey. Sharing your answers with us will help our editorial staff understand who you are and what activities you enjoy.

To thank you for your participation, we would like to send you up to 4 books and 2 gifts – **ABSOLUTELY FREE!**

Enjoy your gifts with our appreciation,

Pam Powers

SEE INSIDE FOR READER'S SURVEY

Get up to 4 Free Books!

Romance ⬥ **Historical**

We'll send you 2 Free Books from each series you choose plus 2 Free Gifts!

Try **Love Inspired® Romance Larger-Print** books featuring Christian characters facing modern-day challenges.

Try **Love Inspired® Historical** novels featuring Christian characters confronting challenges in vivid historical periods.

Or **TRY BOTH!**

YOUR READER'S SURVEY
"THANK YOU" FREE GIFTS INCLUDE:

▶ 2 lovely surprise gifts ▶ Up to 4 FREE books

PLEASE FILL IN THE CIRCLES COMPLETELY TO RESPOND

1) What type of fiction books do you enjoy reading? (Check all that apply)
- ○ Suspense/Thrillers ○ Action/Adventure ○ Modern-day Romances
- ○ Historical Romance ○ Humor ○ Paranormal Romance

2) What attracted you most to the last fiction book you purchased on impulse?
- ○ The Title ○ The Cover ○ The Author ○ The Story

3) What is usually the greatest influencer when you <u>plan</u> to buy a book?
- ○ Advertising ○ Referral ○ Book Review

4) How often do you access the internet?
- ○ Daily ○ Weekly ○ Monthly ○ Rarely or never

YES! I have completed the Reader's Survey. Please send me 2 FREE books and 2 FREE gifts (gifts are worth about $10 retail) from each series selected below. I understand that I am under no obligation to purchase any books, as explained on the back of this card.

Select the series you prefer (check one or both):

❏ **Love Inspired® Romance Larger-Print** (122/322 IDL GMRL)

❏ **Love Inspired® Historical** (102/302 IDL GMRL)

❏ **Try Both** (122/322/102/302 IDL GLYY)

FIRST NAME	LAST NAME

ADDRESS

APT.#	CITY

STATE/PROV.	ZIP/POSTAL CODE

barn. He could see her in his imagination, standing on her tiptoes to get as close to the kitchen window as she could, and calling to him. *Mamm* had called to *Daed* the same way, every dinnertime that he could remember.

When he reached the front of the barn he saw Sadie's horse and buggy tied to the hitching rail by the back door. The surprise would have sent him into a bad mood a few months ago, but now… What had changed? He quickened his pace toward the house. The difference was simple. He looked forward to seeing Mary.

Mary, her sister and Sadie had brought a big bowl of potato salad and some cold ham. Esther had set the table for the six of them, and they crowded together in the kitchen. Another reminder of the past, when all his sisters and Bram lived at home. He squeezed into his seat against the wall and pushed away the prickly memories.

Sadie sat next to him, then fussed. "This chair is too short for me, Mary. Will you trade places?"

"I'll give you mine, Sadie," Esther said, jumping up and picking up her chair to move it around the table.

But the older woman waved her away as Mary moved from one seat to the other. "That's all right. This will work fine." She sat down with a smile and a slight wink in Samuel's direction.

Mary leaned over. "She's up to her tricks again," she said, keeping her voice low.

Samuel shrugged. "It doesn't matter. I don't mind if you don't."

That brought a smile as she turned away and concentrated on straightening her silverware.

After dinner, Samuel took the chairs out into the shady part of the yard while the girls cleaned up the dishes.

"There is something different around here," Sadie said as she made her way through the rough grass toward him. "What have you changed?"

Samuel nodded in the direction of the bare dirt patches next to the barn. "I sold the hogs."

"That's it." She nodded, satisfied. "That change certainly improves the place." She gestured, taking in the farmyard and the fields beyond. "With the hogs gone and cattle in the pasture out there, the farm looks more like it did when Abe was alive."

Samuel had sat on a chair near hers, leaning on his knees, but when she mentioned his grandfather he had to ask, "Why was *Daed* so different from *Grossdawdi*?"

Sadie didn't answer right away. She watched the cattle make their way to the shady corner of the pasture, then turned to him. "Sometimes folks make decisions that take them down wrong paths." She waved at a fly that had landed on her apron. "Your *daed* was full of rebellion as a young man. Hated the farm and everything about it. But when Abe became ill, he seemed to settle down. Came back to the farm. Married a fine girl. Started a family." She patted his hand. "Your *mamm* was a good woman, you know that?"

He nodded and waited for her to go on.

"But that rebellion seemed to continue under the surface, and then the drinking started." Her smile dimmed and her eyes became moist. "But I don't need to tell you this. You remember what he was like."

Samuel reached into the grass to pick a dandelion and twirled it between his fingers. "Do you think I'm like him?"

"In some ways." Sadie's head tilted as she watched

him. "You look a lot like him. But you act more like Abe. You remind me more of your grandfather every year."

A buggy turned into the driveway, followed by a second, larger one. As they pulled up, Judith and Esther ran out of the house.

"Annie!" Esther said. "It's *wonderful-gut* to see you."

Samuel rose from his seat and helped Sadie to her feet. Another surprise. His stomach turned as he saw Bram's family climbing down from the second buggy. A truce with his brother was one thing, but was he ready to spend the afternoon visiting with these folks from Eden Township?

"Samuel, good to see you." Annie's husband walked toward him, hand outstretched, and Samuel had no choice but to welcome him with a firm handshake.

"Glad you stopped by—" Samuel paused, trying to remember his name.

"Matthew." The shorter man grinned, his brown eyes bright and his brown beard bobbing as he nodded his head. "When you stopped by to see Annie a couple weeks ago, you made her so happy. She's been bubbling with joy ever since."

Samuel looked from Matthew to Annie. She and her sisters stood in a circle with Mary and Ida Mae, fussing over the little boy Esther held in her arms. They both seemed to have forgotten the day Samuel had thrown them out of the house.

Bram's wife joined the group and Bram headed toward him and Matthew, carrying a young boy and trailed by a girl and the boy Samuel had seen when he stopped by their farm. Would he ever remember their names?

Bram nodded at Matthew and Samuel as he came

close. "We hoped you would be at home this afternoon. Ellie and Annie wanted to visit."

His brother's voice held a note of caution.

"*Ja*, sure, we're glad you came." Samuel worked up a smile. "Look at the girls over there. Who would they have talked to if you hadn't come?"

The little girl pulled at Bram's sleeve and he stooped down, setting the small boy on his feet.

"May we see the cows?" She pointed toward the pasture.

"That is up to Uncle Samuel. They're his cows."

Samuel swallowed as the girl's big brown eyes turned toward him. Uncle. He was an uncle to these children. Four of them, and from the looks of Annie and Bram's wife, there would soon be two more.

"You can look at them from the fence, but don't go into the pasture. These are young steers, and not very friendly."

"Johnny, will you take Susan to see the cattle? But listen to Uncle Samuel."

As the children ran toward the barn, Bram grinned. "You sold the hogs?"

"How could you tell?"

Bram took a deep breath. "The whole place is different. The hogs were—"

"Dirty? Smelly? Stinking?"

His brother nodded. "All three. What made you change?"

His stomach turned again, facing Bram's questioning. Why couldn't he just leave it alone? Nobody invited him to come by and poke his nose in where he wasn't wanted. Then he looked past the men at the circle of women, still standing at the edge of the drive, talking up a storm. He would be polite and make the best of things for their sakes. He could do that.

"It just seemed like a good thing to do." He started toward the house as the girls drifted their way. "I'll get some more chairs so we can visit."

Bram started after him. "I'll help."

Samuel turned on him, his stomach clenching. "I can do it." He felt the growl creeping into his voice. "Stay here with the others."

His brother took a step back, a troubled frown on his face. "Sure, Samuel. If that's what you want."

He stalked into the house. He didn't need Bram's help. He didn't need Bram telling him what to do. He didn't need Bram in his life at all.

Stomping up the stairs to fetch a couple chairs from the girls' rooms, he glanced out the window toward the group on the lawn. Judith and Esther were smiling. Annie laughed at something Ellie had said. Even Mary looked at ease and happy.

Why did he have this anger surging inside him?

Samuel sat on one of the chairs and buried his face in his hands.

There was a wall between him and his brother. Something about the man set his nerves on edge. Always had. But it seemed that Bram didn't feel the same way, laughing and joking with the others. Leaving him out.

Samuel rubbed his hands over his face again. Sadie was wrong. He was too much like *Daed* and not at all like *Grossdawdi* Abe.

Mary kept a close eye on Sadie as the afternoon wore on, but she seemed to keep her energy, participating in the conversations and even walking with Ellie's youngest, Danny, to see the cows in the pasture.

They hadn't had another bad day like the Tuesday they had all gone into Shipshewana together, but she and Ida Mae had been vigilant about keeping their aunt rested, and they hadn't tried an outing like that one since.

As the Eden Township folks prepared to head home later in the afternoon, Annie took Mary aside.

"I was glad to see you visiting the family this afternoon."

Mary had to return Annie's infectious smile. "My sister and I have gotten to be friends with Judith and Esther."

"That's good." Annie smoothed her apron over her rounded stomach. "When I was at home, we didn't see people from outside the family very much. Once *Mamm* passed away, we didn't go anywhere except to church." She gave Mary's hand a squeeze. "I'm so happy they have friends close to their own ages."

"They've been good friends for us, too." Mary glanced at Ida Mae as she and Sadie chatted with Ellie. "It's difficult to move to a new area."

Annie nodded. "For sure, it is."

As the families got into their buggies, Annie gave Mary a quick hug. "*Denki*. And whatever you're doing for Samuel, it's working."

"I'm not doing anything for him. We're just getting to know each other."

Annie laughed. "As long as I've known him, he has never sat and visited with folks the way he did today." She looked around and took a deep breath. "And the farm is so pleasant. I've never seen it looking so…so…right."

She beamed when she found the word she wanted, then climbed into the buggy with Matthew.

After the buggies had disappeared down the road, Mary looked for Samuel, but he had disappeared.

"He went to get Chester for you," Judith said. "Unless you aren't ready to go home yet."

"We had better get Sadie home before she gets too tired." Across the yard Sadie struggled to pull a chair toward the house, but Ida Mae stepped in to help her. "We should stay and help you straighten up, though."

"Don't worry about it," Judith said. "We had a good visit, and you're right. Sadie needs a rest. If she stays here, we won't be able to stop her from helping."

Samuel came from the direction of the barn with Chester and hitched him to the buggy. When he was done, he headed back toward the barn without saying a word. Mary seemed to be the only one who noticed, though, as Sadie and Ida Mae were saying their goodbyes. Samuel disappeared into the barn, but Mary could see him lingering near the doorway, as if he was watching them. Back to his old grumpy self.

Mary waved to him, but he only turned away. She climbed into the buggy next to Sadie. They called goodbye to the girls as they started the short drive home.

Sadie sighed. "Now that was a fine visit."

"I was surprised to see Annie and Bram and their families come by," Ida Mae said from the back seat. "They haven't been here before, have they?"

Sadie shook her head. "Not since Annie was married, I think. But she loved the idea when I suggested it."

Ida Mae leaned forward. "You suggested it?"

"When we were at Annie's for the quilting. I told her

that the girls would love a visit some Sunday afternoon. They need to be close to their family."

Mary shifted the reins to her left hand and gave Sadie's shoulders a hug. "You're always so thoughtful. I'm glad we came to live with you."

She left her arm around Sadie as Chester turned into the drive without any direction and stopped at the end of the walk leading to the back door.

Ida Mae jumped out of the buggy and reached up to help Sadie down. "I think that horse could go anywhere without a driver. He just reads our minds and takes us where we want to go."

Sadie chuckled. "Anywhere he wants to go, you mean. He knows it's time for his oats." She walked to the horse's head and patted his nose before heading up the sidewalk.

Her steps were halting, as if walking was difficult. Chester headed toward the barn and his supper, but Mary's mind was still on Sadie. Perhaps it was time for her to start using a cane. She would hate to see the elderly woman suffer from a fall when they could prevent it.

After taking care of Chester for the night, Mary checked on the chickens. The new henhouse still smelled of fresh sawed wood and whitewash. The hens gathered around her when she let herself into their yard, knowing the routine as well as she did. She filled their waterers as the hens chose their roosting spots, then she closed the door and latched it. No foxes would get these chickens.

The sun still lingered in the sky as she went in the back door, but Ida Mae had lit the lantern over the kitchen table. Sadie sat in her chair, leafing through a magazine as Ida Mae stirred a pot of soup on the stove. Mary stifled the sigh that rose. She didn't want to complain about the bounty of food in the cellar, but this was the third time they were having canned bean soup in the last four days.

Ida Mae had also brought a jar of canned peaches up from the cellar and Mary picked it up. Bits of cinnamon stick and cloves floated in the juice.

"Spiced peaches? This is a treat."

"I found them with the jars of regular peaches, and I thought they would make a nice change." Ida Mae reached into the cupboard for a bowl to pour them in. "I have to say, though, that it will be nice when the garden starts producing. My mouth has been watering for fresh tomatoes."

"And we haven't had any since September." Mary bit her lip as memories from last fall flooded her mind. It was September when she had pestered *Mamm* and *Daed* to let her take a job in town, at the little diner next to the hardware store. If she hadn't taken that job, she would never have met Harvey Anderson. She gripped the edge of the counter as gray clouds swirled, and she counted, silently, staring at the edge of the cabinet.

"You're doing it again." Ida Mae had her fists balled on her hips and was staring at her.

The swirls disappeared as Mary faced her sister. "Doing what again?"

Ida Mae glanced at Sadie, who was ignoring them, and leaned closer to whisper, "Every so often, for the past few months, your face goes blank and you look like you're going to faint." She bit her lip as her eyes welled with tears. "You're scaring me. What is wrong?"

Mary took a step back. "I'm all right. It's nothing for you to worry about."

"But I do worry. First I lose Seth in that horrible accident, and now I'm afraid that you're going to have an apoplexy or something." She wiped her eyes with the corner of her apron. "I don't want to lose you, too."

Mary tried to smile as she took Ida Mae's hand and squeezed it. "I'm not going anywhere."

Her sister held on to her hand. "But you already have. We used to talk about everything, but now..."

"You're right." Tears filled Mary's eyes and she blinked them away. When they were girls, she and Ida Mae shared all their secrets. Their dreams. Every moment of their days. "I've never let you talk about Seth."

"And we've never talked about what happened to you."

Mary swallowed. "What happened to me?"

"When you came home that day in February with your clothes all dirty, and you had been crying. I waited for you to tell me, but then...well, Seth's accident, and then moving here to Indiana..." She held Mary's gaze and didn't look away. "I miss how close we used to be. Whatever happened, we need to talk about it. It has put a wall between us, and I don't want it there anymore."

Mary took a deep, ragged breath. Her secret was a burden that weighed her down, but could she share it with Ida Mae?

"After supper. We'll talk after supper."

When Sadie's buggy disappeared down the road, Samuel turned his attention to his chores. The afternoon had been torturous, sitting with the family and pretending everything was going well.

After he poured oats into Tilly's feed box, he went to the pump and started filling the water trough again. The steers crowded around as the fresh water gushed from the spout, and Samuel's sour mood lifted. The steers were a good investment, so far. They grazed on the rich spring grass during the day, relieving him of the chore of cooking mash and making slop for the hogs. The oppressive atmosphere around the farm had lifted with the clean odor of the pastured cattle. The change had been a good one.

As he pumped, he thought back on the afternoon. Bram had been friendly. Pleasant, even. He and Matthew had visited together the way longtime friends did, with inside jokes and speaking of folks Samuel had never met. Was that what had turned his mood sour?

The trough finally full, Samuel lowered the handle with a clang. He leaned on the fence and watched Tilly push her way through the herd of cattle to get some of the water. After dipping her nose into the cold water, she lifted it and looked at him, water dripping from her chin.

"Hello, Tilly-girl." Samuel kept his voice soft, in the tone she liked.

She took a step closer and laid her chin on his shoulder, soaking his shirt. He patted her cheek and smoothed the hair along her neck under her mane. Her affection over the last few weeks continued to take him by surprise. He had never had an animal that liked him. *Daed* had never allowed dogs on the farm, and the barn cats were all half wild. Tilly's willingness to be near him hammered against that place in his head that told him that animals were only dumb creatures, created to be used. Nothing more.

He stroked her neck once more. *Daed*'s voice again. He tuned it out.

Had it been *Daed*'s voice that had made his temper

rise this afternoon? Made him see Bram and Matthew as enemies?

Tilly stuck her nose back in the water for another drink and Samuel headed toward the house. He picked up the two chairs remaining in the yard and carried them inside, his mind still on the afternoon. He still didn't know what had bothered him so much about the afternoon visits from Bram and Matthew and their families. The girls had enjoyed spending time with them.

Maybe it was the bond he had seen between the folks from Eden Township. He was the odd one out. Again.

And he hadn't said goodbye to Mary.

Esther and Judith were working in the kitchen as he walked in.

"Supper will be ready in a few minutes."

Samuel set the chairs around the table. "I'm not hungry."

He was too restless to sit and eat.

Esther glanced at him, looking more like *Mamm* than ever.

"I forgot to send Sadie's bowl from the potato salad home with them. Would you take it over when you go in the morning?"

Samuel grabbed the bowl. "I'll take it over now. The walk will do me good."

As Esther and Judith exchanged glances, he could tell that his attempt to keep the growl out of his voice hadn't been successful. *Ja*, he needed the walk over to Sadie's.

He took the path through the fields. Darkness had fallen while he had been in the house, and now only a pale gray sky remained of the day. Light glowed from Sadie's windows, and he could see the three women in the kitchen. Mary gathered dishes from the table as Ida

Mae helped Sadie into the back bedroom. He knocked on the door, and Mary hesitated.

"It's only me," Samuel said. "I have Sadie's bowl."

She opened the door. "*Denki.* I had forgotten that we took it over to your house this morning." She took a step back. "Do you want to come in?"

Samuel leaned in. "I don't want to disturb your supper."

Mary waved him in. "We've finished, but there are a few spiced peaches left. Sit down and I'll get a dish for you."

Samuel hung his hat on a peg near the door and sat down. Sadie's kitchen was always bright and clean, but this evening, in the lamplight, it was an island in the dark.

He smiled as Mary set the peaches and a spoon in front of him. "These smell delicious."

Mary sat in a chair next to him. "I don't know who made them, but they are very good."

Cutting into the peach half with the edge of his spoon, Samuel took a bite and nodded as the sweet juice filled his mouth.

"Good. Very good." He took another bite and looked at Mary. "I didn't come over only to return the bowl."

Her eyebrows went up.

"I guess I need to apologize. I never thanked you for coming over today, and bringing dinner to share."

"We had a lot of fun getting to know some more of your family."

Samuel moved the rest of the peach half around in the juice. "*Ja*, well, they were a surprise."

"You don't sound like it was a pleasant surprise."

He peered at her. "I didn't expect them to be there, that's all."

"I watched you talking with Bram and Matthew. They get along well together."

The restlessness came back at the mention of the two men and he pushed away from the table. "They do. The peaches were good."

She followed him out to the back porch. "What did I say to chase you away?"

He turned his hat over in his hands, then stuck it on his head. "Nothing. It's nothing."

"It's Bram and Matthew, isn't it? They're friends with each other and you feel left out."

"I'm not some schoolboy who wasn't chosen for the softball team."

"But you are Bram's brother, and you don't act like you are."

His throat constricted and his words came out as a growl. "We're not brothers. We only happen to have the same parents."

She was silent then, and he turned to leave. But she came after him.

"Wait."

He stopped at the bottom of the porch steps and looked up at her. The scent of cinnamon and vanilla wafted toward him.

"No matter what has gone on between the two of you in the past, you have to admit that Bram is trying. He came over to see you today. Doesn't that tell you he wants to be friends?"

"You don't know what it was like, growing up with our *daed*."

She came down one step and her head was even with

his. "I don't know what it was like for you growing up, but Sadie has told us some things about your family. I understand that your father was a hard man to live with."

He shrugged. "You're right."

"But that is the past."

He felt a weight drop off his shoulders at her words. She was right. He took her hand in his. "And I'm not my *daed*."

She didn't pull her hand back, but squeezed his, leaning close. "You're not your *daed*."

If Mary thought Ida Mae might forget the promised talk, she was wrong. When she came back inside after saying good-night to Samuel and making a final check on the chickens, Ida Mae was sitting at the kitchen table with a pan of light brown fudge and two cups of mint tea.

Ida Mae smiled when she saw Mary. "Remember how we used to sneak downstairs after *Mamm* went to bed and made fudge?"

"Where did you find the sugar?" Mary slipped into her chair and took the spoon her sister offered her.

"I used some from the sugar bowl, and then added some honey. I couldn't find any chocolate, though, so it's a vanilla fudge."

Mary spooned some of the warm candy into her mouth. "Mmm. More like caramel."

"I cooked the sugar and butter together before I added the milk, but I wasn't sure how it would turn out."

"Perfect."

Ida Mae took a bite on her spoon and held it up, admiring the rich color. "So. Tell me what happened last February."

Mary swallowed as she turned her cup of tea around

on the saucer. "It is something terrible. Are you sure you want to hear?"

Her sister put her spoon down and took both of Mary's hands in hers. "I'm here to listen. And it can't be as terrible as what I've been imagining."

Mary looked at her and Ida Mae sucked in her lower lip. "Or maybe it is."

"There was a young man. A boy, really." Mary took a deep breath. "He worked at the store next to the diner where I worked last winter."

"I don't remember any Amish boys working there."

"He wasn't Amish."

Ida Mae waited for her to go on.

"He…was friendly at first." She swallowed. "And he would ask me to meet him in the alley behind the diner after work. He said he would buy me a soda pop."

"Did he?"

"The first time." Mary remembered the fuzzy feeling of the pop sliding down her throat. "I liked it. It was orange."

"But then?"

"We met every Friday night, after the stores closed, and before I walked home. He was funny. Told jokes. When he tried to put his arm around me one time, I told him I couldn't do that. And he laughed and said I'd learn to like it."

"Did he stop?"

"That time he did. But then the next week he told me how pretty I was, and how I should take off my *kapp* so he could see how long my hair was…" She stopped. Her voice was shaking and Ida Mae squeezed her hand.

"Were you in love with him?"

"Maybe." Mary blinked back the tears that sprang into her eyes. "I don't know. I don't think so."

"Did he kiss you?"

Mary couldn't look at Ida Mae. "He did much more than kiss me." Tears tickled her cheeks as they tracked down to her chin. Her voice shook, but she kept on, feeling the burden of her secret lift as she shared it with her sister. "That night in February, he wouldn't stop. He wouldn't listen to me. He pushed me down to the ground…"

Ida Mae scooted her chair over and pulled her close in a hug. "Shh. It's all right. You don't have to tell me more."

"Every time something reminds me of it, I…" She hiccupped. "I start shaking, and I feel like I'm going to faint."

"What can I do to help you?"

Mary leaned her head on her sister's shoulder. "You've been through a terrible time, too. How can I ask you to help?"

Ida Mae pushed Mary up and looked into her eyes. "Because we've both been through terrible things. We need each other."

Mary swiped at her cheek. "And I've been shutting you out. I was afraid that when you learned how shameful I had been…"

"What is shameful about being a victim?"

"If I hadn't asked *Daed* to let me work in town, and if I hadn't been so friendly with…with Harvey…" She swiped at another tear. "I know I led him on, making him think I was a different kind of girl—" She sniffed. "I'm so ashamed of what I did."

"Don't." Ida Mae's lips pressed together. "Don't blame

yourself. I've been blaming myself ever since Seth died. I wanted to go on a picnic with him that day, but I never told him. If I had made him go with me, he wouldn't have been in that accident."

Mary shook her head. "Seth's accident wasn't your fault. You didn't know he was going to fall into that machine."

"*Mamm* finally convinced me of that, just before we left home. But don't you see? You're trying to blame yourself for the terrible thing Harvey did. It isn't your fault. It's his."

"But if I hadn't…"

"Don't make excuses for him." Ida Mae brushed a lock of Mary's hair behind her ear with a tender touch. "He made you trust him. He took something that didn't belong to him. It isn't your fault."

Mary squeezed Ida Mae's hand. "Tell me again, which one of us is the older sister?"

"Will you tell Samuel?"

"Why would I tell him?"

Ida Mae shrugged. "You are good friends with him, aren't you? And the way he looks at you…"

Mary's stomach turned. "What do you mean, the way he looks at me?"

"He's in love with you."

"He can't be." Mary shook her head. "He can't."

"Why not?"

"Because I'm never going to fall in love. I'm never going to get married."

Ida Mae twined her fingers in Mary's. "Is that what you really want? What about the dreams we had as girls?"

Mary watched her sister's face as Ida Mae struggled

to keep a smile. "Have you given up on yours, now that Seth is gone?"

She shook her head. "Seth was the best thing that ever happened to me. I still can't imagine living my life without him. But then I think about Ruth, in the Good Book. Her husband died, but she was faithful and honored her mother-in-law, and look what happened to her." Her smile became peaceful. "She married a good, honest man who loved her. Don't you think God could have something like that in our future?"

"For you, for sure." Mary smiled at her sweet sister. God would have another young man who would be perfect for Ida Mae.

"And for you, too."

Mary shook her head. "Not for me. No man wants a woman like me for a wife. I'm content with what He has given me. Sadie and I will be happy together."

Ida Mae squeezed her hand again. "Samuel may have something to say about that."

Chapter Nine

It was Thursday morning, and Samuel had propped the chicken coop doors open while he cleaned out the litter and mess from the winter. He had let the chickens run into the yard to scratch and feed on whatever they found, and they clucked with every bug they ate. He leaned on his shovel in the doorway and watched them.

While he still had the hogs, the hens had stayed in their yard. The hog wallow with its flies and leftover slops was too tempting for the hens, but it was a dangerous place for them. More than one chicken had ended up being a meal for the hungry sows.

He went back to shoveling soiled bedding into the wheelbarrow, but his conversation with Mary on Sunday evening kept intruding, just as it had all week. Did Bram want to be more than friends? Could they be real brothers? Could they leave the past behind them? The idea was tempting. Starting over. Clearing out the old and starting fresh.

After the chicken house was cleaned out, Judith and Esther brought out a bucket of sudsy water and some old brushes, and the three of them scrubbed the roosts, nesting boxes and floor.

Judith coughed. "Do you think the hens will appreciate all of our hard work?"

"We will when we come out to gather the eggs in the morning." Esther gave the roost another swipe, then swished her brush in the bucket.

When they finished, Samuel gave the floor a final rinse with a pail of clean water and they retreated to the fresh air of the barnyard. The girls went to change their clothes while Samuel got the bucket of cracked corn to scatter for the hens, grinning at their eager clucking.

Just as he finished, Sadie's buggy came up the lane and stopped outside the house. Setting the empty pail inside the henhouse, he met Mary just as she stepped down. He frowned to banish the smile. She didn't need to know how happy he was to see her. Since she and Ida Mae had taken over his chores at Sadie's, he missed seeing her every day.

"What brings you by?"

She waved a paper. "I got a letter from Ellie."

Ellie? "Bram's wife?"

"She said on Sunday that she had a hen sitting on some eggs, and she would give me some of the chicks when they hatched."

Samuel couldn't stop his grin. She looked like a young girl, she was so excited. "She wrote to tell you they have hatched."

"She said I could come and get them, but I don't know where they live."

"So you want me to take you?"

"Would you be able to? I have a dinner packed, since it's so late in the morning. We can eat it on the way."

Samuel crossed his arms. "What if I'm busy?"

"Then Esther or Judith could go with me. But I thought you would like to see your brother." She leaned closer to him and lowered her voice. "I thought you'd like to show him that you aren't always as grumpy as you were on Sunday afternoon."

Scratching his jaw, Samuel eyed Mary. Her cheeks were dimpled, as if she was laughing at him.

"Was I that bad when they were here?"

"Not that bad, but not as friendly as you could have been. Sadie says you've become a new man over the last few weeks."

"Humph." He tried to scowl, but Mary's smile broke through. "All right. Let me change out of my work clothes, and then I'll take you. Come on in and visit with the girls while you wait."

Mary went into the kitchen with Judith and Esther while Samuel washed up on the back porch. As he changed into clean clothes in his room off the kitchen, he could hear their voices, but couldn't make out the words. Were they talking about him? About how Sadie said he had changed?

He looked down at the soiled work clothes he had piled on the floor and tucked his shirttail into his clean trousers. If only getting rid of his unpredictable temper was as easy as changing his clothes. He had fought that temper all Sunday afternoon, but it hadn't shown itself since. Would seeing Bram again start it all over?

Not if he could help it.

Samuel paused before he opened the door leading to the kitchen. That was the problem. He couldn't help it. He fingered the doorknob. *Mamm* would tell him to pray about his temper, and for help as he talked to Bram this afternoon. Could he do that? Would the Good Lord even listen? He raised his eyes toward the ceiling.

"God, if You're there," he whispered, "help me keep my temper today. Don't let Mary see me at my worst."

No answer.

When he opened the door, a trio of faces met him.

"We're going to go over to Sadie's while you and Mary visit Bram and Ellie." Esther's smile was brighter than he had ever seen it. "Mary said they're sewing a new quilt top today, so we're going to help."

Samuel looked from one to the other. Before Mary and her sister had moved here, Esther and Judith had never visited their neighbor. They rarely left the farm, except to go to church or a quilting.

Esther's face fell. "Unless you don't want us to."

That's when he realized he was frowning. "*Ach*, I want you to. I'm glad you're going."

"We'll be home before supper," Judith said.

"If you want to eat supper there, that will be fine. I'll fix something for myself when Mary and I get home."

The girls stared at him.

"What's wrong? Have I sprouted wings or something?"

Judith chewed on her lower lip. "Do you know how to fix your supper?"

"For sure, I do." Samuel looked around the kitchen. How hard could it be? "There's a loaf of bread, and we have butter in the cellar, right? I'll fix myself a sandwich."

Esther grinned. "If you're certain you don't mind…"

He flapped his hands at them. "Go to Sadie's. Have fun. Don't worry about me."

Judith squealed and ran up the stairs to her room and

Esther gave him a quick hug before heading to the front room, where she kept her sewing basket.

Samuel grabbed his hat from the hook by the door and looked at Mary. She was smiling as she followed him out the door.

"That was very nice of you," she said, as she climbed into the buggy seat. She sat on the passenger side and handed him the reins as he climbed in.

He shrugged his shoulders. She didn't need to make it sound so noble.

"It wasn't anything. I just thought they would have fun." He turned Chester onto the road and they headed west.

"Think about it," Mary said. "When is the last time the girls ate supper someplace besides home?"

Samuel searched his memory. "I have no idea. They always stay at home."

She nodded. "They stay at home because they need to take care of you. You just gave them an entire afternoon of not having to worry about you."

He felt a frown lowering his brow. "I'm not such a bother."

"Maybe not, but you're there. You need to be fed, your clothes need to be washed, your house needs to be cleaned…"

Samuel raised a hand to halt her words. "I understand." He grinned at her as he turned Chester south at the next intersection. "So I did a good thing?"

She smiled and leaned back in the seat. "*Ja.* A *wonderful-gut* thing."

Mary relaxed in the seat and watched the scenery go by. Chester trotted along, his hooves tapping out a comfortable rhythm on the road. Buggy wheel tracks stretched along the dusty ribbon as far as she could see. She still hadn't gotten used to the straight-as-arrow roads and flat land of her new northern Indiana home.

"So, Sadie has been talking about me?"

Samuel's voice startled her out of her thoughts.

"Not in a bad way." Mary brushed some dust off her skirt. "She likes you very much, you know."

He sat a little straighter. "That's good, because I like her, too." He used the whip to brush a fly off Chester's back. "She has always been good to me, even when…"

His voice trailed off, as if he thought he had said too much.

"Even when what?"

"When *Daed* was at his worst." Samuel glanced at her. "Has Sadie told you about him?"

"Only that he could be difficult, and that he had some problems."

Chester trotted on.

"*Daed* was a drunk."

Samuel had said it quietly and with no emotion. It took a minute for Mary to realize what he meant.

"You mean he drank alcohol? How often?"

"All of the time. But sometimes he got angry when he drank. Those were the bad times." He looked at her. "Sadie always knew, somehow, and would come up with some chore for Bram and me to do at her place, to give us an excuse to be away from home."

"What about the girls?"

"*Mamm* took care of the girls. She protected them."

Mary bit her lip and stared at the side of the road. She couldn't imagine a family like that. A sudden thought made her stomach clench.

"Sadie has said that you had learned some bad habits from your *daed*…"

"You want to ask me if I drink?"

She nodded.

"*Ne*. Never. That's one thing Bram and I agreed on when we were young. We promised each other that we would never touch alcohol."

"Has it been hard to keep that promise?"

He shook his head. "Not for me. I have a bad enough temper that I never want to add drink to it. I saw what it did to *Daed*, and to *Mamm*."

They rode in silence until they passed the next intersection. Mary tried to imagine what a young Samuel had been like. She didn't have to imagine the warm refuge Sadie had given him. She had felt that welcoming safety herself.

"Enough about me. Tell me about your family."

Mary smiled. "*Mamm* and *Daed* have always been good parents. *Daed* is a minister in our church. There are eight of us children. I'm the oldest, and then Ida Mae. We have another sister and five brothers."

"Do you all get along?"

"Sometimes the boys squabble, but *Daed* puts a stop to that. Whenever they start arguing, he gives them a chore to do."

He chuckled. "That sounds like a good idea." He nudged her with his elbow. "What about you? What brought you to Indiana?"

Her insides went cold and she rubbed her fingers together. "You know. We came to take care of Aunt Sadie."

"Sadie has a lot of relatives who could have taken care of her. Why did you and Ida Mae come?"

Mary's finger began to hurt, so she rubbed a different

one. "Ida Mae's beau died in an accident. She wanted to move here, where the memories wouldn't be so fresh."

Chester's hooves clip-clopped on the gravel while she waited for Samuel's next question. Ida Mae had said she should tell him her secret, but she couldn't. She couldn't face the shame of telling him.

"Why did you come? You must have had a beau, too, didn't you?"

He watched her, waiting for her answer. Then he smiled when she shook her head.

"I...I don't have a beau. I thought Ida Mae would need me to be with her."

"Was it hard to leave home?"

"Ne...ja..."

Her throat filled as she panicked. He must think she was lying. She turned slightly away from him as she watched a herd of cows in a field. He had been open with her, telling her about the hurts from his past. But this secret...it was too fresh. And Samuel was still a man. She couldn't tell him, and she couldn't lie.

He laughed. "Which was it? Hard or easy?"

She could feel the wall between them, tall and thick as if she had built it out of bricks. She had nearly lost the close relationship she had with Ida Mae because of keeping her secret. Would she ever be able to be close to anyone, any friend, as long as she hid her past?

"Something happened, back in Ohio. Something that made me want to leave home." She took a deep breath as he took her hand in his. "Please don't ask me to tell you."

"I know someone hurt you. I can see it in your eyes sometimes."

Mary nodded. "Someone did hurt me, but it is over. I will never see him again."

"Him?"

His face was growing red as he stared at her.

"Please don't ask me any more about it. It's in the past, and I want to leave it there."

Chester trotted past Annie and Matthew's house. Matthew's work horses grazed in the pasture next to the barn.

Samuel sighed and sat back in the buggy seat. "If you don't want to talk about it, that's all right. But if you ever need someone to listen to your story…" He smiled at her. "Sadie is a good listener. And if you don't want to tell her, then I hope I can be as good a friend as she is."

Mary smiled her thanks as Chester crossed the next intersection.

Samuel pointed across the fields with his buggy whip. "There's Bram's place."

"By the creek? It's pretty, isn't it?"

"Ja." He sighed again. "Very nice."

As Samuel drove up Bram's lane, he felt that envy creeping back in. The house and barnyard were neat and orderly, and early summer flowers turned the yard into a lovely riot of color. Bram's wife, Ellie, stepped out onto the porch to greet them, and the two older children came running from the barn. What had Bram done to deserve this kind of life?

But he tamped down the irritation as he pulled Chester to a halt at the hitching rail by the house. He wanted this day to be a good one for Mary, and if he didn't control the direction of his thoughts, he would spoil it for her.

Mary jumped down from the buggy as soon as it stopped and went to greet Ellie. As Samuel tied Chester, the oldest boy approached him.

"Hello, Uncle Samuel."

"Hey there, Johnny."

Behind the boy, the little girl, Susan, peeked at him. He smiled at her, and she grinned back. Maybe Bram had never told them about his brother and how grumpy he could be.

"What have you two been up to today?"

Johnny thumbed over his shoulder. "We're helping *Daed* in the barn. Bessie is having a calf soon, so we're building a special pen for her."

"You're helping Bram?"

"*Ja*, for sure. I always help him."

The boy's chest swelled as he said this, and Samuel looked past him as Bram emerged from the barn. Their *daed* had always said that boys got in the way, and they would learn as they got older. But Johnny had been helping the last time he was here, and this time, too. That was something Bram had never learned growing up, and another reminder of just how far his brother had slipped out from under their father's shadow.

Bram joined Johnny and Susan, putting a hand on each of their shoulders.

"Samuel. I didn't expect to see you today."

Samuel tilted his head in Mary's direction. "Mary didn't know how to get here, so she asked me to drive. She said Ellie had written to her about some chickens."

"*Ach, ja.* The chickens." Bram tousled Johnny's hair. "And we're building a calf pen in the barn. Do you want to join us?"

"Can we play with the baby chicks?" Susan asked, looking up at Bram.

"For sure." Bram turned to Samuel as they ran to their mother. "I guess I've lost my helpers."

"Are they any good? I mean, you know how *Daed* said we were never a help to him."

Bram started back toward the barn and motioned for Samuel to follow him. "I've come to realize that *Daed*'s way wasn't the best way. What did we learn from the way he raised us?"

Samuel rubbed the back of his neck as he walked. "I suppose we didn't learn much."

Bram gave a short laugh. "I learned a lot of things I wish I hadn't. Like how to fear him, and how to be a bully. I learned how to get out of work by finding the easiest way to do things rather than the best." He picked a stalk of grass growing next to the barn door and snapped it in two. "I don't want Ellie's children—my children—to learn the same from me."

"But…" Samuel stopped and picked his own grass stalk. "How did you do it?"

"What?"

Samuel gestured around them at the barn, the yard, the sounds of the children calling to each other. "How did you know that there was any other way than what *Daed* taught us?"

Bram leaned against the doorway of the barn and crossed his arms. "I suppose the first time I thought I could live differently was when I bought a horse from Ellie's father, John Stoltzfus. You haven't met him yet, have you?"

Samuel shook his head.

"Some homes are like ours was. You just feel like you have to leave. To get away. The Stoltzfus farm is what a home should be. It reminds me of that time we visited *Mamm*'s parents when Annie was born. Do you remember that? The two of us spent a week with them."

Samuel smiled as the memory came back again. "It was a good week, wasn't it?"

"I want my home to have that same feeling of welcome. Of peace. So, I have spent a lot of time with Ellie's parents and their family, and I try to love and discipline my own family the way John does his."

Bram walked over to the half-built calving pen. "Would you hold the other end of this board while I nail it on?"

Samuel picked up the end of the board and held it while Bram hammered some nails into the other end. They worked together as Bram finished building the pen, then picked up a few nails that had fallen onto the floor.

"Now we're all set for Bessie to have her calf." He grinned at Samuel. "I appreciate you giving me a hand."

Samuel shrugged. "For sure. You would do the same for me, wouldn't you?"

Bram studied him. "I would. Because that's what brothers do."

"And we didn't get into an argument, even though you did use three nails where I would have used two." Samuel felt a grin starting.

"Two would have gotten the job done, but three makes it more secure." Bram grinned back as he put his tools away. "I was surprised to see that you had company when we got to the farm on Sunday. I'm glad the girls have friends." He turned to Samuel. "Or is one of Sadie's nieces more than a friend?"

Samuel felt his face heating. "What do you mean?"

"You know what I mean. You and Mary seem quite friendly today, with you driving her down here and everything."

Samuel's stomach started turning as if the puppies

were back, raising a ruckus. "I don't intend to be too friendly with anyone."

Bram closed his toolbox. "Why not?"

The churning in his stomach closed in on itself. "I'm too much like *Daed*."

"Who said?"

Samuel shrugged. "Everyone. I could see it in your eyes when you stopped by the farm last year. Men at church just laugh when I say I want to do something to be part of the community. And…" And his temper. Always going off when he least expected it.

"And you storm off when things don't go your way," Bram finished for him. "I saw that on Sunday afternoon." He wiped his hands on a rag and tossed it on the workbench. "You don't have to be that way. Look at you now. You aren't angry with me, are you?"

Samuel shook his head. Bram was right. At other times, he would have closed off the conversation by now, with all of Bram's prodding.

"You're changing. I can see it."

"But not enough. I can't control my temper, and I can't ask any woman to live…to live like *Mamm* did."

Bram stood at the barn door, combing his fingers through his beard and watching a pair of barn swallows dance over the corn field.

"One thing I've learned is that if you try to change on your own, it's nearly impossible."

"How else can I do it?" Samuel could feel his temper pulsing.

"Ask God to help you."

"As simple as that?" His words came out with a growl, but then he remembered. His prayer that morning had been for God to help him keep his temper, and here he was, talking with Bram, and his temper was controlled.

"As simple as that."

Samuel looked at him sideways, not sure how to ask the next question. "You believe that God will do that?"

Bram grinned, still watching the swallows. "I know as sure as I'm standing here that God will do that if you ask Him."

Chapter Ten

Mary held the box of chicks on her lap as Samuel drove home. The fifteen Rhode Island Reds from Ellie would be a welcome addition to the young flock.

They passed Annie's house and continued north, but Samuel was silent. Ever since they had left Bram and Ellie's, he had stared straight ahead through Chester's ears as if she didn't exist.

"The chicks are a wonderful gift, don't you think?"

Samuel grunted.

"Ellie has nice children. She said they love Bram, and he is a good father to them."

Samuel rubbed the side of his nose.

"The children certainly like having the old folks around. They are Ellie's first husband's aunt and uncle. Did you know that?"

No response. Mary sat back in her seat and watched the roadside.

When Samuel pulled to a stop at an intersection, she tried again.

"What did you and Bram find to talk about?"

He looked at her as if he had forgotten she was there.

"Hmm." He clucked at Chester to signal him to go on. "We talked about the children."

He had finally given her a response.

"What about them?"

Samuel glanced at her. "Bram wants to raise them differently than how he and I were raised."

"I'm sure you'd want to do the same thing if you had children."

He nodded. "If I ever have children."

"You don't think you'll find a nice girl to marry and raise a family?" Mary's fingers grew cold. Had Samuel given up on the same dream that she had?

"I never thought about it much. I've always thought I was too much like my *daed*, and I didn't want to have a family like his."

Mary remembered the sad tone of his voice as he had spoken of his father on the way to Bram and Ellie's farm.

"You don't have to be like him. Bram isn't."

He lowered his brow. "I'm not Bram."

"You aren't your *daed*, either. I've told you that." She shifted in her seat to look at him. "Who are you, Samuel?"

"I'm not sure." He glanced at her again. "I've spent too much time trying to not be *Daed*, I guess."

He drove past his farm and on to Sadie's. When he turned in the drive, a strange buggy was tied near the house.

"Who could that be?"

Samuel's voice was a growl. "That's Martin Troyer's rig."

He pulled to a stop in the drive behind the other buggy. "I'll take care of Chester if you want to go in to see your visitor. Esther and Judith might be eating supper here, too."

Mary shook her head. "*Ne*, I'll go to the barn with you." She clutched the box of chicks, thankful for their presence. "I have to get these peeps settled in."

She had no idea what Martin was doing there, but she wanted to put off going into the house as long as possible. She would find a way to keep busy in the barn or the henhouse.

Samuel nudged her with his elbow as he clucked to Chester to continue to the barn. "Don't you want to keep those chicks in the house until they're older?"

Mary looked down at the box. "I forgot that I need to keep them by the stove for a week or so. But I still want to check on the other chickens."

"Martin might be waiting for you." Chester walked into the barn and stopped. Samuel got out of the buggy and reached for the chicks so Mary could climb out.

"Why would he do that?"

Samuel shrugged, not meeting her eyes as he handed the peeping box back to her. "He's a bachelor, and there are two single women living here."

Mary stared at him. "You don't mean that you think he came courting?"

"You won't find out until you go in."

As Samuel started unhitching Chester, Mary glanced back at the house. The sun was lowering into a bank of clouds in the west and Ida Mae had lit the kitchen lamp. If she was fixing supper already, that meant Sadie had invited Martin to stay. Her knees started to shake at the thought of a man sitting at their cozy kitchen table. Unless...

"Samuel, would you stay to supper?"

He had hung the harness on its rack and was brushing Chester.

"You want me to eat with Martin Troyer?"

She didn't want to beg, but Samuel's presence might keep the conversation off the subject of exactly why Martin Troyer was visiting a home with two single women.

"Please do. We can make a party of it, with your sisters and Sadie." She smiled, willing her chin to stop quivering. "You can visit with Martin."

"What makes you think Martin and I have anything to talk about?" He opened Chester's stall and led him in.

"Please, Samuel. For me."

He looked at her then, his eyes dark in the shadows of Chester's stall. He met her in the center of the barn and took the box of chicks.

"All right. I'll stay for you." He carried the box under one arm and took her elbow with the other. "For you, I'll even try to control my temper."

When Mary stepped into the kitchen, the first thing she noticed was Ida Mae's face. Tight and pale with a pained smile. Judith and Esther sat on either side of her, and Sadie was at the end of the table watching Martin, who sat with his back to the door.

"My farm is quite large," he was saying, "and I have a full barn of dairy cows. My brother and I work the farm together."

Samuel hung his hat on the peg next to Martin's and planted his hand in the small of Mary's back, propelling her forward to the empty chair at the end of the table.

"Good afternoon, Martin," he said as he pulled the kitchen stool over and placed it at the corner between Mary and their visitor. "I was surprised to see your buggy here."

Martin smiled at Mary before turning to Samuel, his eyebrows raised. "No more surprised than I am to see you here."

Martin leaned forward so he could see past Samuel's bulk and catch Mary's eye. "As I was saying, my brother and I have a dairy farm. And to be plain—" He broke off and glared at Samuel before scooting his chair up. "Neither one of us is married." He grinned. "Just a couple of bachelors. And we thought we should learn to know you girls a bit better."

Samuel shifted on his stool and moved the box so it cut off Martin's view of Mary. She looked up at him and he gave her a wink.

Ida Mae grabbed Mary's hand under the table and squeezed hard enough to send shooting pains up her arm. Judith and Esther were both scrunched small in their chairs, looking at their laps. None of them looked happy. How long had Martin been here?

"I don't think—" Mary started.

But Martin kept talking. "We thought a picnic on Saturday would be a good way to get acquainted. Just us four. You could pack some fried chicken, and potato salad. And Peter loves boiled eggs." He scooted forward again to see around Samuel. "What do you think?"

Mary exchanged glances with Ida Mae. There had to be a reason for them to decline.

"This coming Saturday?" Samuel said, placing a hand on Mary's shoulder. "I was going to ask Mary to spend the day with me."

He squeezed her shoulder, letting her know he was giving her an excuse to refuse the invitation, but Mary wouldn't make any commitments without talking to Ida Mae.

Martin's teeth ground together. "I don't see what concern this is of yours, Samuel Lapp. Isn't it time for you to leave?"

Mary glanced at Sadie. The older woman was quiet for once, watching the exchange between the two men with a little smile, as if she was enjoying herself.

"I was invited to stay for supper." Samuel's voice was quiet, without the hard edge Martin's frown invited.

Martin looked from Mary, to Ida Mae, to Sadie. But none of them said anything. The aroma of roast ham filled the kitchen, and a pot of potatoes boiled on the stove. If Ida Mae hadn't invited him to supper, Mary certainly wasn't going to be the one to do it, no matter how rude it looked.

Shoving his chair back, Martin finally stood and reached for his hat.

"I'll come back another time, when you aren't so busy," he said, stepping toward the door, "and when you're ready for better company." He glared at Samuel.

"You're welcome anytime," Sadie said. "Isn't he, girls?"

"For sure," Mary said. She got up to close the door behind him. "Anytime."

Martin turned as he reached the top of the steps.

"Think about my invitation."

"I'll let you know what we decide."

Martin looked from Mary to Samuel, still sitting on the stool with his back to the door. "If I were you, I would think hard about the kind of company you keep." His voice was quiet, so it wouldn't carry back into the kitchen. "I can offer you a much better life than a Lapp can."

Mary forced a polite smile. "I'll keep that in mind."

"And I will be back on Thursday for your answer. I've been watching you at church, and I like how you care for Sadie. You seem to be a good Amish woman, just the type of girl I want to be my wife. We'll do well together."

A sickening turn to her stomach forced Mary to clutch at the doorknob. "You are wasting your time. I don't intend to marry."

He gave her a self-assured grin. "We'll see about that." He stepped off the porch and untied his horse. "We'll see."

Mary watched him leave, willing her knees to stop quivering. When she had seen Martin at church, she had no idea that he might have been watching her. The thought made her stomach turn again. He didn't seem to be the type of man who would give up his suit easily.

Even though he had been invited to supper, Samuel had no intention of outstaying his welcome. Once the sound of Martin's buggy wheels disappeared down the drive, Samuel set the box of chicks on the table and took his hat from the peg by the door.

"I'll be getting home. I don't want to horn in on your hen party." He grinned at Judith's giggle.

Mary, still standing by the door, brushed his sleeve with her hand. "You can still stay, even though Martin left."

"I have work to do at home, but I'll do your chores before I leave."

Mary followed him out the door. "You don't need to do that."

She seemed nervous. Had Martin's visit frightened her? He started toward the chicken house on the far side of the barn and she followed.

"I heard Martin talking to you as he left. Did he insist that you and Ida Mae go on that picnic he had planned?"

"He said he wants to marry me."

Samuel put his hands on his hips, facing her. "You can't think that Martin Troyer would make a good husband. What made him think you would consider such a thing? How many times has he visited you? How much have you talked together?"

"I don't know." She shook her head. "I've never even talked to him before."

A dull roar started in Samuel's ears, echoing the thunder that rumbled in the distance. "He wouldn't just ask you out of thin air." But why would Mary lie to him?

"He said he had been watching me at church meeting, and he liked what he saw. I guess he and his brother want to spend time with Ida Mae and me to convince us to marry them."

Samuel rubbed his day's growth of whiskers. Martin Troyer. If that man came courting his sisters, he would throw him out on his ear. He was old enough to be their father.

"I hope you told him to forget the idea."

She drew herself up to her full height and her eyes narrowed. "Why?"

"Because he's not the man for you."

She took a step closer to him and he backed away. "You are not the one to tell me who I should consider and who I shouldn't, Samuel Lapp. You are not my father or my brother."

"But I'm…" What? Her friend? He leaned toward her. "I don't want to see you make a bad decision. You don't know this man like I do."

"Aren't you the one who told me I should get married

rather than start a business?" Her eyes narrowed farther. "Maybe I should think about taking your advice."

Had he said that? He stared at her. Probably, and she remembered even if he didn't. But she couldn't...she wouldn't marry that bully.

He wouldn't let her.

"Go on in the house and visit with the girls. I'll do your chores for you."

She shook her head. "I'll do them. I don't need you or any other man telling me what to do."

Samuel's face grew hot in the cool evening air. The wind whipped in a moisture-laden gust. "I said I would do your chores. You need to learn to accept help when it's offered."

Her fists perched on her hips. "You're telling me what to do again."

He held his hands up in surrender. "All right. You do it your way." He took two steps back as the thunder rumbled again. "I told the girls to stay all night if it's still storming after supper." He turned to take the path home. "But don't forget what I said about Martin."

Glancing back, he saw her silhouette in the dusk, her fists still on her hips, watching him go. He took off his hat and slapped it against his leg as he walked. That woman was the most stubborn female in the world. He had known sows who were easier to handle than her.

Reaching home, he went to the barn to do his chores. The first task was pumping the water trough full. As he pumped, he watched the sky. Clouds gathered in the west, blocking the last pale blue of the sky. A flash of lightning lit the darkness with a brief glow. He counted the seconds before the quiet rumble of thunder reached him. By the time the rain started, he should be in the house for the night.

He finished filling the trough, then went into the barn. As he poured a cupful of oats into Tilly's feed box, she came in from her pasture. She sniffed the grain, then pushed against his chest with her nose before taking a mouthful of the oats. She raised her head, watching him as she chewed. He closed her door to keep her in out of the storm for the night, and fastened the shutters on the windows. He gave Tilly a last pat before leaving the barn. After he blew out the lantern and hung it from the hook by the door, he checked the latch on the big main doors then headed to the house.

The wind had picked up, and the storm was closer. Lightning flashed again, followed by a crack of thunder. He watched the storm as it rolled in, the black clouds building on each other as the wind pushed them, backlit by lightning that was nearly constant. A picture of his building temper.

As the first large drops plopped on his hat, he ran the rest of the way to the back porch and cover.

He shut the back door against the storm and hung his hat on the hook. The house was quiet and still. Heat radiated from the kitchen stove as Samuel lit the lamp above the table. He grabbed a towel and took out the Dutch oven. Even though he had told her he would fend for himself, Esther had made a pot pie. A thick crust, golden brown, covered the chicken and gravy. The aroma of stewed chicken filled the kitchen when he poked the crust with a fork.

Taking a dish from the cupboard shelf, he cut into the crust and laid it on his plate. Then he spooned the rich gravy, chicken and vegetables over the crust and held it close, breathing in the aroma.

Sitting at the table, he lifted a forkful of his supper, then paused. He was alone in the house. He couldn't remember the last time he had been alone in this house, if he had ever been. Someone had always been here... *Mamm*, one of his sisters, Bram...

The doorway to the living room was an empty hole, black between flashes of lightning. His bedroom door was shut, and the door to the back porch was, too. The kitchen light showed the bottom three steps going up from the doorway next to the stove, but then darkness lurked beyond the lamplight.

He ate the food on his fork, his chewing loud in his own ears between the rumbles of thunder. The storm passed overhead, leaving behind a steady rain that could last for hours. The girls would stay at Sadie's tonight, and he was on his own.

Washing the dishes took no time, except for the minutes he spent watching raindrops hit the window, then slide down to the sill. Over and over, one after another. Just like the generations of Lapps who had lived in this house. Abe's father had built the house nearly a hundred years ago. Then *Grossdawdi* Abe, then his own father, and now him. Who would live here after him?

Samuel wiped out the Dutch oven with an oiled rag and set it on the stove. Banking the fire, he left the kitchen. He took the lamp with him into the living room and found the new *Farm and Home* magazine. Settling into the rocking chair with the lamp on the table beside him, he leafed through articles about shearing sheep, the new electric fence someone in New Zealand had developed, poultry waterers and a different butchering technique for hogs.

Tossing the magazine onto the table, Samuel leaned back in the chair, rocking himself with his toe. The house was quiet. Too quiet. But when Judith and Esther married and moved away, this would be his life. Quiet evenings alone in the dark, silent house.

As the wind picked up, the old house creaked, as if it was complaining about the quiet, too. The house was full of memories. So many folks had been born and died within these walls.

He pulled his thoughts back from that road. Very few of his memories were good ones, but there had been some worth thinking about on a stormy night. Like when he was small, and *Daed* would come in from doing chores in the winter, laughing as Samuel and Bram would rush to lick the snow off his coat sleeve before it melted. He remembered *Mamm* in the kitchen and the warm stove on cold mornings. He remembered jokes, stories, games…he remembered that there had once been life in this house. Life that was gone now, and no one could bring it back.

Leaning his head back against the rocker, he closed his eyes. Sadie's kitchen had been full of that life this evening, and the girls were there enjoying it. And Mary… His eyes popped open. He couldn't let Mary wed that Martin Troyer. He couldn't. But how could he stop her?

The storm hit with a rush of wind carrying big, plopping drops of rain. Mary ran from the barn to the house, but by the time she reached the back porch, she was soaked. Her *kapp* hung by its ties from her neck, and her hair clung to her wet skin in long, dripping ropes. She lifted her skirt and apron together and wrung out a few drops of water, but it was no use. She needed to change into dry clothes before supper.

She opened the kitchen door into a world of light and happy conversation. Esther and Ida Mae were laughing over something as they sprinkled chopped raisins into cake batter. Judith sat at the table while Sadie showed her how to do a knitting stitch. They all looked up when Mary came in.

"You're wet," Ida Mae said. "Is it raining that hard?"

"For sure it is." Mary stepped over to the stove and spread her hands out to the heat. "And with the storm as strong as it is, Judith and Esther will be staying the night with us, *ja*?"

"We were just talking about that. Supper is nearly ready, but you have time to change." Ida Mae tilted the bowl so that Esther could scrape the cake batter into the pan. "Put on your nightgown and some warm socks."

"To eat supper?"

Judith grinned. "Why not? No one will be here except us."

Esther nudged Mary aside with her elbow so she could put the cake in the oven. "Perhaps we should all put our nightgowns on. Ida Mae said you had an extra one I could borrow."

Sadie laughed. "That sounds like fun. I haven't done anything like this since I was a girl."

By the time everyone met back in the kitchen, the thunderstorm had passed overhead and left a steady rain. Ida Mae dished up ham and scalloped potatoes while Judith and Esther set the table. Sadie sat in her usual place, with a quaint *kapp* on her head.

"What are you wearing, Aunt Sadie?" Judith asked.

"My night *kapp*. I know girls don't wear them anymore, but I don't feel dressed without one."

Mary had combed and braided her wet hair, and the other girls had long braids hanging past their waists, too. Ida Mae had been right. Mary had gotten her long flannel nightgown from her chest and loaned her summer cotton one to Esther. The warm, dry fabric felt wonderful against her chilled skin, and the warm socks were beginning to take the icy feeling out of her toes.

In fact, between the warmth of her night clothes and the filling heat of her supper, Mary began to get sleepy as she sat at the table, listening to the conversation. But then Judith mentioned Martin Troyer's visit.

"Are you going to go on that picnic he invited you to?"

Ida Mae glanced at Mary, then shook her head. "I'm sure he and his brother are nice men, but…" She bit her lip.

Mary felt a guilty nudge inside. She had only thought what Martin's invitation meant to her. She hadn't considered Ida Mae's feelings at all. Was her sister ready to spend some time with a man?

"I'm not too sure about Martin," Esther said. "He always seems to be bragging about something."

"His brother, Peter, is a hard worker, but that's all I know about him." Judith cut her ham into bites. "He's very quiet, and doesn't enter into conversations much."

Mary took a biscuit and spread some jam on it. "What do you know about them, Sadie?"

"Like the girls said, Martin is a talker and Peter isn't. Martin was right about their dairy farm, though. Their father started it, and the boys have taken it over and are doing well with it. They're hard workers, for sure."

Ida Mae leaned back in her chair. "You called them boys, but Martin seemed to be pretty old."

"He may seem that way to you, but to me he's still a boy." Sadie tapped her finger on pursed lips. "He must be Samuel's age...*ne*, that can't be right. Martin's mother was a Zook, but not related to the Eden Township Zooks. She was Myron's Betza's sister..." Suddenly Sadie smiled. "Martin was born the same year as my brother, Solomon's, youngest. So, that would make him forty years old, and his brother, Peter, must be thirty-eight."

Martin Troyer was the same age as *Daed.* "And they are both bachelors?"

Sadie nodded. "The dairy farm has kept them busy. Too busy for starting a family, it seems. I'm not sure what put it into Martin's head that he should come courting."

Ida Mae stood and started gathering the dirty dishes. "No one said anything about courting. Martin only asked if we would want to go on a picnic."

Mary rubbed at her finger. Ida Mae hadn't heard her conversation with Martin on the back porch. But she seemed to be interested. Perhaps they should accept the invitation, for Ida Mae's sake. But Mary's stomach clenched. She couldn't think of marrying Martin Troyer. She would never put herself in the position of being alone with any man again. Especially an overbearing man like him. But what did Ida Mae think?

Judith and Esther took Sadie into the front room while Mary and Ida Mae washed the dishes and *redd* up the kitchen for the night.

Ida Mae chewed her bottom lip as she shaved soap flakes into the dish pan. "Do you think we should go on the picnic with Martin and Peter?"

That was the comment Mary had been waiting for. It

sounded like Ida Mae was in favor of getting to know the two men better.

She poured warm water into the dishpan and kept her voice casual. "If you would like to." She smiled as Ida Mae glanced at her. "It's an opportunity to get to know them better. And who knows? We might even like them."

"Would you consider marrying a man so much older than you are?" Ida Mae swirled the dish rag in the water to melt the soap flakes.

"It happens pretty often," Mary said, thinking of the number of families she knew where the husband was several years older than his wife. "Especially when the man is a widower and has young children to care for."

"But these two have never been married. What if there is something wrong with them? How many girls have they tried to court that have turned them down?"

Mary couldn't tell if Ida Mae was worried about the men's characters, or if she felt sorry for them.

"Sadie said they have been working very hard on their farm. It sounds like they would be good providers."

Her sister chewed on her bottom lip again as she washed the four plates and handed them to Mary to dry.

"I guess we could go on the picnic. What would it hurt?"

It was Mary's turn to chew on her bottom lip. She could do this for Ida Mae. She would do anything to see her sister happy and looking toward the future again.

"You're right. What would it hurt?"

Chapter Eleven

Samuel couldn't listen to Preacher William's sermon that Sunday morning. Martin Troyer sat two rows in front of him, next to Peter, and two rows in front of them, on the women's side, were Mary and Ida Mae. It seemed that Martin and Peter weren't listening to the sermon, either, since they were both staring at the girls. He recognized the slow burn of jealousy for what it was, and didn't care. Martin had no call to be thinking of marrying a girl like Mary.

At least Mary didn't notice. Her attention was on the preaching.

Samuel forced his attention back to Preacher William's droning voice. It was too bad preachers weren't called on the basis of their speaking ability. Focusing on the sermon, Samuel heard him stress that a man must die to sin and be united with Christ.

Samuel's gaze drifted to his hands, calloused and with a bruise on one thumb where he had hit it with a hammer yesterday. Yesterday. When Mary and Ida Mae had gone on that picnic with the Troyers and he had heard the Troyers' buggy going by on the road. He flexed his fingers, feeling the dull pain of the bruise creep into the palm of his hand.

The congregation shifted in their seats as Preacher William sat down and Preacher Jonas stood. The first thing he did was to read from the German Bible the story of how the Pharisee, Nicodemus, had talked with Jesus in the garden at night. Samuel tried to think of something other than the familiar words, but Jonas's voice wasn't the kind you could ignore.

Preacher Jonas had a habit of looking the people of the congregation in the eyes as he spoke, and for some reason, he focused on Samuel this morning. Samuel shifted on the bench and glanced behind him. Every man's gaze was focused on the preacher. When he looked back at Jonas, the preacher had shifted his focus to the other side of the room, but then came right back to Samuel.

"Ye must be born again," said Jonas with a smile.

A smile on the man's face? After Preacher William had only talked of death?

Samuel focused on his shoes, polished for this morning's meeting. The messages in the sermons were confusing. He glanced at Mary. She watched Preacher Jonas, sitting straight on the bench, her hands in her lap. He looked at Martin. He was also watching the preacher, as if the man was talking only to him.

Tapping the bruise on his thumb, Samuel kept his gaze focused on the black coat in front of him, waiting for the preaching to end.

Dinner after the preaching was intolerable as Samuel watched Martin watch Mary. The man was blatant in his attentions to her, even rising once to help her carry a heavy platter to one of the tables. He should be embarrassed, mooning on like a love-sick cow.

Samuel snorted and left the house. He would wait for the girls by the buggy, and then they could go home. Maybe he should have stayed home today and let the girls ride with Sadie, then he wouldn't have had to witness that display of Martin's.

He leaned on the Hopplestadts' pasture fence. Conrad was one of those farmers who never let anything on his farm look run down, but the pasture fence had been repaired badly. Samuel bent down to examine it. The broken fence wires had been patched with baling twine, and the patch was nearly worn through.

"Hello, Samuel."

Preacher Jonas's voice took him by surprise.

"Preacher." Samuel shook the hand the other man offered.

Jonas leaned on the fence next to Samuel. "You barely touched your dinner, and now you're out here by yourself instead of visiting with the rest of the congregation." He turned to look at him. "Is everything all right?"

Samuel shrugged. "For sure, everything is fine."

"That's good." The preacher looked out over the pasture. "The grass is good and rich this year. Not like last year at all."

"We've had some good rain."

"*Ja*, for sure. We have much to be thankful for."

Samuel picked at the broken bit of fence wire.

"You seemed uncomfortable during the sermon."

"Preachers notice things like that?"

The older man laughed. "*Ja*, for sure." He gestured toward the horses in the field. "When you look at these horses, what do you see? A bunch of animals? Or do you see that some are grazing and some are standing, drowsing in the sun? It's like that when you're in front of a congregation. We see who is paying attention to our words, who is thinking of something else and who is fighting to stay awake."

"So, which one was I?" Samuel grinned. At least he wasn't sleeping.

"You seemed to be listening at first, but then you were trying hard not to listen."

Samuel didn't answer.

"I had to ask myself, why? Why is Samuel Lapp trying so hard to ignore God's word?"

"It wasn't God talking, Preacher. It was you."

"When I read from the Good Book, I'm reading God's words. And when I expound on those words in a sermon, I pray that I'm communicating God's message to His people."

Samuel picked at the fence again. "I'll tell you why. It seemed that Preacher William had one kind of message, and then you were saying the opposite. How am I supposed to figure out who is right?"

Jonas picked a stalk of grass and started pulling off blades. "The messages weren't contradictory. They go together, like a hand in a glove."

"So we die, and then are born again?"

The preacher smiled. "That's right."

"Who? Who could die and then come to life again? You're not making sense."

Jonas sighed. "Have you ever listened to a sermon in your life, Samuel?"

Samuel dug into a clump of grass with the toe of his shoe.

The preacher grabbed his shoulder and gave it a squeeze. "Try listening to the entire sermon the next time, all right?"

Samuel nodded. "I'll try."

Jonas shook his head. "No one can ever accuse you of being a liar." Then he laughed. "I just wish all church members were as honest with themselves as you are." He plucked another blade of grass. "In a few weeks we'll have the church council meeting. Someone has asked that you be disciplined."

An icy hand clutched at Samuel's stomach. Disciplining meant standing before the congregation and being asked to repent.

"What for?"

"We've received an accusation that you are harboring ill will toward another church member." Jonas paused, then said, "Is this something you need to repent of before the congregation?"

"Who am I supposed to be angry with?"

"Martin Troyer."

Samuel sighed. "I guess it is no secret that his words goad me to anger, but I don't wish him ill."

"You would not rejoice if his dairy cows became ill and he couldn't sell the milk?"

Samuel's eyebrows rose. "Is that what I'm accused of saying?"

"Something similar."

"I have never thought such a thing, and I certainly never said it."

Preacher Jonas threw the grass stem away and leaned on the fence post, staring out at the horses. "Then we have one man's word against another's."

Samuel's temper rose. "You can't believe this—"

Jonas interrupted him with a raised hand. "I don't know who to believe, but I've never known you to be other than truthful."

"Tell me, is it Martin who made this accusation?"

The preacher shook his head. "And at this point, I don't want to tell you who did."

Jonas sighed again, his shoulders bent as if he carried the weight of the entire congregation on them. With a start, Samuel realized that was exactly the burden he bore.

"Preacher William, Bishop Kaufman and I need to discuss this. But I hope you will do everything you can to make amends with Martin. You are brothers in Christ, and must act that way. I will say the same to Martin."

Samuel shifted his feet. He was being asked to do more than just talk to Martin. He must support him in his work and find a way to be friends with the man. Must he even encourage Martin's courtship of Mary, like a friend and brother would?

"Is something wrong?"

"There's a girl..."

Jonas nodded. "I thought there might be when I saw the direction of Martin's thoughts this morning." He glanced at Samuel. "What are your feelings for Mary?"

"I don't have feelings for her. I just want to make sure she's happy, and safe, and that she marries someone better for her than Martin Troyer."

Jonas laughed. "But you don't have feelings for her."

Samuel shook his head. He didn't—couldn't—harbor any feelings for any woman.

The preacher clapped him on the shoulder. "I hate to tell you the bad news, but it's obvious to me that you are in love with her."

"Love?" His voice turned into a growl. "I'm not in love with anyone. I just don't want Mary to be hurt."

Jonas grinned. "Maybe if you tell yourself that

enough, you might believe it. But I think you're wrong."
He leaned closer to Samuel. "Ask yourself this, then.
How will you feel when you are at her wedding if you
aren't the groom?"

Samuel glared at him. This preacher had a knack for
reading his mind.

Monday morning dawned with a glorious blue sky.

"A perfect day for laundry," Sadie said. She stirred the
tubful of white clothes with an old washing bat. Mary
thought it was probably a hundred years old, as stained
and warped as it was, yet Sadie wielded it like she was
David fighting the giant laundry tasks.

Ida Mae ran an apron through the wringer and
dropped it in the basket for Mary to hang on the line.

"It feels like it might get warm enough today to set
out the tomato plants. What do you think, Mary?"

Before Mary could even think of an answer, a farm
wagon turned into the lane. Her stomach sank when she
saw Martin Troyer driving. Peter rode in the back of the
wagon with a cow.

"Good morning!" Martin pulled his team to a stop
and climbed into the wagon to help Peter. "We brought
you a present."

Mary and Ida Mae both stared as Peter and Martin
unloaded the cow from the wagon. Martin handed the
lead rope to Mary. Meanwhile, Sadie had come up behind them.

"That's a cow," she said.

The Jersey stared at Mary with huge brown eyes as
she chewed her cud.

"It's a cow," Ida Mae said.

"*Ja*, for sure." Martin grinned. "A cow."

"Y-you said y-you could sell b-butter along with your eggs," Peter said. He smiled as he watched Ida Mae.

"We thought you could put her to good use." Martin said, petting the animal's neck. "And the butter would bring in a good income, just like you said."

Mary shook her head. "We can't pay you for her."

Martin grinned wider. "We don't want to sell her. We're giving her to you." He glanced at his brother. "Right, Peter?"

The other man nodded, his eyes still on Ida Mae. "*Ja, ja, ja.* She's a p-present."

"Do you want us to help you get her settled? You have a stall for her, don't you?"

Sadie took the rope from Mary. "We can put her in the second stall, and she can share Chester's pasture." The old woman started toward the barn, the cow following her.

Mary looked from Sadie's retreating back to Ida Mae, who shrugged.

"We don't know how to thank you," she said. "But we really can't take her—"

Peter climbed into the wagon and Martin followed him. "You have to take her. She's yours." He clucked to the team and turned them around in the space in front of the barn. He waved as the wagon passed the house on the way down the drive. "We'll see you again soon. We're looking forward to another picnic."

Ida Mae slipped her arm through Mary's as she stared at the retreating wagon. "What are we going to do now?"

"I guess we have a cow. We'll have to ask Sadie if she has any milking equipment, because that cow will need to be milked this evening."

They started toward the barn.

"Do you know anything about taking care of cows?" Ida Mae asked.

"I know as much as you do, and that's from helping *Daed* do the milking. But beyond the day-to-day feeding and milking, I don't know what to do with her."

"She'll need to be freshened sometime…"

Mary stopped her sister's words as they entered the barn. "We'll worry about that when the time comes."

When the time came, they would need to find a bull. And then decide what to do with the calf. And then… Mary shook her head. One step at a time.

Sadie had let the cow into the stall next to Chester's and was patting her nose. "Nice *Schmetterling*. Good *Schmetterling*."

Mary and Ida Mae exchanged glances.

"Sadie," Mary said, keeping her voice even, "why are you calling her a butterfly?"

Sadie grinned at the girls. "I know she isn't a butterfly. I thought *Schmetterling* would be a nice name for her. Her eyelashes are so long, just like a butterfly's wings."

"I feel funny, accepting a gift like this from Martin and Peter," Ida Mae said, stroking Schmetterling's face. "We hardly know them."

"You'll get to know Peter, and then fall in love with him," Mary said. "You know he wants to marry you, and that's why he gave you the cow."

Ida Mae's mouth dropped open. "I'm not going to marry Peter. It's Martin who wants to marry you. He brought the cow to you."

Mary shook her head. "And I'm never going to marry Martin, no matter how many cows he brings us."

"Then you need to make sure he knows that."

"I've told him." Mary shrugged. "He won't listen to me."

Sadie stroked the cow's soft ears. "Those Troyers never listen to anyone. Once they have their minds made up, they're going to get their way, unless someone steps in to stop them."

Ida Mae groaned and covered her face with her hands. "Is there no way to get out of marrying them, then?"

"You won't have any trouble with Peter," Sadie said. "Martin is the hardheaded one. Once Mary has dissuaded him, Peter will follow."

"How can we convince Martin?" Mary asked.

Sadie smiled, looking as crafty as a fox. "I don't think you'll need to worry about that. Meanwhile, we have a cow, and we need to take care of her."

"Do you have anything like a milking pail? Or a stool?"

"I have all that in the cellar, in a box in the corner. I had a cow until a few years ago, and milked her every morning and evening. She was a fine cow, but not a Jersey like this one. Jerseys give rich milk, and we'll be able to make a lot of butter to sell."

Mary's mind started churning. How much butter could she make from Schmetterling's milk? If her milk was as rich as Sadie said, probably more than enough to pay for the cow's keep. She scratched Schmetterling's ears. She would have to find a way to thank Martin, without making him think it was time to start planning a wedding.

"Chester's pasture is too small for both animals, though. Can we make it bigger?"

"Ach, ja." Sadie gestured out the back door of the barn. "Abe gave me ten acres. All we need to do is move

the fence back behind the barn. We can go all the way to the line of trees along the fence row back there, where it was before I sold my cow." Sadie started out the side door of the barn. "Come along and I'll show you."

She led the way around Chester's pasture to the far side, walking between the new chicken coop and fence. When she reached the corner fence post, she stopped.

"Who has been plowing back here?"

The space between the back fence and the tree line had been plowed in neat rows, and corn shoots were already growing in the black soil.

"Samuel said that Dale Yoder was going to plow a corn field for him. He must have thought this was part of Samuel's farm."

"We need to let Schmetterling graze. She needs a pasture." Sadie's brow puckered as she tried to think through the problem without success.

Mary gave her shoulders a quick hug. "Don't worry about it. We'll fence in the space and she can eat the corn shoots until the grass grows again."

Ida Mae took Sadie's arm and turned her back toward the house. "Let's finish our laundry and get out the milking pail to use this evening. And Mary is right. We'll just move the fence and use the field. Samuel probably doesn't know that Dale planted it."

Mary hung back as Ida Mae and Sadie walked toward the house. The corn shoots fluttered in the slight breeze. They would need to fence off about three acres on the end of the planted field that stretched from here to behind Samuel's barn. Moving the fence wasn't something the three of them could do on their own, but she could ask Samuel to help. They would have a good laugh over Dale's mistake.

She hoped.

* * *

Samuel gave the pump handle one last push, sending a spurt of water into the watering trough. He wiped his forehead with his handkerchief and leaned back against the fence post, looking up at the derelict water pump tower again. When the windmill had stopped working five or six years ago, *Daed* had left it where it stood. Winds had battered the mill blades and a few hung from the broken spokes.

If he could get the windmill going again, he'd save himself a lot of work.

Shoving his hat back on his head, he walked over to the sixteen-foot tower and pushed against it, then pulled on it. Steady as the day it was built, years before his time. He put a foot on the crossbar, hearing *Daed*'s voice in his head.

"You boys stay away from that tower. First thing you know, one of you will fall off and break your leg."

Samuel grinned. *Daed* had been right. Bram had climbed up about ten feet before he missed his footing. He didn't break his leg, but he was bruised and sore. Neither of them had said anything about the fall, though. Bram said that *Daed*'s punishment for disobedience would be worse than the bruises he already had.

Testing the steadiness of the tower once more, Samuel started the climb. Right about where Bram had fallen, rungs had been nailed to the vertical tower beams to form a ladder. The rest of the way up was easy, and he soon reached the top. He pried the cover off the gearbox. He had never seen how the mill worked, but it shouldn't be too hard to figure out. Opening his knife, he pried away some of the old hard grease, crusted with dirt that had blown in over the years.

Reaching over to the vanes, Samuel tried moving the wheel, but the complex tangle of gears didn't budge. It was frozen tight. The mill had worked once, though, and maybe he could get it working again. He scraped dirt and rust away from the nuts and bolts, checking for any damage. It looked like it only needed to be taken apart and cleaned. If he could get the gear mechanism down to the barn, he could do the job properly.

"Samuel!"

Mary was below him.

"What are you doing up there?"

"Checking to see if the windmill can be fixed." He started down the ladder.

"Do you think you can do it?"

Her skirt swirled around her legs as the wind freshened, and she stood with one hand shading her eyes against the sun. He had never seen a prettier girl. He dropped to the ground and grinned at her.

"Well? Do you think you'll be able to get it going?"

"*Ja*, for sure." Samuel wiped his greasy hands on his handkerchief and tucked it back in his waistband. "It's dirty and the vanes need repairing, but I think I can do it."

"It would sure help you keep the watering troughs full, wouldn't it?"

He patted the tower. "It sure would." Then he turned his attention to Mary. "What brings you here today?"

"We have a cow, and we need your help."

Samuel had started walking with her toward the barn and his toolbox, but now turned and stared at her. "A cow? Why did you buy a cow?"

Her eyes shifted away from his. "We didn't buy it. It was a gift."

He could guess who the gift was from. "A gift? With strings attached?"

"I don't think so."

She answered so quickly that he could tell the possibility was on her mind.

"You should have refused to take her."

"We tried." Her gaze went from the cattle in the field to the windmill. "But they wouldn't hear of it."

"And 'they' are the Troyer brothers?"

Mary nodded and finally met his eyes. "Sadie thought we should keep her, since there's no arguing with a Troyer, as she put it."

Samuel started toward the barn again and Mary came after him.

"We'll get a lot of good butter from her milk, and we'll be able to sell it along with the eggs."

"So you're still determined to make this business idea of yours work?"

Her eyebrows went up. "For sure, and it's working already. We're paying back the money Mr. Holdeman loaned us for the lumber and supplies, and we're making a bit extra, too. The chickens are doing well, and in a few months when the new chicks are grown, we'll have even more eggs to sell."

Samuel went to his workbench and opened the toolbox, but she followed him, moving around so she could see his face.

"I plan to go to the auction again tomorrow to buy more hens. Having the cow means that we'll be able to support ourselves that much sooner."

"You don't need to do all that work. I can support both of our families. That's the way *Grossdawdi* Abe wanted it, and that's the way it will be."

She stared at him, her lips pressed together. He found his gloves, put them in the toolbox and went back outside, the heavy wooden box bumping against his knee as he walked. She trotted behind him to keep up, but he didn't shorten his stride. She wasn't going to listen to reason.

"But I don't want you to support us. Ida Mae and I can take care of Sadie on our own. We don't need your help."

Samuel had reached the base of the windmill tower, but at her words he turned back. "You need my help," he said, pointing his finger and jabbing with every word, "and you're going to accept my help. I can do this. I can take care of all of us."

"I don't want your help." She spoke through gritted teeth.

A sudden thought almost made him laugh. "Then why did you come over here?"

Mary's face grew red and she stamped one foot. "All right. I came to ask for your help. But as a neighbor, not…not as someone who has to take care of us."

He turned around and leaned against the tower. "What do you need my help with?"

"We need a bigger pasture since we have both Chester and Schmetterling."

"Who?"

"The cow. Sadie named her." She swiped at a lock of hair that had escaped her *kapp*. "We need to move the fence to enlarge the pasture. It shouldn't be too hard."

Samuel set his toolbox on the ground. "And just where are you going to move the fence? The new chicken coop takes up the only space."

"We want to use the back part of Sadie's land. Dale planted corn there, but I'm sure it was a mistake. He must not know where your land ends and Sadie's begins."

"There was no mistake." Samuel rubbed the back of his neck. *Grossdawdi* Abe had handled the transfer of the land for Sadie's use, but the deed was clear. The ten acres still belonged to the Lapps. Sadie must not have told Mary of the arrangement.

"You told him to plant corn on Sadie's farm?"

"Actually, it isn't Sadie's land."

Mary stared at him for a full minute, her eyes widening, then narrowing as she took this information in.

"Sadie said it is. It was her idea to move the fence to make a larger pasture."

"You're not going to ruin good acres of growing corn."

She bit her lower lip. "I'll admit, it isn't the best pasture, but the grass will grow back."

Samuel felt the pounding in his ears before he heard it. His fists flexed. There must be a way to solve this problem before he lost his temper completely. He sent a quick look up at the white clouds hanging in the deep blue sky. Count to ten. He could hear *Mamm*'s voice echoing from his memory. She would tell her boys to count whenever they started one of their many fights.

"One...two...three..."

He glanced at Mary, who was staring at him with her eyes wide. He forced the muscles in his face to relax into a more pleasant expression.

"Four...five...six..."

"What are you doing?"

"Counting to ten. Seven...eight..."

"Why?"

He clenched his teeth. "Because it's better than yelling at you."

"Why would you yell at me?"

"Because you aren't listening to reason." His voice rose and he finished counting. "Nine...ten."

"Do you feel better?"

"*Ja.* I feel better." His voice was a growl.

"Then you'll help us move the fence?"

"*Ne.* I won't help you move the fence!" He started counting again as she turned on her heel and walked away.

Chapter Twelve

After leaving Samuel in the barnyard, Mary stormed along the path leading to Sadie's house. She had never met such an overbearing, stubborn, pigheaded man in her entire life. She knew men could be pushy and high-handed, but Samuel Lapp put all of them to shame.

She slowed when she reached the corner of their barn and paused to catch her breath. Sadie would not understand why she was so upset, and that could make the day end up like a buggy with a wobbly wheel. She and Ida Mae had discovered that keeping their lives calm and peaceful was the key to helping Sadie get through the day without becoming confused or anxious.

Once her breathing slowed, she went into the house. She followed the sound of humming through the kitchen and into the sewing room. Ida Mae sat in the rocking chair, putting the last stitches on a quilt block.

She looked up when Mary stepped into the room. "What has you all flustered?"

Mary pressed cool hands to her hot cheeks. "Does it show so much?" When Ida Mae nodded, she plopped onto the other rocking chair. "Where is Sadie?"

"Lying down for a while. She might be sleeping."

"We have a problem."

Ida Mae laid her sewing in her lap. "What kind of problem?"

"Samuel says that field behind the barn isn't Sadie's."

"Whose is it then? Sadie is sure it's part of her farm."

Mary shook her head. "Samuel thinks it is his, and he has this notion that it's his job to take care of us. Something about his *grossdawdi*. He says he won't help us at all."

Ida Mae picked her sewing up again. "How is he going to take care of us if he doesn't help us?"

Mary pushed her foot against the floorboards, sending the chair into an agitated rocking. "That isn't what I meant. He isn't going to help us move the fence because he says the cornfield is his. He wants us to give Schmetterling back to the Troyers and stop trying to support ourselves." Mary got up and paced to the end of the room and back. "If I didn't know better, I would think he regards us as two more of his sisters, under his thumb and at his beck and call."

Ida Mae laid the finished quilt block on a pile of other blocks on the table and picked up two small triangles to stitch together.

"And if I didn't know better," she said, threading her needle, "I would say he thinks of you as much more than another sister."

Mary spun on her heel to face her sister. "What did you say?"

"Shh. Don't wake Sadie." Ida Mae twisted the thread around her needle to make a knot. "I think he's in love with you."

Mary sank into the rocking chair again, shaking her head. "He can't be."

"You haven't seen the way he looks at you." Ida Mae took five tiny stitches in her seam and pulled the thread through. "And I've seen the looks you give him."

"I don't give him looks."

"You might not think so, but you do."

"But…" Mary bit her lower lip, then went on. "You know that I am never going to marry anyone. How can I? No man wants a woman with my…past…for his wife." She bit her lip again to keep the welling tears from falling.

"So you're not denying that you have feelings for him."

Mary slouched back in the chair and rocked it gently. A swaying branch outside the window caught her eye. She didn't want to think about her feelings for Samuel. She wanted things to go on the way they had been. When did life get so difficult?

"All right. I think I like him." She rocked her chair harder. "At least I do when he isn't being so…so…"

"…much like a man?" Ida Mae grinned at her.

The grin swept Mary's melancholy mood away and she smiled back. "Even so, I'm never getting married."

"Martin Troyer would marry you, even if he knew… what happened. It wouldn't matter to him."

Mary shuddered at the thought of being married to Martin. The thought of his hands holding hers, of being alone with him… Dark clouds swirled and she took a deep breath. "I can never, never marry Martin. He wouldn't be…patient, or tender or thoughtful. He only thinks about himself."

"And you know this from one short picnic?"

With a nod, Mary leaned forward in her chair. "You have seen how he treats Peter. If he can be so thoughtless and selfish with his brother, how do you think he would treat a wife?" She leaned back and rocked again. "Any woman married to him would be little more than a slave."

Ida Mae looked up from her sewing. "I'm so glad we don't have to go on another picnic with them."

"Are you sure you want to refuse Peter so quickly?"

Ida Mae threw a scrap of cloth across the space between them as Mary covered her mouth to keep a burst of laughter from escaping. Then she looked at Ida Mae's red cheeks and couldn't help it. They both giggled with hissing whispers.

"Don't wake up Sadie!"

Ida Mae laughed. "I…I'm…not the one…who's making all the noise." She glanced at Mary and the giggles started again.

"We have to tell Martin and Peter that there will be no more picnics," Mary said when she finally caught her breath.

"You'll have to do it." Ida Mae's face was bright pink from laughing.

"Why me?"

"Because if I tell Peter, it won't do any good. Martin will never pay attention to what he says."

Mary nodded. "Martin won't listen to either of you. But what makes you think he'll be any different with me?"

"You're strong and stubborn. You'll make him listen."

"I'm not sure being stubborn will be enough." Mary sighed and laid her head against the back of the chair. "Do you think we should give back the cow?"

"After Sadie already named her? I don't think we'll be able to."

Mary rocked while Ida Mae sewed in silence for a few minutes. The sound of a buggy horse clip-clopping on the road drifted in the open windows. The trotting horse slowed, then stopped.

Ida Mae put her sewing on the table. "Someone is here."

She went to the back door while Mary stayed sitting in the rocker.

Voices drifting from the kitchen told her that their visitor was Effie Hopplestadt calling on Sadie. Since the season had turned to early summer, the weekly quiltings had ended until after the garden produce was stored away in the fall. But Sadie's friends still dropped in on her regularly.

Sadie must have heard Effie come in, because her voice joined the others, but Mary still sat and rocked. She should get up and greet Effie, but her mind kept going back to Ida Mae's comment that Samuel was in love with her.

Mary closed her eyes. Samuel wasn't in love with her. If he was, he wouldn't have argued with her the way he had this morning. But if someone had to be in love with her, he wouldn't be a bad choice. Much better than Martin Troyer. That man caused her thoughts to go down dark paths.

Samuel, though… Even if they did argue, she still looked forward to talking to him every day.

A smile crept its way onto her face as she gazed out the window. *Ja*, she looked forward to seeing him again.

Samuel's mood worsened as the sun sped toward noon. After Mary left, he climbed the tower and unfastened the wind wheel from the shaft, lowering it with a rope until it laid on the ground in three pieces. Then he worked at the bolts holding the gearbox to the platform until they finally came loose and the gearbox was ready to follow the wind wheel to the ground. He tied the rope firmly and lowered it, bracing himself on the ladder.

Only then did he let himself look toward Sadie's farm, but Mary wasn't coming back to apologize.

"Leave it to her to find a way to ruin the cornfield," he said to Tilly as he climbed down the ladder. "She'll probably move the fence herself, and get hurt in the process."

His feet touched the ground and Tilly's ears swiveled back and forth.

Samuel untied the gearbox from the rope, lifted it and started toward the barn.

"Don't look at me that way, Tilly-girl. I know you're on her side."

He glanced back once to see Tilly standing with her hip cocked and her ears swiveled toward her tail. *Ja*, those women stuck together.

Once the gearbox was on the work bench, Samuel spent the rest of the morning dismantling the gears and shafts and cleaning the old grease off the mechanism. Kerosene helped dissolve the gummy residue and he soon had the pieces apart and cleaned.

After dinner, he got his grease pot and started putting the machine back together.

"Hello, Samuel."

Samuel turned to see Preacher Jonas.

"Esther told me you were working in the barn cellar."

"Good afternoon and welcome."

Samuel grabbed a rag to clean his hands but Jonas stopped him.

"Don't let me keep you from your work." He stepped closer to see what Samuel was doing. "I didn't know you could repair machines like this."

Samuel held a bolt up to the light to check the size. "I've never tried before. But the windmill hasn't worked for years and I thought it was worth seeing what was wrong with it." He set a gear in place and tightened the bolt.

Jonas watched as Samuel placed another gear so that it interlocked with the first one. Cleaned and with fresh grease, the pieces went together easily.

"Where did you learn how to do that?"

"Rebuild a gearbox?" Samuel shrugged. "I just remember where the pieces go." He set the shaft in place and turned the mechanism. "It looks like it's working." He tightened a couple of the bolts and spun the shaft. The gears moved like clockwork.

He picked it up and started toward the mill tower. "I could use your help."

"For sure. What can I do?"

"I'll climb up with the rope while you tie the gearbox and wheel pieces to the other end. Then I'll be able to haul them up as I need them, without having to climb up and down this tower."

Jonas helped as Samuel reassembled the windmill mechanism and reattached the wheel. He climbed down the tower and released the brake, and both men watched as the mill turned into the wind and picked up speed.

"You're certain you've never fixed a windmill before?" Jonas asked.

"I've never fixed any machine before."

"You seem to have a knack for it. That would have

taken me a week of fruitless toil, and then it still wouldn't run."

Samuel's chest warmed at the other man's words. Praise for a job well done. He had never heard anyone say anything like that before. Not to him.

He cleared his throat and wiped the grease off his hands. "You didn't make the trip over here to help me with a little chore."

Jonas was still watching the mill turn in the wind. "I came to tell you that your name won't come up at the council meeting. Your accuser will be repenting instead. It turns out that he was spreading a tale to get attention for himself."

"Who?"

"Peter Troyer." The older man looked at Samuel as he said the name. "Don't harbor hard feelings toward him. He is truly repentant for the trouble he caused."

Samuel waited for the roar in his ears and the pounding in his head that always signaled that his temper was flaring, but it didn't come. Instead, he saw Peter's face in his mind, a little bit homely and perpetually sad.

"I'm not angry with him. But I feel sorry for the man. He is always in his brother's shadow." Samuel rubbed at a stubborn grease spot on his left palm. He knew what it was like to live in someone's shadow, never seen for who he was. Always judged by someone else's actions.

"I hope that you will tell him that you forgive him after he repents in front of the church."

Samuel nodded and Jonas watched the mill again.

"I wonder if you'd do something else for me."

"For sure."

"Some of the others in the community have windmills that are giving them problems. Vernon Hershberger for one. His mill creaks and groans with every turn, but with his broken leg, he can't hope to climb the tower to fix it. There are other older members, too, who could use the help of someone who knows what he's doing. Would you consider going around to the different farms? Give a hand to whoever needs it?"

Samuel shrugged. "That shouldn't be any trouble. I'll go over to Vernon's in the morning and see what's going on there."

That put a smile on Jonas's face. "You know, the Samuel Lapp of a few months ago would have found some excuse to stay home."

"The Samuel Lapp of a few months ago didn't know he had anything to offer." Samuel grinned back. "Anything I can do to help, I'd like to."

Jonas clapped him on the shoulder before he started back toward his buggy. "Someone has been having a good influence on you. You should keep spending time with her."

Samuel's grin widened. Perhaps he would invite Mary to go to the Hershbergers' with him tomorrow. That would help them get past their disagreement about the fence.

On Tuesday morning Samuel pulled into Sadie's drive. Those puppies were back in his stomach, rolling over each other as they tried to fight their way out. He laid a hand on his waist to try to quiet them down, but then Mary came from the henhouse with a basket of eggs and they started all over again. She blushed when she saw him but continued to the house without a greeting.

Samuel climbed down from the buggy and met Mary at the door, opening it for her.

"Mary, I—"

She walked into the house without even looking at him. Sadie peered out the open door from her seat at the table and beckoned him into the kitchen. When he shook his head, she came out onto the porch, closing the kitchen door behind her.

"What are you doing out here?"

"I was going to talk to Mary, but she doesn't seem to want to see me."

"You're going to let a little thing like that stop you from talking to her?"

Samuel shrugged. "What can I do? She just walked right by without even looking at me."

"You need to go after her. Don't let her treat you like that."

He grinned. "This is your niece we're talking about, not some misbehaving horse."

Sadie's eyes twinkled. "You go after her. She wants to see you, but she's afraid for some reason."

"Probably because I yelled at her yesterday."

The elderly woman patted his arm. "So the two of you had a disagreement. That won't stop you." She turned to go back into the house.

"Stop me from what?"

But she continued into the kitchen as if she hadn't heard him. He had no choice but to follow her.

Ida Mae was washing dishes, but Mary was nowhere to be seen. The basket of eggs sat on the kitchen table.

"Good morning, Samuel," Ida Mae said. "Do you want me to find Mary for you?"

His teeth ground together, but he couldn't decide if he should get angry or not. "If you just point out the way she went, I'll go find her."

Ida Mae grinned. "Back there," she tilted her head down the short hallway off the kitchen. "She went into the sewing room."

Samuel hung his hat on the hook by the door and headed that way. As he passed Sadie's seat at the table, she smiled and sipped her coffee.

The room was airy and bright. A table for cutting fabric was in the center, and near the window were two rocking chairs. Mary stood at one of the windows as if she was waiting for him.

"Why didn't you talk to me?" Samuel stopped, cautious. "You walked right past me as if I wasn't there."

"I won't talk to you until you apologize."

Samuel put his hands on his hips and stared at the floor. *One...two...three...*

"Oh, no, you don't." Mary stepped across the room toward him. "You stop counting and apologize to me."

He gritted his teeth. *Four...five...*

"Well?"

Bah! Women!

"I apologize for..." Samuel scratched his head. "What am I apologizing for?"

"For being pigheaded and not helping us move the fence so Schmetterling could have the larger pasture she needs."

Samuel met her eyes. Instead of the stormy anger he expected, she was almost smiling.

"You didn't move that fence on your own, did you? Because if you let that cow destroy my corn—"

"There is no need to get upset. We haven't moved any fences. Not yet."

The light coming in the window made her face glow as she turned toward him. She was beautiful.

"Samuel, are you going to apologize or not? That's why you came over here, isn't it?"

She had him so turned around he was surprised he could remember his own name.

"I'm going over to Vernon Hershberger's to repair his windmill. I thought you might want to come along."

"Why would I want to go watch you look at a windmill?" Her toe started tapping. "Especially since you haven't apologized to me yet."

Samuel stifled a groan. A noise from the kitchen sounded like Sadie laughing.

"All right, all right. I apologize for…" He raised his eyebrows at her.

"For refusing to help me move the fence."

His eyebrows went down. "I apologize for making you angry so that you stormed off." His own toe started twitching. "Now, will you come with me or not?"

She crossed her arms and looked out the window. Her cheeks became pinker by the minute. Her profile was perfect, with her nose turning up a bit at the tip. He could watch her all morning.

"I need to go into Shipshewana today to sell the eggs we've collected."

"We can go to Shipshewana, too. We'll make a day of it."

Her eyes narrowed as she turned to him. "What do you mean?"

"We'll take a picnic for a lunch we can eat at the park in town. And then if I get done at Vernon's early enough, maybe we'll take a drive down by Emma Lake before we come home."

"Why?"

He shrugged, wanting her to agree to the outing, but

refusing to force her into it. "We're friends, aren't we? And I don't want us going on the way we did yesterday."

"So we're just two friends spending the day together?"

Samuel grinned. "Maybe I'll make you climb up Vernon's windmill tower with me."

"I won't climb any tower, but I'll go with you. Who knows? We might even have a good time." She started toward the kitchen. "I have to clean the eggs and pack a picnic first."

Samuel watched her skirt swish around her legs as she went down the hallway.

"I'll wait."

The drive to Vernon Hershberger's farm, just a mile or so south of Shipshewana, was enjoyable. Mary had sold four dozen eggs and a pound of butter. At this rate, she would have her debt to Mr. Holdeman paid off in only a couple months.

Samuel didn't speak much as he drove, but when they went by a pasture with some mares and foals, he pointed them out to her.

"There are a bunch of new work horses for someone."

One of the youngsters trotted along the fence as they passed, nose in the air.

"They are very cute, aren't they?"

He nodded. "They look fine. The dams are in good shape, which means the foals should be healthy and strong."

Mary remembered the empty stalls in Samuel's barn. "Do you think you'll ever have a team again?"

He was silent as they went past the horses and came to a field filled with growing corn. "I haven't thought much about it. Horses cost money, and there isn't very much of that for anyone these days."

Samuel turned Tilly into the next farm lane. Mary didn't have to look for the windmill. The contraption creaked and groaned from the top of the tower next to the barn.

"This is the Hershbergers'?"

"*Ja.* Are you ready to climb that windmill with me?"

Samuel jumped out of the buggy and reached for Mary's hand to steady her as she climbed down. His grip was firm, but tender.

"I think I'll visit with Myrtle and the children while you're working."

He grinned. "If you're sure you want to."

Mary spent the time visiting with Vernon's wife while Samuel worked on the windmill. Vernon could get around with his crutches and had gone outside to watch Samuel.

"What can I do to help?" Mary asked. She picked up Myrtle's toddling one-year-old who was about to fall into the table leg.

"If you can just hold her while I get this bread in the oven, that would be *wonderful-gut.*"

Myrtle slid five loaf pans in the oven and closed the damper to keep the heat regulated. Just as she straightened up, a crash of wooden blocks came from the front room, along with a crying voice.

"It never ends," Myrtle said.

Her smile kept Mary from being too worried as they went into the front room, where Troy and David, two and three years old, were playing with blocks. Troy's face was red with anger as Myrtle sat next to him and took the little boy on her lap.

"See?" she said, pointing at the blocks. "David is setting them back up again. There isn't anything to cry about."

"He cries because I knocked his tower over," David said.

"Why did you do that?"

"Because he knocked my barn down."

"Did pushing his tower over help you fix your barn?"

David sat back on his heels, shaking his head.

"You both need to put the blocks away. It's nap time."

The boys obeyed and then followed Myrtle up the stairs.

"I'll be right back," she said.

"Don't hurry."

Mary held the little girl, Rosie, in her arms, rocking her gently. The baby settled in against her shoulder and grew heavier with every minute. Soft breathing told Mary that the little girl was asleep.

She stood in the middle of the room, swaying slowly. She took in the two comfortable chairs, the heating stove along the wall, the toys set neatly on shelves, and the table between the chairs with a copy of the Good Book and the *Christenflicht*, the book of prayers. The aroma of baking bread drifted in from the kitchen, and from the stairway came Myrtle's soft voice as she helped the boys into their beds for their afternoon naps.

Tears welled in Mary's eyes and she buried her nose in Rosie's curls. This had been her dream. The home, the children, the husband…a man who cherished her and their life together. Lately she had felt the pull of that dream again, but she pushed it away. A man like Martin would never be part of her life. And Samuel…if he knew her secret, he wouldn't want to go beyond being friends.

She breathed in the little-girl scent and closed her eyes. Somehow she would have to learn to be content loving other people's children.

After Myrtle took Rosie into the downstairs bedroom to lay her down, she came back to join Mary.

"*Ach*, nap time is my favorite part of the afternoon," she said, dropping into a chair. "Sit down and we can have a nice, uninterrupted visit. I miss the weekly quiltings, even though I didn't make it very often this winter. I was glad to meet you and your sister at the last one, though. How are you getting on with Sadie?"

"We're adjusting." Mary took the other chair and relaxed. "Sadie usually doesn't need much care at all, but we're there in case she does need us."

"I'm happy you came today, but I was surprised to see you with Samuel Lapp." Her face turned bright red and she laughed. "I guess Samuel is the one I'm surprised to see. When Preacher Jonas stopped by yesterday and told Vernon that Samuel would help him with the windmill, I had a hard time believing it."

Mary's mind went back to her first Sunday in Shipshewana, when Martin bullied Samuel about helping Vernon with his plowing.

"The men got the fields plowed and planted?"

"They did it all in one day. It is such a blessing to be part of a close church like ours. With Vernon's injury, we would never have been able to get all the work done."

Myrtle sat up and looked out the window. "There's Samuel climbing down the tower." She stood up. "Let's go see if he's done."

Mary followed her friend out into the barnyard, where Samuel and Vernon stood, watching the wind wheel spin in the breeze without any squeaking or moaning. Vernon turned as his wife came to his side.

"Listen to that quiet," he said. "No more shrieking during storms."

Samuel stood with his arms crossed, and Mary could tell he was pleased.

"You could have engaged the brake if it got too bad."

Vernon shook his head. "I thought about it, but we need the pump to keep working. Myrtle couldn't spend her time out here pumping water, and I have been in no shape to get around, either." He hobbled the two steps over to Samuel and put out his hand. "*Denki*, Samuel. You have a gift for working with machines. I had no idea."

Samuel shook Vernon's hand. "Neither did I, until I tried to repair my own wind pump."

"I appreciate everything you've done."

Mary watched Samuel's face as his expression flitted from denial to acceptance and then to irritation as his brow lowered. Was it so hard for him to accept the thanks of a friend?

Samuel finally nodded and turned to get in the buggy, pushing Mary ahead of him.

"Goodbye, Myrtle." Mary waved as she stepped into the buggy. "I enjoyed our visit."

Myrtle waved as Samuel slapped the reins on Tilly's back and headed down the lane toward the road.

"We left awfully fast."

Samuel still didn't say anything, but drove with his gaze set on the road ahead.

"That was a good thing you did, using your skill to help Vernon and Myrtle. But why did we leave so quickly?"

"I don't like it when folks start thanking me like that, as if I'm something special." Samuel hunched his shoulders. "I suppose you're used to it."

Mary let his words sink in as Tilly trotted south. Samuel was right. There were things she did well, and she helped others whenever she could. But she never thought about it beyond knowing that was the way the people of the community lived together.

"That feeling you get when you help others might be new to you," she said, laying a hand on his arm, "but I think you'll learn to like it."

Chapter Thirteen

Samuel kept driving south until they reached the county road leading to the little town of Emma. As he turned Tilly at the corner, he dared to glance at Mary. She had been silent for the last two miles, ever since she said he might learn to like helping others. With a sigh, he concentrated on the road ahead again.

She couldn't know how wrong she was. He was a Lapp. He had seen the surprise in Vernon's eyes when they arrived at the farm. And then the man had been so suspicious that he had watched Samuel's every move. Nothing had changed. He still lived in *Daed*'s shadow.

"It's such a beautiful afternoon," Mary said.

He nodded.

"Look how green everything is. Summer is getting close."

"It's green because of the rain we've had, and the warm nights. It makes the grass grow."

She nodded, smiling at him. "That's what I said. Summer is getting close."

He felt a grin coming in spite of his sour mood.

"Emma is just ahead. Do you want to stop at the store for a soda pop?"

Mary stiffened. He felt it in her elbow that brushed against his as they sat next to each other in the buggy seat.

"There's nothing wrong with a soda pop, is there?"

She took a deep breath, her eyes closed.

"Mary?"

Her eyes flashed open and she stared at him. "I...I guess we could have a soda."

He pulled Tilly to a stop outside the general store. "What flavor do you want? Grape? Orange?"

Her hands shook. "Not orange. Grape. Or strawberry. Anything but orange."

Samuel hesitated before taking the bottles of pop from the cooler on the store's broad front porch. Something was wrong. Mary sat in the buggy seat, staring at her lap. Her lips were moving as if she was reciting something to herself, or...counting. She continued her strange behavior as he used the bottle opener on the outside of the cooler.

He went into the store and laid a dime on the counter, nodding to the clerk, then hurried back to the buggy.

"Here you go."

She stared at the bottle of grape soda he handed her.

"I chose grape. It's my favorite."

Mary finally took it from him, but she didn't drink it. He turned south and drove out of town to the little lake that lapped against the shore, just yards from the road. He slowed Tilly to a walk. Mary still hadn't taken a drink of her soda, and she still hadn't said a word.

She startled when he drove Tilly off the road into the grass where someone had set up a bench under a tree.

He pulled the hitching weight out from under the buggy seat and fastened it to Tilly's bridle. The short rope would allow the horse to graze in the shade while he and Mary talked. He went back to the buggy and held Mary's pop bottle while she climbed down, then he led her to the bench. It was time to find out what was going on.

"Now," he said as he handed the bottle back to her. "Tell me what's wrong."

She stared at him. "Who said anything is wrong?"

"As soon as I mentioned getting some soda pop, you changed. You haven't even taken a drink." He tipped his own bottle up to drain the last of his grape soda. Just as he thought, she was going to deny that anything was amiss.

She passed her bottle from one hand to the other.

He leaned toward her. "Whatever it is, it's making you into someone other than the Mary I know. I've suspected for a long time that someone has hurt you, and now it's time for you to tell me about it."

She shook her head. He took the bottle from her and set it next to her on the bench.

Samuel tried again. "My *mamm* was a wonderful, gentle, kind woman." Thinking about her made his eyes itch. "But she was the victim of *Daed*'s temper."

Mary looked at him.

"She never told anyone, but we children knew." He cleared his throat. "I wonder how different her life would have been if she had confided in Sadie, or her parents or someone."

Mary sniffed. "I've told Ida Mae about it."

He was right. There was something wrong.

"I'm glad you told your sister, but it's still bothering

you, isn't it?" He scooted closer to her. "We're friends, aren't we?"

She nodded.

"You can tell me anything. I want to help you."

"Ida Mae said I should tell you, but you'll never want to see me again." Her voice was raspy, almost a whisper.

He slid so he was next to her on the bench and took her icy hands in his. "I don't think you could say anything that would cause that."

She glanced at him. "It's terrible."

"I thought it would be."

She chewed on her bottom lip.

"Why is the soda pop a problem?"

"He...he bought some for me. Orange."

He? Samuel's head started pounding, but he kept his voice quiet.

"Orange soda?"

She nodded.

"Who is he?"

"A man...a boy I met when I worked at a diner back home."

"An Amish man?"

She shook her head. Samuel squeezed the cold fingers and sat back a little, relaxing. She was only embarrassed because she had let an *Englischer* buy a soda pop for her. The way she had been acting, he had thought the problem was much worse.

"There isn't anything that bad about sharing a soda pop—"

"We didn't just sh-share a soda." She took a deep, shaky breath. "He...took advantage of me. He forced himself on me."

She pulled her hands from his grasp and walked

down the grassy lawn to the edge of the lake, but Samuel couldn't move. Could he have heard her right? This wasn't about sharing a soda with an *Englischer*.

Ice filled his arms, his legs, his core. Everything was frozen as he watched her stand on the shore of the lake with her back to him. He sank his head into his hands and a moan escaped. What could he say to her? How could she live after experiencing that... The ice fled as quickly as it had formed and the anger came roaring in. His fist slammed on the bench, knocking the soda bottle off, spilling the grape pop onto the ground, where it disappeared into the grass.

Never to be recovered.

Mary still stood looking out over the lake as he walked up behind her and grasped her shoulders with both hands. He pulled her back against him.

"It wasn't your fault." He whispered the words, close to her ear as his cheek brushed her *kapp*.

A tear dripped from her chin as he put his arms around her.

"You don't have to be nice to me. I can guess what you must think." She stepped away from his embrace, but he grasped her hand.

"I don't hate you."

She sniffed. "But now, every time you look at me, you'll think about what happened. What I did."

A stone dropped in Samuel's middle. If he ever needed the Good Lord to hear his prayers, now was the time. He needed to say whatever she needed to hear.

He turned Mary around and tipped her face toward his. "*Ne*, that isn't true. Every time I look at you, I'll think about what a strong woman you are. You have suffered, and survived, and you will never suffer like that again. I promise."

She buried her face in his shirt and he held her close, tucked under his chin.

Mary kept her arms folded tight as she rode in the buggy, her knees pressed together and as far away from Samuel as she could get. If they were closer to home, she would get out and walk the rest of the way, but the only thing worse than sitting in the same buggy as Samuel would to be alone. Vulnerable.

Why had she told him her secret? Mary chewed her lower lip. She knew why. The soda pop had brought back such strong memories. Memories that clamored for release. And in a way, she felt better. A tight knot inside her had loosened and she could breathe easier.

But things would never be the same between the two of them. Samuel would never feel relaxed and comfortable around her again.

Thunder rolled from the west, and the breeze gusted, rocking the buggy. Samuel urged Tilly to a faster trot and glanced at Mary, the creases around his eyes showing that he was concerned. Even worried.

"A storm is coming, but I'm going to try to make it home before the worst of it hits."

Lightning flashed in the distance and Tilly's ears went back. Samuel kept a firm grip on the reins and paid attention to his driving instead of her.

Tilly jumped at the next crack of thunder, and Samuel leaned forward, concentrating on his driving.

"That storm is getting closer. Will you roll down the rain curtains? I don't want to risk taking my hands off the reins with Tilly as skittish as she is."

Mary untied the rolled curtain on her side and low-ered it, snapping it into place all the way down. But to reach the other one, she would have to get past Samuel somehow.

"Do you want me to drive while you do your side?"

He shook his head, his gaze on the road ahead. "Here." Samuel lifted his arms so she could climb over him, under the reins, but she hesitated. "Come on, scoot over there before Tilly gets spooked again."

She had no choice. She ducked under his outstretched arms and stepped over his legs while he slid to her spot on the buggy seat. Now she could reach the curtain and fasten the snaps, and they were closed in the cozy buggy just in time. Big raindrops pelted the roof.

Samuel said something, but she couldn't hear him over the noise.

"What?" she shouted.

He leaned toward her and spoke close to her ear. "We're almost to our farm. I'm going to stop there until the storm is over and take you home after."

She nodded, showing she understood. Tilly trotted faster, but Samuel still gripped the reins, keeping her from breaking into a full gallop. If she panicked, they would be in trouble. But Samuel's firm grip told the horse he was in control and she trusted him.

Samuel turned up the lane, past the house and on to the barn.

He pulled Tilly to a stop in front of the closed barn door. "You hold her until I get the doors open, then let her go in. Whatever you do, don't let go of the reins."

Mary nodded, grasping the leather reins in shaky hands. Just as Samuel unfastened the rain curtain, light-ning flashed again, sending Tilly into a half rear, her front feet striking at the barn door. Samuel sent Mary a worried look, but she smiled, trying to look confident.

Samuel opened one of the doors, and then the other, sliding them out of the way. As soon as the opening appeared, Tilly tried to leap into the shelter, but Mary was ready for her. Bracing her feet, Mary leaned back on the reins, keeping the frightened horse under control. Tilly walked into the barn, straining at the reins the whole way, but Mary didn't let up until Tilly reached the gate of her stall and Samuel took her bridle, stopping her.

Mary climbed down from the buggy and shook her arms, releasing the tense muscles. The barn echoed with the pounding rain on the roof high above them, but Samuel grinned at her in the dim light. He looked triumphant, as if they had defeated a monster rather than escaped a rainstorm.

"You did a *wonderful-gut* job," he shouted. "Will you close the doors while I take care of Tilly?"

Mary slid the big doors closed while Samuel lit the lantern to chase away the shadows. He unhitched the buggy, then removed Tilly's bridle and slipped a halter over her head. Tying her to the hitching post, he got a towel from a pile nearby. He crooned to Tilly as he wiped her face dry and gave her an old apple from a bucket. He cared for her as tenderly as he would a child.

As tenderly as he had held her when she confessed what had happened. Samuel didn't seem to hate her, and hadn't turned away from her, even when he had learned the worst about her.

Shivering, Mary moved toward him, craving the security of his strength and the warmth of his company.

"Can I help?"

"For sure. I'll take the harness off while you rub Tilly down."

"She's soaked through to the skin. Do you have some warm mash for her?"

"I'll heat some up in the barn cellar." The thunder boomed, sounding like the center of the storm was above their heads. "If the storm ever lets up."

They worked in silence since talking was nearly impossible with the rain pounding on the roof. By the time Mary had toweled off Tilly's back and was working on her front legs, the rain had eased. Samuel had hung the harness on its pegs and had wiped each strap, then he grabbed another towel and started rubbing down Tilly's hind legs.

When they were done, he led Tilly into her stall and poured a measure of oats into her feed box while Mary opened the small door next to the big barn door. The thunder and lightning had passed, but rain still poured down in steady streams. Samuel joined her and peered out.

"Look there." He pointed to the west, where a shaft of sunlight had broken out of the clouds. "The storm is nearly over. We'll wait for a few moments, then we can go to the house."

Mary shivered in her damp clothes and Samuel moved closer. Was he going to hold her in his arms again? Part of her recoiled from the thought, but another part remembered his solid strength and the complete safety she had felt by the lakeshore. The first time she had truly felt safe in months.

He knew her secret, but he hadn't shunned her. His acceptance had softened her heart and she leaned toward him, longing for his strong arms around her.

Samuel, standing behind her, rubbed her upper arms, then pulled her close.

"You're cold." His breath was warm and moist in her ear.

"Not very cold."

"Enough to give me an excuse to put my arms around you."

She turned in his arms and looked up at him. She had to know, to hear him say it again. "Do you want to do that, knowing…what you know about me?"

He wiped at her cheek with his thumb. "I told you, I don't blame you for what happened."

It was too good to be true. "You say that now, but what about the future?"

"I've told you about my *daed*."

She nodded.

"What you went through has left you wounded. What *Daed* did to my *mamm* left its mark, too."

Mary saw the pain on his face as he relived the memories. His arms dropped to his sides as he gazed out the door at the rain.

"Sometimes it was a black eye. Once it was a broken arm. Other times the bruises were hidden, but I knew they were there." He sighed. "I wish I could have helped her."

"You were only a boy."

"I'm not a boy anymore." His hand shook as he reached for hers. "I couldn't protect *Mamm*, but perhaps I can stand between you and your past." He didn't look at her, but shut his eyes, as if pushing away his own memories.

Mary drew back a little, looking into his face. "I've told you that you aren't your father, and this is proof. He didn't protect and care for your mother, but when you heard of my problem, that's the first thing you wanted to do." She reached up and traced a line down his cheek to his chin. "You are a gentle and tender man, Samuel. And I...I trust you to take care of me."

He looked at her then, his smile grim. "Don't trust me too far, Mary. I may not be my *daed*, but—"

She rose on her toes and kissed his cheek. "You aren't your *daed*. I see a lot of Bram in you, and from what Sadie says, your *grossdawdi* Abe, too. I do trust you."

He kissed her then, pulling her to himself and claiming her with a kiss so light she almost didn't feel it. The kisses continued to her cheek, her ear, and then he tucked her under his chin, surrounded by his arms.

"I will try my best."

Samuel picked his way around mud puddles the next morning. Last night's storm had been powerful, and it had brought plenty of rain. Tilly stood in the pasture, her side to the rising sun, hip cocked and head down. Her ear flicked at a fly, but there was no other movement.

The stock watering trough was full, so Samuel threw the brake, disengaging the windmill. The wheel would still spin in the wind, but wouldn't pump the water, wasting it.

The next chore was cleaning the harness after the soaking it got in last night's rain. Samuel pushed the big barn doors open and pulled Tilly's harness down from its pegs. He laid it on the workbench and grabbed the can of saddle soap off the shelf, setting to work. Methodically, he detached each piece of harness and rubbed the soap into it, cleaning and conditioning the leather. As he worked, his mind drifted right back to Mary.

He had told her that he didn't hate her for the attack, that she wasn't to blame. But that unknown man…had he been punished for causing Mary such grief? Did he even know how much he had hurt her? Someone should do something. He should do something.

Rubbing harder at the harness, he pushed that thought from his mind. Samuel stretched and rolled his shoulders, trying to relieve the tension that had crept in. He wanted to protect her, but who was he protecting her from? She hadn't said who her attacker had been, only that it was a young man in Ohio. No wonder she jumped every time a strange man came near. She was worried that the scoundrel would try to follow her to Indiana.

By the time he finished cleaning the harness and had put it away, he had run through five or six possibilities of what would happen if a strange *Englischer* started nosing around. And by the time he finished cleaning Tilly's box stall he had imagined every outcome, from Mary's panicked flight to another community where he would never see her again to her welcoming smile when the man showed up.

When that scene flitted through his imagination, he slammed his fist into the post next to the stall, making the entire barn quiver.

Suddenly, he had to see Mary. Last night, after the storm, he had walked her home. But even though she had let him hold her hand, there had been no more kisses. He had to know…had he imagined the sweetness of holding her in his arms? The closeness he had felt was something he craved. He wanted to be that close to her again. Every day.

He washed quickly in the watering trough, splashing water in his hair and scrubbing his hands. A tune found its way out in a whistle as he strode along the path. His steps quickened as he imagined the smile that would light Mary's face when she saw him.

When he reached Sadie's, Martin Troyer's buggy was in the yard and voices came from the barn. He headed that way, but stopped just outside the door. Martin was inside with Mary facing him.

"I told you. Ida Mae and I won't go on any more picnics with you." Her voice sounded strained. Tired.

Martin took a step closer to her. "The picnic isn't important. I've learned everything about you that I need to know. I'll ask Bishop to announce the wedding next week, and we can marry in July."

Even from this distance, Samuel saw the panic in Mary's eyes. She shook her head.

"I've been waiting a long time to find someone like you," Martin said. His voice had become tender, almost petulant. "You will be the perfect wife for me. You're young and strong. We'll have a big family with plenty of sons and daughters to carry on after me."

Mary shook her head again as Martin stepped closer and took her hand. "I don't want to marry you."

"You'll have everything you need. And when your sister marries Peter, you'll even have her close by."

Martin grasped her shoulder, but Mary shrugged his hand off and stepped back until she was pressed against the center post.

"I won't marry you." She shook her head. "I won't."

"Why not?" Martin stepped closer to her, trapping her against the post. "Don't you see? You're perfect for me." He traced the line of her jaw with a stubby finger.

Mary wrenched her face away from him.

Samuel had seen enough. He stepped into the barn.

"I think she has refused you, Martin."

The older man jumped at the sound of his voice, dropping his hands and taking a step away from Mary. The grateful look on her face gave Samuel the courage he needed.

"I think it's time for you to leave."

"This isn't any concern of yours, Lapp." Martin's face grew red. "This is between me and Mary."

"It is my concern, because Mary and I are friends." Samuel felt the familiar, tight burn pushing its way into his head, but ignored the warning. "I heard her say she doesn't want to marry you, but you aren't listening to her."

Martin turned toward Samuel as Mary moved away from him, toward Chester's stall.

"She's a woman who needs someone to take care of her." Martin's voice rose as he spoke. "I can do that for her better than anyone, whether she thinks so now or not. She'll learn."

Samuel's head throbbed. He took a step closer to Martin, clenching his fists.

"She's a woman who knows her own mind and she will marry the man she chooses."

Martin laughed. "And who will that be? You? That just proves what I was saying. She needs someone to help her and guide her so she doesn't make a terrible mistake."

Samuel grabbed Martin's shirt and yanked him close.

"The mistake would be marrying you, Troyer." The words roared in his ears. Over Martin's shoulder he saw Mary let herself into Chester's stall, putting a barrier between them.

Martin tried to push him away, but Samuel's grip on his shirt was too tight.

"When she accepted the cow, she accepted me." Martin's eyes narrowed as he leaned toward Samuel. "It has already been decided and there is nothing you can do about it."

Samuel lifted his fist, pulling Martin up with it. The other man's feet scraped the floor as he tried to regain his footing. "Take the cow and leave."

Martin's face hardened. "You're just like your old *daed*, Samuel. Just like him. You're a bully and always will be." His lips thinned as he dropped his voice to a whisper. "And Mary knows it. You've lost any chance you had with her."

Samuel's grip loosened on Martin's shirt and he backed away. His heart was a heavy rock plummeting toward his feet. Martin was right. He was his father's son.

Martin straightened his shirt. "Mary can keep the cow. She'll come around."

Samuel looked toward the stall where Mary stood, staring at him with eyes wide.

Martin pushed past him. "*Ja*, for sure. She'll come around."

Samuel barely heard the other man leave. He only saw Mary slip through the outside door of the stall and disappear.

Chapter Fourteen

Mary ran around the end of the barn, wiping away tears as she went. Slipping through the gate into the pasture, she ran to the far corner, where a creek cut through and trees grew in a small grove. She jumped across the narrow stream and pushed her way through the branches until she reached the fence, hidden from prying eyes.

She had never seen Samuel when he was angry. Not like this. She bit her knuckle raw when the memory of his uncontrolled rage washed over her. If that anger was ever directed at her, she would be helpless. As helpless as she had been in the barn with Martin. As helpless as she had been in the alley… She sank to the ground as the tears overwhelmed her. Cold mud seeped through her dress, and she welcomed it, trying to keep the memories at bay. But like a barn door flung open in a stormy wind, the carefully tied and bundled thoughts flew where they would.

Samuel's angry shouts. Every groping touch of Harvey's hands. The hot look in Martin's eyes. The stones of the alleyway pressing into her back. Damp, steaming breath on her neck… She tried to wrench her thoughts away, but they wouldn't obey her. She couldn't stop the tears. Her hoarse sobs took over, wrenching her body until she was sick, and still they continued until she gave up fighting against them.

Until every one of the memories had flown through her consciousness, leaving her empty of everything except the shame. The dreadful shame. The shame that made her want to bury herself in the cold mud.

She knelt on the ground, her forehead against a tree, but her thoughts went no further than the hollow pit deep within her.

"God in Heaven…"

How could she even pray? She had no words.

"Mary!"

Samuel was calling her. Looking for her. She wiped one cheek, and then the other, trembling. How could she face him?

"Mary?"

She looked up at his voice, tender and quiet. He had found her hiding place. He dropped to his knees beside her, but she turned away from him.

"Leave me alone." She buried her face in her hands. "Go away and leave me alone."

A dead stick cracked as he moved closer.

"I'm so sorry—"

"Samuel…" Mary swallowed. She was going to be sick again. "I told you to go away. I don't want to see you."

"What I did back there—" He sniffed as if he was trying to hold back tears. "I lost control, and I'm sorry."

She stood with jerky movements. She hadn't been afraid of Samuel since she learned to know him, but now his angry expression filled her mind, blotting out the man kneeling before her.

"You think you're going to fix this, but you aren't. Don't try. Don't ask about it. Don't talk about it."

His face grew pale. Her hands shook and she clasped them together. She hadn't made him angry, she had hurt him. Her heart wrenched, but she couldn't...she couldn't reach out to him. She couldn't survive when his expression twisted into the hunger she had seen on Martin's face. And it would change, because he was a man, with the same hunger for what every man wanted. The clawing, grasping hunger...

She turned and ran, splashing through the creek and to the house. Ida Mae and Sadie were in the kitchen, but she flew past them and up the stairs, slamming her bedroom door shut and throwing herself on the bed.

The tears flowed as if she had never cried before. Her stomach roiled. She covered her head with her pillow and sobbed into the quilt on her bed. She would never, never know the tender love of a man. Never know what it was like to be cherished as someone's wife. She would never be anyone's mother. In one horrible night, Harvey Anderson had stolen that from her, and Samuel had only proven that she could never trust any man.

Anything good that might have come out of her friendship with Samuel was gone. Destroyed. Because every time he held her close, she would relive the horror of his rage against Martin.

The sobs ended, but the despair remained. She threw the pillow off her head and sat up, wiping her hot cheeks with the heel of her hand.

"Are you all right?"

Ida Mae had pushed the door open far enough to peek through.

Mary shook her head, making it throb.

"I'll get you a cool cloth, and we'll talk."

Mary took a deep breath. "I don't want to talk."

The door pushed open farther and Sadie walked into the room. "Go get a towel." She waved Ida Mae away and sat on the bed next to Mary, sighing as she lowered herself onto the mattress.

"You didn't need to come all the way upstairs."

"I find it difficult, but not impossible." Sadie smoothed the hair off Mary's forehead. "You need us, so we came."

Ida Mae came back with a damp towel and Mary held it on her face, drinking in the coolness.

"How did your dress get so muddy?" Ida Mae asked.

Mary had forgotten the mud. She stood, moaning as she saw that the mud from her dress had soiled the quilt. She buried her face in the towel again.

Sadie pulled her back down to sit on the bed again. "Tell us what is wrong."

"I'm all right, really."

"Your *kapp* is crooked," Ida Mae said. She reached to straighten Mary's *kapp* and the hairpins fell out.

Sadie brought a small stool closer to the bed. "Sit here and I'll brush your hair while you tell us what is wrong."

Mary succumbed to Sadie's attention and relaxed on the stool, fingering the towel she still held. Sadie took long strokes with the brush that eased away all the remaining tension, leaving Mary as weak as the towel in her hands. She gave it back to Ida Mae and picked up her *kapp* from the bed where Sadie had laid it. Mary turned it in her hands. She had worn it for as long as she could remember, from the time she was a little girl. Every woman she knew wore a *kapp*, only to be removed at bedtime, and she had done the same…until the night Harvey had attacked her. Then it had fallen off as she struggled with him.

She fingered each pleat in the fine fabric.

"Sadie, why do we wear our *kapps*?"

"It is a sign of our submission to God and to our fathers or husbands. It is a sign of our humility."

Humility. The concept was as familiar to her as her *kapp*. It went hand in hand with submission…she held back a shudder as she considered ever needing to submit to a husband. She was right to remain single.

Mary shook her head. "I don't feel very humble, or very much like submitting to any man."

Sadie chuckled. "Whether you feel humble or not, you must act that way. God calls us to always put others before ourselves. To obey. To serve. And to put Him above all." She finished brushing and started gathering Mary's hair into a bun. "We are to enthrone Him, not ourselves. The *kapp* is the symbol of that submission, of putting ourselves under His authority."

She took Mary's *kapp* and pinned it in place with the last of the hairpins.

"What if it doesn't work?"

"What do you mean?" Sadie sat down on the bed again and Ida Mae joined her.

Mary bit her lip and glanced at Ida Mae.

Her sister grasped her hand. "I told Sadie what happened to you. I know you wanted to keep it a secret, but Sadie asked what was bothering you—"

Mary patted her sister's knee. "That's all right. I'm

glad you both know." She drew a deep breath that caught at the end. She wouldn't start crying again.

"I mean," she said, looking at Sadie, "the *kapp* is that sign, but doesn't that mean that God is supposed to protect us?"

Sadie's eyes grew wet and she bowed her head.

"*Ach*, Mary, you're learning what submission to God truly is."

She raised her head again and took Mary's hand in her own worn one. Mary stroked the soft, fragile skin with her thumb.

"You are asking where God was when you needed him the most." She grasped Mary's hand tighter. "He was right there with you, suffering with you. And He is with you now, ready to help you understand. Our Lord suffered and died so that we could come to Him and be forgiven of our sins."

Mary shrugged. "I've heard that my whole life, in church and at home. What does that have to do with what…what happened?"

"When you can forgive that man for what he did to you, you will begin to understand the forgiveness God extends to us." Sadie leaned closer. "Humble yourself, and submit to what God is teaching you through these circumstances."

Mary pressed her lips together, thinking of Samuel's angry face as he had held Martin in his grip. "How can I do that? How can I just forgive and forget like nothing ever happened?"

Sadie shook her head. "You will never forget. But you must forgive, whether the man who attacked you is repentant or not. Forgiving him has nothing to do with him, and everything to do with you. Let God turn this terrible event to your good rather than making you fearful and bitter."

Mary sniffed. Fearful, *ja*. She had lived in fear ever since that night. But bitter? Unbidden, memories came of harsh words to Ida Mae, and to Samuel. Uncharitable thoughts about Sadie. And Martin…she had reserved her most bitter thoughts for him.

She gave Sadie's hand a gentle squeeze before releasing it.

"I think I need to spend some time alone."

Sadie gave Mary a gentle hug, then she and Ida Mae left the room, closing the door quietly behind them. She sat, considering Sadie's words. Forgiving Harvey…that would take more strength than she possessed, but perhaps she could in time.

But Samuel was different. She would see him often, perhaps daily. He had asked for her forgiveness. Could she do that? Could they ever be friends once more?

Mary changed her soiled dress for her clean one and lay down on the bed again. Tears came, but not the anguished, violent tears of earlier. These tears fell like a gentle, cleansing rain until she fell asleep.

On Friday, Samuel was surprised to see Ida Mae drive Chester up the lane to the house. He met her at the hitching rail and caught Chester's reins to hold him while Ida Mae stepped out of the buggy.

"You're on your way to town?"

Ida Mae smiled at him. She was nearly as pretty as Mary, with blue eyes instead of brown. But some unnamed sadness haunted her expression most days.

"I'm taking the eggs and butter into Shipshewana, and I thought Judith or Esther would like to go with me."

She glanced toward the house. "Mary is brave enough to make the trip by herself, but not me. I'd rather have company."

"I haven't seen Mary for days." Not since she had told him to leave her alone. And he had, even though he worried about her every minute. "Is she feeling all right?"

"She has been staying close to home, taking care of the chickens and everything. And the cow, Schmetterling, takes a lot of her time."

He backed away. "I see."

Ida Mae took a step closer to him. "Sadie thought you might like to stop by some time. Maybe tomorrow?"

Samuel rubbed his chin. "Sadie thought so?"

Ida Mae just smiled and started toward the house with Samuel following.

"What about Mary? Does she want me to come by?"

Mary's sister paused. "She hasn't said so, but I think she misses you. I think she would like to see you again." She put her hand on the doorknob, then turned to him. "Tomorrow. After morning chores are done."

Samuel headed back to the barn and the work that was waiting. Sadie and Ida Mae both thought Mary wanted to see him, but he knew better. He had seen the frightened look in her eyes. She feared what he had become when he let the rage take over.

He took the manure fork from its place on the wall and headed toward Tilly's stall, but stopped when his vision became too blurred to see where he was going. He wiped at his eyes with the back of his hand. The weight of what he had done bowed his shoulders as he opened the gate to the stall. He stared at the soiled straw. What was the use? Why even try to clear it out? It would only have to be done again tomorrow.

For the first time, he understood *Daed*'s need to drink. To obliterate the pain of what he had become, what he had done. What hope was there if he couldn't control the rage that lurked inside him?

A call came from outside the barn. "Samuel?"

Bram. What was he doing here? Samuel wiped his eyes again and picked up the manure fork before Bram walked into the barn.

"There you are." Bram voice was pleasant. Carefree. "I was passing by on my way to town and thought I'd stop in to say hello."

Samuel shoved the fork under the straw and lifted, balancing the load. If he didn't turn around, if he didn't look at Bram, maybe his brother would get the message that he didn't feel like talking.

"Esther sent me out to get you. She has some bread fresh out of the oven, and she put a pot of coffee on. She thought you'd like to take a break while we visit."

Samuel grunted as he carried the loaded fork to the manure pile outside. When he came back in, Bram was waiting for him, leaning on the stall gate.

"If I didn't know better, I'd think you were back to your old self."

Samuel glared at him. "I never stopped being my 'old self.' I'm the same as I've ever been."

A frown passed over his brother's face. "What has happened?"

Samuel shoved the fork under the next section of wet, soiled bedding and carried it out to the pile. Bram was still waiting for an answer when he came back in.

"Who says anything has happened?"

Bram reached over the gate and grabbed his sleeve.

"Put the fork down and talk to me. You're as grumpy as an old hen."

"I'm not grumpy. This is just the way I am."

Bram stared at him and Samuel gave up. He leaned the fork handle against the side of the stall and faced Bram.

"I lost my temper and acted as bad as *Daed* ever did. Worse."

"So you slipped back into his old habits."

Samuel nodded. "I can't trust myself not to do it again."

"Is that why you've stopped keeping company with Mary?"

"Esther's been talking about me?"

Bram rubbed his thumb along the top of the gate. "Actually, she asked me to stop by and talk to you. She's worried about you."

Samuel shrugged, trying not to care. "There's no reason to be worried. I'm a Lapp. Our father's son. It's just the way I am."

"I used to think you were, too. But as we've gotten reacquainted I can see that you're nothing like him."

Samuel picked at a loose splinter on the wall of the stall. He couldn't look his brother in the eye. "How can you say that?"

"We both know what drove *Daed*. It was the alcohol. I don't know why he drank, but he did, and it controlled him." Bram reached over and grasped Samuel's arm. "You aren't like him. You can ask for help. You can control your temper."

A short laugh escaped. "Obviously, I can't. You weren't there." Samuel shook his head. "You didn't see the look on Mary's face when I threw Martin out of the barn." Just like *Daed*, he had ruined everything that was good in his life.

Bram's eyebrows rose. "Mary? So you do care about her."

"If I did, I ruined it when I lost my temper." He leveled his gaze at Bram. "You know I can't ask anyone to live the way *Mamm* did."

Bram didn't answer right away and Samuel didn't blame him.

"So you made a mistake."

"A big one."

"Have you asked for forgiveness?"

Samuel picked at another splinter in the wood. "I thought so. But Mary hasn't spoken to me since then."

"Not from Mary. From God."

It was Samuel's turn to be silent. He hadn't asked God for help, and he hadn't asked Him for forgiveness, either. It was no use anyway.

"You haven't, have you?"

Samuel shook his head.

"Then you have some work to do. Ask God for His forgiveness and His help. Then go apologize to Mary. Ask her to give you another chance."

Samuel bowed his head. "I can't risk it. I know that eventually I'll lose my temper again. It's best that Mary and I just call it quits. She'll find someone else." Even as he said the words, he felt them knife through his heart.

"You can't give up, Samuel. Let God take control of your temper and your life. Submit to Him." Bram squeezed his arm, then pushed away from the gate. "I'll leave you to it."

Samuel watched him leave. Bram was wrong. There were just some things a man couldn't trust to anyone else, even God.

* * *

Samuel woke before the sun came up the next morning. It had been a long night as he spent several sleepless hours arguing with God. Every time he had made up his mind to ignore Bram's advice and give up on Mary, Bible verses and snatches of sermons would echo in his mind. The theme of all of them was trust.

He finally gave up, sitting on the edge of his bed and reaching for his clothes. He would give God one more chance. He would trust Him with Mary's safety and his own sanity. Glancing at the ceiling, he had said one simple prayer. "Help me."

But he still wasn't in a hurry to face Mary. He dawdled at his chores and breakfast until Esther took his plate away.

"Whatever it is you don't want to do, just get it over with."

He pushed himself away from the table. "That's easy for you to say."

She piled his plate on top of hers and Judith's and took them to the sink. "So what is it that you don't want to do?"

"I need to go over to Sadie's, but I'm not sure Mary wants to see me."

Her eyebrows rose. "You don't think Mary wants to talk to you?"

He shrugged and took his hat from the peg. "I guess I'll find out."

Esther's giggle followed him out the door and down the steps. He stalked down the worn path through the fence row. Esther could laugh all she wanted, but she hadn't seen Mary's face when she told him to leave. He couldn't see any way back to the friendship they had shared before.

When he reached Sadie's yard, the only person in sight was Ida Mae, working in the garden. When she saw him, she pointed in the direction of the new chicken coop.

Samuel walked in that direction, following the sound of excited clucking and Mary's voice calling to the hens. As he rounded the corner of the chicken coop, she saw him and fell silent.

"Good morning," Samuel said.

She finished spreading the rest of the grain over the ground, then came out of the pen, closing the gate behind her. "I didn't expect to see you."

"I know." He ran his thumbs up and down his suspenders. "The last time we spoke, you told me to leave you alone. Do you still mean it?"

Mary swung the empty grain bucket in her hand. "I don't know."

"Ida Mae said she thought you missed me." He took the pail from her and set it next to the gate. "Do you want to go for a walk? Just down to the creek?"

She bit her lip, and then shrugged, never looking at him. He held the fence wires apart for her, and then he looked at the pasture. Instead of stopping at the corn field, it extended all the way to the woods, the fence enclosing a good three acres of his corn field. The young corn plants were gone, and he could imagine how the cow and Chester had found them sweet and tasty.

"When did you move the fence?" He struggled to keep his voice even.

"Dale and his son came over and did it for us yesterday afternoon. He said he was sorry he had planted corn on Sadie's land."

Samuel started counting inside his head, hoping Mary wouldn't notice. "On my land. Dale planted the corn on my land."

She faced him. "Aren't these three acres part of the ten that your *grossdawdi* gave to Sadie? She said it was."

"He gave her the ten acres to use, but we still own it. Someday, when Sadie is gone, this land will be part of our farm again."

Mary stared at him. "Does Sadie know this?"

"She did at one time. But the way she forgets things, I have no idea what she believes."

"Then it sounds like we should move the fence back."

Samuel had lost track of his counting. He didn't need it. He was in no danger of losing his temper. "The corn is already gone, and you are right. You need the pasture for the cow." He lifted his hat and wiped his brow. The day was growing warm. "There's no use making Sadie upset. *Grossdawdi* would never have wanted that to happen."

Mary was quiet as they continued to the corner of the pasture where the creek cut through. "He must have loved her very much, the way he made sure she was taken care of." She plucked a wild carrot flower and twirled it between her fingers.

"I think he regretted what happened between them. Even though he had married *Grossmutti* and was happy with her, he always had a soft spot for Sadie."

They had reached the creek and Mary jumped across it. Samuel followed her.

"Are all the Lapp men like that?"

Samuel watched her profile as she leaned against a

sycamore tree. If she never loved him, it didn't matter. He would still care for her and protect her.

"I think they are."

She picked some more of the wild carrots and started making a chain of the flower stems.

Samuel plucked one of the flowers and let it bounce at the end of its stalk. "I came to apologize. I…I lost my temper the other day."

Her hands stilled, holding the half-finished chain.

"I frightened you, the way I lost my temper with Martin."

She nodded. He picked the flower in his hands apart. "I don't know why I lost control. I was angry about what you told me…what happened to you…and then when I saw Martin…"

Mary wove another flower into her chain.

"I had the thought that I could go and take care of that man in Ohio. Make him pay for what he did."

Her eyebrows went up. "That wouldn't change anything."

He shrugged. "I only want to fix things, to make it better."

She plucked a flower. "Even if you wiped Harvey off the face of the earth, it wouldn't change what happened. I still have to live with…with the shame." She bit her lip. "No one can make this better."

He moved closer to her and brushed a fly off her shoulder. She tensed.

"Maybe you need to go on with your life. Leave those memories behind you."

"I tried that when I came here. It doesn't work."

"You came here to hide. To escape. Not to go on."

She finished the flower chain and turned it between her fingers.

"You're right. When Sadie invited Ida Mae and me to come here, I jumped at the chance. Anything to get away. But the memories followed me." She dropped the flowers onto an old tree stump. "It's no use."

Samuel leaned toward Mary, catching a scent of chicken feed and fresh straw. "What can I say to make things better?"

She turned away from him, toward the house. "Nothing. Don't say anything."

As she walked away, Samuel waited as a hot stone burned in his chest. But it wasn't anger. The stone settled. A weight of sorrow only Mary's forgiveness could ease.

Chapter Fifteen

A week later, the thunderstorms were still coming almost every day.

On Thursday night, a storm had kept Samuel awake until nearly midnight. And then sometime during the night, another storm blew in, the rolls of thunder bringing Samuel fully awake again.

His bedroom was close and hot with the windows closed. When the earlier storm had come through, he had gone around the house, slamming the sashes down against the rising wind. As he had stumbled back to his bed, he had heard the girls closing the windows upstairs.

Thunder boomed again, only seconds after the last roll. Samuel held his clock up to the faint light coming through the window. A flash of lightning illuminated the dial enough for him to read it. Three o'clock.

He settled back into his pillow and tried to sleep again, but to no avail. Between the thunder and Mary...

Samuel sat up, planting his feet on the throw rug next to his bed, and ran his fingers through his hair. Mary had filled his thoughts for the past week. More than that. Ever since she had first come from Ohio.

A loud boom shook the house and Samuel jumped to his feet. Lightning had struck something close. His first thought was Sadie's barn, and he got dressed as quickly as he could. Shoving his feet into his shoes, he found himself praying, "Not Mary. Protect Mary…"

He ran out the kitchen door, past Esther and Judith standing at the bottom of the stairway in their night-dresses and out to the back porch. The glow that met him was what he had feared, but Sadie's barn was safe. The glow was coming from his barn. The lightning had struck the cupola and flames were tailing in the south wind. The smoke stung his eyes, even from across the barnyard.

Esther had followed him to the porch. "Samuel! The barn!"

He pushed her back. "I know. I know. Stay back. I'm going to get as much out as I can."

"The roof is burning. It's going to fall in."

He heard Esther's words screaming after him, but he was already at the barn door. Tilly was inside, shut in her stall to keep her safe from the storm, but now she was trapped.

The barn door latch stuck. He hit it with his fist, then rammed the door with his shoulder until it broke. By the time he reached Tilly's stall, the haymow was on fire. Embers drifted down around him. He stared at the thick tree trunk, the center post that carried the weight of the whole structure. Flames ran down it, toward him.

Tilly's scream brought him to his senses, and he swung her stall door open. She ran past him, eyes wide and white in the firelight, out the door to safety.

A crash from above made him look up. One end of the roof had caved in. Waves of heat washed over him.

He ran for the harness and threw it onto the buggy. He made a grab for the buggy shafts, but there was another crash and the wall of heat and flames threw him backward. He scrambled toward the door, watching in horror as the lacquered roof of the old buggy burst into flames.

He turned and ran out the door, his eyes on his sisters. Their white nightdresses waved in the wind. The wind that was sending flaming sparks toward the house.

The cattle. Samuel turned to look toward the pasture. The windmill was burning, standing like a torch, and in its light, he could make out the steers in the far corner of the pasture, huddled together. Upwind of the fire, they would be safe.

He grabbed Judith in one arm and Esther in the other, holding them close. The fire roared and he shouted so they could hear him.

"Go to Sadie's house. I'm going to go to the neighbors for help."

"We need to get dressed!" Esther tried to pull away from him.

"It's too late. Look!"

As they watched, the fire engulfed the old, rotten shingles of the roof. The house would be gone before they could do anything.

"Go to Sadie's," he yelled. "You'll be safe there."

Esther grabbed Judith's hand and the girls ran down the path. The path he had taken so many times. He started down the lane toward the road, toward Dale Yoder's, but a strange noise made him look back. The roaring had turned to a groaning sound as the old barn twisted, then collapsed on itself. The apple trees between the barn and house were burning, and the chicken coop… Samuel sank to his knees as the chicken coop disappeared in the flames.

It was too late. Too late to save anything.

As the fire claimed the house, Samuel struggled to his feet and retreated from the blaze. He thought of all the things that the fire was consuming. The room where he and the other children had been born. *Daed*'s old desk. *Mamm*'s rocking chair. The kitchen table.

He buried his face in his hands. The steps that had claimed *Mamm*'s life.

And now the fire was destroying everything. Everything.

Another crash as the roof of the house collapsed into the second floor, and then he felt ashes pelting him.

Looking up, he stared in disbelief as the rain began to fall. Heavy, wet, raindrops. He held his face up to the cleansing rain, letting it cool his burning skin.

A distant pounding woke Mary up. The first thing she saw was light on her bedroom ceiling. It couldn't be the dawning sun. The light was too red…

Fire. She sat up in bed and reached for her robe. Through the top pane in her window she could see the angry red flames pulsing against black smoke. Fear stabbed like lightning when she saw that Samuel's barn was on fire.

When she opened her bedroom door, the pounding was louder. Someone knocking at the back door. She ran down the stairs just as Sadie opened her bedroom door.

"What is going on?"

Mary continued through the kitchen to the door. "There's a fire at Samuel's."

Judith and Esther were at the back door in their night-dresses.

"Come in, come in." Mary opened the door and ushered them into the kitchen, where Sadie had already lit the lantern above the kitchen table.

The girls clung to each other as Sadie pumped water into the coffee pot. Ida Mae appeared at the bottom of the stairs.

"What is happening?"

"Our barn caught on fire." Esther coughed, then went on. "Samuel went into the barn to let Tilly out—" She coughed again.

Samuel. Dread filled Mary with a cold spiral. If something happened to Samuel—

"Is Samuel all right?"

Judith nodded. "He got Tilly out of the barn, but the fire was so hot…"

"…and it spread to the house."

Sadie handed Esther a glass of water and sank into one of the chairs. "The house?"

"Everything caught fire so quickly, there was nothing we could do." Esther took another swallow of water. "Samuel wouldn't let us go back in to get our clothes, or anything."

Mary slipped out the back door as they continued talking. Esther and Judith would be all right. Sadie and Ida Mae would take care of them. But Samuel…

She ran down the path toward the Lapp farm in the rain, her bare feet slipping in the mud. Where was Samuel?

When she came through the opening in the fence row that opened into the Lapps' farmyard, she stopped. The scene in front of her was horrific. The barn was gone and

only a pile of smoldering rubble remained. The house…
two walls still stood, but they were burning, even in the
rain. The rest was a pile of black beams and crazy an-
gles. One pane of glass hadn't broken, but reflected the
flames. Smoke and steam rose everywhere.

The rain let up as the storm moved on, but Mary
couldn't see Samuel anywhere. She walked toward the
destroyed house, careful not to get too close. Smoking
embers lay all around, and she was barefoot. When she
reached the lane that led from the road, past the house
and to the barn, she stopped. As the brief shower of rain
ended, the remaining house walls burned stronger, lend-
ing light and heat.

"Samuel! Where are you?"

Her voice met silence.

The wind pushed the storm to the east and the morning sun lightened the sky behind the breaking clouds. The
gray, predawn glow revealed more of the destruction…
and a man hunched in the lane. Mary picked her way
through the debris until she reached him. She knelt and
laid her hand on his back. He didn't look at her.

"Are you all right? Are you hurt anywhere?"

His shoulders shook as if he was crying in deep, silent sobs.

"Samuel, it's me, Mary. Talk to me."

He stood and pulled her to him in a strong hug, and
she realized that he wasn't crying, he was…laughing?

"It's gone." He gestured with one arm to take in the
scene before them. "It's all gone."

Mary took a step back. "Why are you—"

"Laughing?" He hiccupped, then laughed again. "It's
gone." The laugh turned into a sob, and he reached for her
again. "I'm not going insane," he said into her ear as he

held her close. "It's just that this farm…the memories… the work…it's all gone."

Mary looked into his face. The growing light was reflected in tears that streamed down his cheeks.

"I know. It's terrible."

He shook his head. "Not terrible."

"But you've lost everything." Mary couldn't look at the destruction the fire had caused. She jumped when one of the house walls fell in with a crash.

"There it goes, burning up like chaff." Samuel watched, sober now, as the greedy flames fed on the newly exposed beams.

"But the barn, the house—"

Samuel shook his head. "The girls are safe, and Tilly is grazing over there along the road. What have we really lost?"

"What will you wear? What will you eat? The fire has burned up everything." She stared at him. Did he lose his mind along with everything else?

"You don't understand."

He turned them both away from the fire, toward the rising sun in the east. Mary heard horses trotting on the road. The neighbors had seen the smoke in the morning light and were coming to help.

"At first I thought that my life was over. You're right, we lost everything. But I also lost this burden. God freed me from *Daed*'s legacy, and now I can go my own way. I can start over new and fresh. Clean. All the things that were holding me back are gone."

Samuel cupped her cheeks in his large hands, gazing into her eyes.

"I'm glad you came. I've been wanting to tell you

how sorry I am. Can you forgive me for being so over-bearing and stupid?"

Mary searched his face, looking for any sign that he had lost touch with reality, but she only saw weariness and peace. She nodded and he smiled.

"You're the most beautiful sight I've ever seen." His thumb traced her cheekbone. "Don't you have anything to say?"

She felt her own smile answering his. "Only that I'm sorry, too. When the girls came to the house and told us about the fire, and that you had gone into the burning barn—" Tears sprang into her eyes. "I was so afraid for you. What if I lost you, and I had never told you—?" She bit her lower lip. Amish girls didn't say the things she wanted to say to Samuel.

He lifted her chin. "Never told me what?"

Mary straightened her shoulders. She didn't care what she was supposed to do or not do.

"If I never told you that I...love you, I would be sorry for the rest of my life."

He leaned close and brushed his lips against her cheek. "It's all right. I'm all right."

"But we've wasted so much time with my silliness."

"It wasn't silliness." He tugged the braid hanging down her back. "I'm just glad you aren't going to marry Martin."

She pulled her braid out of his grasp. "Who says I'm not?"

He grinned and brought her close to him again. "I do."

His kiss was tender, yet demanding. As if she was the only answer to his longings.

But he broke off the kiss all too soon.

"Folks are coming, and we shouldn't be together like this. You had better go home and get dressed."

Mary looked down. She had forgotten she was still in her nightclothes.

As she left, she heard Dale Yoder ask, "Samuel, is everyone all right? Where do you need me to help?"

When she reached the opening in the fence row between the two farms, she glanced back. Buggies had crowded into the lane and more were stopped along the road. Even an automobile was making its way to the farm. Clean up was already underway.

By midmorning, the barnyard was crowded with neighbors and church folks. Mary, Sadie and the girls had made a batch of doughnuts and had brought over baskets full of them, along with pots of coffee.

Samuel leaned against a makeshift table someone had put together out of lumber they had brought and held a warm doughnut in his hand, but he had no appetite. Once the initial shock had worn off, the reality of the fire began to set in. There was no feed for Tilly or the cattle. It had been destroyed. There were no clean trousers for him to change into, so he wore his wet, ash-encrusted pants with holes burned in them where embers had landed. He had thought he would wash the grime off his hands…but the soap was gone. The bars of soap Sadie had helped Judith and Esther make last winter.

Everything they had worked for was gone. Every bit of food they had stored. The chickens. The hams hung from the beams in the cellar. Everything gone.

He took a bite of the doughnut, but it tasted like ashes.

"Here's some coffee for you." Mary held out a steaming cup. "You need to eat and drink something."

Samuel took the cup she offered, looking into her eyes. "Are you all right?"

Her brows peaked. "I should be asking you that question."

"You looked upset this morning."

"I was." She broke off a piece of his doughnut and popped it in her mouth.

He leaned into her strength. The moment when she had come to find him in the midst of the chaos was the point he clung to as his world collapsed around him.

He brushed a crumb off her chin. "I would never be able to survive this without you."

She held him with her gaze. "You won't need to. I'm here."

Samuel let his gaze scan the crowd of people. Some were carrying buckets of water to the areas of the house and barn that were still smoldering. Others picked through the rubble, but found nothing worth saving.

Mary threaded her hand through his elbow. "I was concerned because I didn't know where you were. I didn't know if you were hurt or not." She squeezed his elbow. "And here you were. You had lost everything."

Samuel sipped the hot coffee. "Not everything." He pressed his elbow against his side, trapping her hand. "I didn't lose you."

She smiled and ducked her head. "I'm not that important."

"Now that all of this is gone—" he gestured toward the ashes "—I can see what the most important things in my life are. The girls are safe, you're safe. Nothing else matters."

Another buggy pulled up the lane. Bram and Matthew got out.

Mary took his cup and the doughnut. "You need to go talk to Bram."

"I know." He glanced at her. She looked very kissable in the morning light. "The coffee was good."

Matthew spotted Samuel and made his way toward him, but Bram stood in the lane, staring at what had been the house and barn.

Samuel met Matthew halfway across the yard. "I wasn't expecting to see you this morning." He shook Matthew's offered hand.

Matthew gripped Samuel's shoulder. "I don't think you expected any of this, did you?"

Samuel shook his head. "How did you folks hear about the fire?"

"News travels fast. Someone told Bram, knowing it was his family's farm, and Bram stopped by to get me. We came to help." Matthew glanced at the crowds. "At least, to do what we can."

"I'm not sure what there is to do. As far as I can tell, there is nothing to be saved except the livestock."

Matthew's eyes widened. "You lost everything?"

"Everything."

Bram joined them. "I can't believe this. How did it happen?"

"During the storm last night, lightning hit the cupola on the barn, and the place went up faster than I could think."

"The house, too?"

"The wind blew embers from the barn to the house. The roof must have been dry and rotten, it caught so quickly."

Bram stared at what was left of the house. "All those memories."

"You still have the memories," Matthew said. "No fire can erase those."

Bram turned away from the devastation. "You're right. The important thing is that you and the girls are all right."

"We're safe." Samuel couldn't look toward the ruined house.

"Were you able to save anything? Clothes? Anything?"

"Only the clothes we were wearing. The girls were in their nightdresses." Samuel gestured toward the circle of women gathered around Judith and Esther. "The clothes they are wearing now are borrowed."

Preacher Jonas came toward them. "Samuel, this is terrible. How are you holding up?"

The reminder of just what had happened overnight made Samuel's knees weak. "It has been a long morning."

Martin Troyer's farm wagon joined the other buggies and wagons along the road, and the Troyer brothers jumped down. The morning was about to get a lot longer.

"You will have the help of the community when you're ready to rebuild," Jonas said. "I've had several offers already."

Samuel's mouth went dry. He hadn't thought of rebuilding yet...and he never would have expected the community to help.

Jonas stepped across the yard to greet another church member, but Bram pulled Samuel aside.

"That's something, isn't it?" Bram's voice was low, meant for only Samuel to hear. "Would they have stepped forward so quickly when *Daed* was alive?"

Samuel shook his head.

"You're changing things." Bram gave him a brotherly squeeze around his shoulders. "You're becoming part of the community."

"*Daed* always hovered around the edges, didn't he?"

"Like a dog waiting for scraps." Bram shook his head. "I don't know what made him be the way he was, but you've shown that you aren't like him."

Samuel spied Martin coming toward him. "Here comes trouble."

Bram's eyebrows went up. "Why?"

"We've had some words about Mary. Martin Troyer is convinced he's going to marry her."

"What does she say about that?"

Samuel grinned. "She's a strong one. Refused him with no way to misunderstand her meaning, but he still insists it's going to happen."

"Is he jealous of you?"

"Most likely."

Martin stopped several steps away from Samuel, raising his voice as he spoke so that everyone could hear.

"Sorry to hear about the tragedy, Lapp."

Samuel faced him. Out of the corner of his eye, he could see Mary watching them. "Not so much of a tragedy, Martin. We only lost the house and barn. The family and the livestock survived. We're thankful."

"I've heard folks saying that you're going to rebuild."

"I haven't thought too much about it yet, but I suppose we will."

Martin took a step closer. "So at the end of it, you'll have a nice new barn to replace the old decrepit one that stood here yesterday."

Samuel shifted his feet. What was Martin getting at?

Preacher Jonas stepped forward. "Are you suggesting something, Martin?"

Martin turned from one side to the other, perusing the audience he had gathered. "I'm just saying that it is nice for Samuel Lapp—" he emphasized the last name "—to enjoy a new house and barn while the rest of us are struggling so much in these hard times."

Samuel heard the accusation in his voice. "I didn't have anything to do with this fire."

"Of course you would say that." Martin grinned, his gaze shifting to Mary and then back. "But we have to wonder, don't we? You were saddled with a real burden when your old father died, and you've been losing ground every year." He took another step closer. "So tell us, Samuel, did you wait for a storm in the middle of the night to set the fire so you could blame it on the lightning? Or was it just a happy coincidence?"

A few voices protested at Martin's accusation, but not enough. Samuel looked around at the small clusters of men talking among themselves. Not enough.

Preacher Jonas stepped between Samuel and Martin. "That is a pretty serious accusation, Martin. There is no proof that Samuel had anything to do with the fire."

Martin's grin faded, then strengthened as he found a few supporters in the crowd. "There isn't any proof that he didn't, either. It seems that this should be a matter to look into."

Jonas quieted the crowd's response to Martin's suggestion. "It was an accident, Martin. This rumor that you're trying to spread needs to stop."

Martin took a few steps back, a satisfied look on his face. Samuel's pulse thumped as Martin joined his friends near the farm lane. If Martin was determined to follow through with his threats, knowing the truth might not be enough to stop him.

Chapter Sixteen

Mary packed the used coffee cups into the baskets the doughnuts had been in and swept crumbs off the make-shift table onto the ground. The crowds had cleared out once Preacher Jonas had come up with a plan to begin preparing the old building sites for the new barn and house. Work would begin tomorrow morning. Saturday.

With a gasp, she remembered that this was Friday, the day to take her carefully gathered eggs to town for the buyer. The butter would keep until next week, but the six dozen eggs waiting in the cool cellar wouldn't be fresh by Tuesday. Ida Mae would have to put up with more puddings and custard. And they would have to pickle most of the eggs. With a sigh, Mary resigned herself to the chore she hated.

"Good afternoon, Mary."

"Martin." He had walked up while she had been thinking about the eggs.

"Can I give you a hand with anything?"

She leveled her gaze at him. "If you want to help me, you can take back that accusation you made about Samuel. You know he didn't set this fire."

He smiled with a touch of a leer. "I don't know that, and neither do you. This is just the kind of stunt a Lapp would pull."

"You don't need to run Samuel down. No matter how you feel about him, it makes no difference in how I feel about you. I've told you that I won't marry you."

Martin put a false pouting expression on his face. "You keep saying that."

"Because it's true."

"You won't find a better situation than I can offer you."

He started ticking off the reasons on his fingers, but she interrupted him.

"I don't care what you can offer me, because you can't offer me what I want."

"And what is that?"

"To be left alone." She picked up the basket full of coffee cups and carried it to the buggy. Chester stood, still hitched to it, head down and tail swishing.

Martin hurried after her. "You don't mean that."

She turned on him. "Don't tell me what I mean." Too late, she remembered her manners. She started over. "I want you to leave me alone. Forget about me."

He spread his hands with an imploring gesture. "But I gave you a cow."

"You can have her back." Mary walked back to the table to get the next basket.

"You don't like her?"

Mary sighed and turned toward him. "I like the cow. She is very useful. But if accepting her means I owe you something, then you can have her back."

Martin's eyes narrowed. "You want her, but you don't want her. It's time to stop playing games. Bishop

Kaufman is going to announce our wedding at church on Sunday. We're going to get married."

An icy trickle went down Mary's back. "I'm not going to marry you, and you can't force me."

Martin stepped toward her and Mary looked for help, but no one was near. He grabbed her hand and pulled her close. His breath smelled like cheese.

"When we are married, you will learn to control what you say. Now—" he wrenched her hand and tears welled "—tell me what I want to hear."

She looked him in the eye. "I will not marry you. Never."

He tightened his grip, but she refused to back down. When Harvey Anderson had forced her against her will, she had been weak. She had caved in to his demands. She had given him control.

But she wasn't that girl anymore.

"Leave now, Martin, and don't come back. I won't marry you, and my sister won't marry Peter. You need to look somewhere else."

Over Martin's shoulder, she caught sight of Samuel walking toward them. Martin turned to see what had captured her attention.

"So that's it. You've chosen that Samuel Lapp over me." He shoved her away. "You deserve whatever he gives you. Peter and I will stop by your place to pick up the cow on our way home." He glanced behind him again. Samuel had almost reached them. "I will enjoy watching you suffer as his wife the same way his mother suffered. Being married to a Lapp is no way for a woman as fine as you to spend her life, but that's your choice."

He walked off toward his wagon and Mary ran to

Samuel. He held her close, but she didn't cry. Martin Troyer wasn't worth crying over.

Samuel held her for a moment, then pushed her back, searching her face. "What did he do? What did he say to you?"

Mary wiped her eyes and laughed. "He said I deserve what I get when I—"

She stopped, biting her lip before the rest of the sentence could escape.

"When you what?"

"Never mind. He's taking Schmetterling back." She looked up at Samuel's puzzled face. "I'll miss the poor cow, and I'll miss the butter we made from her milk, but I won't keep her on Martin's terms."

"He still wants you to marry him?"

"I think I've finally convinced him that I won't."

Samuel picked up the basket of coffee cups and carried it to the buggy, sliding it in the back next to the first one.

"I'm not sure he's going to give up that easily."

"He'll have to get used to it." She sighed and rolled her tired shoulders. "Do you think anyone will listen to his silly accusation?"

"That I set this fire myself?" He shook his head. "I don't know. Some people will believe anything bad they hear about the Lapps, and Martin has his supporters."

"But you've been working so hard to change that ever since the day you helped with the plowing. How many farmers have you helped with their windmills? And didn't you say you spent all day Wednesday at the Hopplestadts' last week, helping build a new fence?"

"It might not make any difference if Martin insists on spreading his rumors."

Mary folded her arms. "If the church won't help you rebuild because of Martin, then we'll do it ourselves."

He grinned. "You and I are going to build a barn?"

"We have Judith, Esther and Ida Mae to help, too."

"Four women and one man are going to build a barn and house without anyone else helping?"

"Why not? You know how, don't you?"

Samuel shook his head and leaned against the buggy. "I don't see Sadie and the girls anywhere."

"They went home a while ago. Sadie was getting tired."

"You and your sister take good care of her." He scratched at the day's growth of whiskers on his chin. "I have to admit, I had my doubts when you first moved here."

"But then you realized that someone else is just as able…even more able to care for her like she needs than you are."

The corners of his mouth twitched and he shrugged. "I've gotten used to it."

He waved to Preacher Jonas as he drove down the lane toward the road, the last of the neighbors to leave after the long day.

"What time are folks coming in the morning?"

"An hour past dawn. That will give everyone the time to finish their chores at home, and then we start clearing out the debris from the barn and house."

"Judith and Esther are staying with us, but where will you sleep tonight?"

"Sadie said I should sleep in her barn. The girls were going to make a bed for me in the loft."

Mary closed the side door of the buggy. "Do you have

anything else you need to do here? You could ride home with me."

"I need to make sure the pasture fence is tight. I don't want the cattle wandering off. I also need to check on Tilly. Dale Yoder put her in with his horses. I'll walk over when I'm done."

It was time for her to go home, but Mary didn't want to leave Samuel alone. She was running out of things to say, though. She stalled one more time.

"Have you thought about rebuilding? What kind of house and barn you'll need?"

Samuel turned to her. "That's been going through my head all day. We need a home, the three of us, but I want to build for the future, too."

"What do you mean?"

He shrugged. "I may decide to get married someday. So, the house will need an upstairs for the children, and a room downstairs."

Mary remembered the day he told her he would never get married. What had changed his mind?

Then she thought about the house she grew up in back in Ohio. "A big laundry porch would be nice. And a cellar."

"And the house should be large enough so we could host church without crowding everyone in too much."

"A modern kitchen, with a pump at the sink."

"With room for a big table."

Mary's eyebrows rose. "Why does it have to be big?"

"For all of the children. I don't want my children squeezed so tightly on a bench that one might fall off during a meal."

"Just how many children do you think you'll have?"

Samuel's eyes were soft and warm as he watched her face. "As many as we can."

She leaned closer to him, drawn by the breathless tone in his voice. "And who will be the mother of all these children?"

He smiled and put his arms around her, pulling her close. "We'll have to see about that."

His kiss, gentle and warm, grew deeper until he broke it off. Then he tucked her under his chin.

"We'll have to see."

Samuel reached the farm just before dawn, after downing a quick cup of coffee and a couple slices of bread and butter in Sadie's kitchen. The air reeked of ashes and soot, damp and acrid. It was the only odor he could smell all through the night. Even the strong cup of coffee hadn't washed it away.

As the rising sun turned the sky rosy pink, the devastation stood out black against the surrounding grass. He peered into the old cellar, something he hadn't been able to bring himself to do the day before. Underneath half-burned beams and floorboards, the canning shelves lay strewn on the dirt floor, every jar broken.

He choked back a sob when he saw *Mamm*'s rocking chair, charred but still together, hanging upside down from a beam. He ventured onto unsteady boards to retrieve it and set it on the ground. He smoothed the seat, wiping ashes off. One arm was burned and blackened, and one of the rockers was broken, but the rest was in one piece. How had it escaped the fury of the fire? Perhaps it could be repaired. He set it to the side, underneath the maple tree in the front yard.

A steer's bawl from the pasture pulled him away from

the house, and he made his way through the orchard, past the shell of the henhouse, to the pump. The watering trough had escaped the fire, but it was dry. He set to work, pumping by hand, turning his back on the skeleton of the windmill and the barn. The steers crowded around, all of them shoving their way in to the fresh water. He pumped hard, working out all the anger and frustration. All the grief. Why did he have to be the one to lose everything?

But at the same time, the relief still lingered. He had tried to push it away, knowing he shouldn't be happy about anything, but the relief of knowing he would never again have to look at the stairway where *Mamm* died. And the barn roof... *Daed*'s death had been just as sudden as he had fallen from that height. Those constant reminders of his failures were gone.

As he finished filling the trough the whisking sound of buggy wheels on the gravel road made him turn around. Preacher Jonas was the first to arrive, along with Paul Stutzman and Conrad Hopplestadt. They tied their horses along the fence away from the burned house. Samuel met them as they crossed the lane to survey the damage.

"Good morning, Samuel," Jonas said, shaking his hand. He sighed. "It doesn't look any better this morning, does it?"

Samuel shook the other men's hands. "Not at all. Except that it seems the fire is out. I haven't seen any smoke from either building."

Conrad gestured toward what remained of the house. "Will we start here, or at the barn?"

"The barn can wait. I only have the one horse, and she's happy sharing Sadie's barn. And the steers won't need shelter. But my sisters need a home, so I thought we'd start there."

Jonas peered into the black hole where the house had once stood. "Are you planning to use the same cellar?" He looked around the barnyard. "There's a nice spot for a house up there on that rise by the maple tree. It's closer to the road, but it will bring the house up and away from the barn."

Samuel nodded. "That would be a good place. And someone suggested a larger cellar, with a window or two. It would be a better cellar for the girls." Sadie had made that suggestion the night before. A light and airy place for the girls to work.

Paul Stutzman rubbed at his beard. "You're going to build a new modern house?" His eyebrows rose as he looked at Samuel. "This fire seems to be a mixed blessing, allowing you to move up in the world."

Something in Samuel's stomach gnawed at him. He had hoped Martin's accusing words from yesterday would be forgotten.

Jonas ignored Paul's comment. "So we have two things to take care of. First we need to do something with the old cellar, and then we need to dig a new one."

Samuel pushed a blackened board in the cellar with his foot. "We could fill in this cellar with the debris from the house and dirt from digging the new one."

"We should let the rest of the house burn down to ashes, then," Conrad said, pushing on a beam. "Some of this is still pretty solid, but not good enough to reuse it."

More buggies pulled in, and soon the yard was filled with as much activity as it had been the day before. Several of the men got together with ropes and maneuvered the larger pieces of the house into a pile and set it on fire.

Smoke billowed into the air once more as others gathered loose boards and pieces to throw on the burning pile, but Samuel saved the rocking chair.

He was carrying the chair to Sadie's barn when he met Mary and the girls on their way to the farm. Each had a covered pan in their hands.

"That smells like breakfast," Samuel said.

"We thought you would all be getting hungry about now," Judith said.

"And we had plenty of eggs to use." Ida Mae grinned at Mary, who was bringing up the rear. "So we made scrambled eggs and sausage."

"What did you find?" Esther asked. "Is that *Mamm*'s chair?"

Samuel nodded. "I think I might be able to fix it."

Tears stood in Esther's eyes, and Samuel suddenly realized that he hadn't been the only one to lose everything. He might be glad some of the reminders of *Daed* were gone, but Esther and Judith had so few memories to hold on to.

"When I do repair it, it will be yours."

Esther's face brightened. "That would be wonderful. *Denki*, Samuel."

They went on their way, but Mary stopped him before she passed by. "That is very thoughtful. Esther will cherish that chair."

The glow from Mary's praise lasted until he rejoined the workers at the farm. Several of the men had brought tools, including picks and shovels, and had started in digging the new cellar.

"Samuel," Preacher Jonas called. "Come help me mark out the walls."

When Samuel reached the work site, Martin was there.

"You finally showed up to help?" Martin's face was twisted in a sneer.

Samuel glanced at Jonas and chose to ignore Martin. The preacher had already put one stake into the ground, but waited for Samuel to place the other corners. Once the stakes were in, they threaded a string around them, forming a square.

Martin's sour stare made Samuel doubt what he was doing. Should he make the house so big? He paced off the area he had marked out. The cellar would be under the kitchen. It didn't need to be large to store the vegetables and canned goods, but if it was bigger, Esther and Judith could do laundry down there in the winter months. He could see it in his imagination, clean and bright with whitewashed walls and windows to let light in. New shelves lining the walls, filled with jars of canned goods. The washtub set in the center of the room with clotheslines strung from the ceiling.

He glanced at Esther and Judith, serving plates of eggs and sausage to the hungry workers. How many times had they apologized to him because the laundry was still hanging in the kitchen at dinnertime on rainy days? And Mary... He looked at the size of the cellar he planned. He couldn't ask her to work in a dark, cramped hole in the ground.

Samuel felt the corners of his mouth ease into a smile. The idea had crept up on him until he couldn't think of anything else. This new house would be Mary's. And his. This house would be for their family...if she would agree.

All through church, Mary struggled to keep her mind on the worship service. After dinner was the council meeting, and she had heard rumors that Martin Troyer was planning to bring something before the church. But he couldn't request for a wedding to be announced without her permission, could he?

She shivered, even though the day was warm. No one could force her to marry against her will, she reminded herself. No one.

Finally, the sermons were over and Bishop started the low tones of the final hymn. Mary closed her eyes as she sang, knowing the words by heart. They spoke to her anxious thoughts. God was her salvation, her protection, the rock of her faith. He never changes, never wavers. When the hymn ended, she was at peace.

After a hurried dinner, the members of the church met again in the house. The usual business of the council meeting was finished, including Peter Troyer's repentance for the rumors he had spread, and folks were shifting restlessly on their benches when Martin stood up to speak. He glanced in Mary's direction, but she averted her eyes, dreading what he might say.

"I have approached Preacher Jonas about this, and the bishop, but neither of them seem to think what I have to say merits any discussion by the members of the church."

Preacher William stood. The old man swayed a bit, and his voice was raspy, but the congregation respected his age and wisdom. "If Bishop and Preacher Jonas have heard what you have to say, then why do you bring it up in the council meeting?"

Martin shifted from one foot to the other, but pressed on. "I want the church to place Samuel Lapp under the *bann*."

At first, Mary sighed with relief. He wasn't going to

bring up any pending marriage. But then his words sunk in. Place Samuel under the *bann*?

"The *bann* is a very serious matter," Preacher William said, raising his hand to call for silence. "What do you accuse Samuel of doing?"

"Samuel Lapp, like his father before him, has repeatedly taken advantage of the goodwill of this congregation. I think he set the fire that destroyed his house and barn last Friday morning to have us build a new one for him."

Bishop Kaufman stood and raised his hands, quieting the murmuring that had broken out at Martin's words.

"This is not the time to discuss this, Martin."

"Then when is the time?" Martin's face reddened as he faced the bishop. "I've tried to bring this up the right way, by going to Preacher Jonas and you, but you won't do anything about it." He took a step toward the bishop and pointed an accusatory finger at Samuel. "This man is taking advantage of the congregation just as his father did before him, and you won't do anything about it."

Bishop laced his fingers together and bent his head. "Sit down, Martin."

Martin looked around the congregation. "Who agrees with me? Shouldn't we look into this travesty? Will we endure more years of bowing to the whims of the Lapp family, bailing them out of trouble wherever their foolish choices lead them?"

Esther, sitting next to Mary, buried her face in her hands. Sadie put her arm around Judith and held her close.

Bishop, his voice as mild as ever, repeated his request. "Martin, sit down and we will discuss this matter." He turned toward Samuel. "You may stay and face your accuser, or you may leave. It's up to you, but I recommend that you stay."

Samuel sat with his head bowed. "I'll stay."

"Before we open our discussion," said Bishop, his head still bowed, "I ask that we enter into a time of silent prayer."

Mary closed her eyes, but couldn't pray. Martin's accusation couldn't be true…but she remembered Samuel on the morning of the fire. His seeming joy in the face of tragedy. Could it be that he did set the fire on purpose? And just as quickly, her thoughts rebelled against the idea. She hadn't known Samuel very long, but he had never given her any reason to doubt that he was completely truthful. He wouldn't destroy his farm. He couldn't.

After the prayer, Bishop Kaufman opened the discussion. Martin made his accusation again, and a couple men added their opinion to support him.

Then men started speaking in support of Samuel, including Preacher Jonas.

"I've gotten to know Samuel quite well over the years," Jonas said, "and I've seen the changes he has made since he lost his father in the accident two years ago. I have never known him to lie, or to twist the truth to his advantage. I think we can trust his version of the cause of the fire."

Other men rose to speak of his willingness to work on their windmills over the past few weeks, volunteering his time to repair or service them before the summer heat came. Samuel fidgeted in his seat when Conrad Hopplestadt rose to tell how Samuel had helped him repair his pasture fence, and had even supplied the fence wire to do the job right.

Then Sadie rose from her seat and Bishop gave her a nod of acknowledgment.

"I know it isn't the custom for women to speak in council meetings, but I've never been much for custom." She smiled as the congregation laughed at this, then became serious once more. "I've known Samuel his entire life, and I knew his father before him. I've never known Samuel to be anything but caring and honest. He has done his best to fulfill his grandfather's desire to care for me into my old age, and he has been a good neighbor and a good friend." She nodded in Samuel's direction, then addressed Bishop Kaufman again. "I don't believe he could set fire to his farm on purpose. He respects his legacy too much to destroy it."

She sat back down while the congregation's voices murmured all around them.

Bishop held up his hand for quiet and turned to Martin. "Do you still want us to vote on whether to place Samuel under the *bann*?"

Martin looked at the faces of the congregation. The men who had supported him during the discussion averted their gazes, then he looked at Mary. She turned her face away, unable to look at him any longer.

"I withdraw my accusation." His voice was quiet. Defeated.

Bishop raised his hands over the congregation once more. "Let us pray."

As the bishop led the people in a prayer of repentance and reconciliation, Mary glanced at Samuel. His head was bowed, fingers steepled in front of his face, and tears flowed freely. How could she have ever doubted that she loved this man?

Chapter Seventeen

By the beginning of July, the new house was finished. After pouring the cement walls for the cellar, the framing had gone up in a single day. Samuel had chosen to make it a larger version of Sadie's house, with two bedrooms upstairs and two on the main floor. The downstairs rooms had removable partitions to open the space for Sunday meeting when it was their turn to host. He and Bram spent most of their time during June plastering the walls and putting down floors. They had been joined by Matthew, when he could come.

Samuel had spent most evenings building furniture in Sadie's barn after working on the house all day. The first thing he did was repair *Mamm*'s rocking chair, making new pieces to replace the charred arm and rocker, and staining the wood a dark brown. Esther was delighted when it was finished, and insisted on putting it in the bedroom she shared with Judith immediately.

"You don't want to wait until we can put it in the new house?" Samuel had asked.

She had shaken her head. "I want it with me. When I sit in it, it's like *Mamm* is with me."

Samuel had built a table with two chairs and two long benches, and two more chairs for the living room. He had also built two bedsteads for Esther and Judith, and a large one for himself. He had smiled as he had measured the wood for the headboard. Large enough for two people, husband and wife.

One or two evenings a week, he took Mary for a buggy ride. Sadie had thought it was scandalous that they would take her closed buggy to court in, and arranged to borrow a proper courting buggy with an open top for them to use. Mary had agreed, so Samuel drove her down the back roads and up the main roads between Shipshewana and Topeka in the open courting buggy. They went all the way west to Goshen, and as far north as Pretty Prairie, near the Michigan state line. Every evening ride was filled with conversation and laughter as he got to know her better.

And as the month wore on, Mary lost that strained look in her face that had been with her since she had come to Indiana. She was happier than he had ever seen her.

When the house was done and the furniture in place, Samuel took Mary to see it for the first time.

"Why have you kept it a secret?" Mary slipped her hand into his as they ambled down the path through the fence row.

"I wanted it to be a surprise."

"You let your sisters go over already, and even Ida Mae."

He shrugged. "I wanted to hear their opinions about certain things."

"But not mine?"

Samuel stopped in the yard where they had the best

view of the new house. It stood on a bit of a rise in the afternoon sunlight next to the shady maple tree. The siding was white, and white shades hung in every window, each of them pulled halfway down to keep the house cool in the afternoon heat.

"It looks just right," Mary said. "And look! You already have a garden planted where the old house was."

"I thought that would be the best way to use that space. It's already level, and the ashes in the soil will make everything grow well."

She hugged his arm. "New life out of ruin," she said. "How appropriate."

"Do you want to go inside?"

Mary let go of him and ran to the back steps and into the back porch.

"This is a wonderful washing porch."

"For summer."

"Esther and Judith will be able to use it in the winter, too, if you cover the screens with boards to keep the weather out."

He grinned. He couldn't wait for her to see the cellar.

Mary led the way into the kitchen, running her hand along the new shelf with the modern cabinets above it. "You built the cabinets yourself?"

"What did you think I've been doing all month?"

She opened the oven door and lifted the stove lids. "Where did you find such a beautiful stove?"

"At an auction. It was a bit rusty, but nothing that couldn't be polished off."

She continued through the kitchen to the bedroom off it, in the same spot as Sadie's room was in her house. When she saw the big bed he had placed there, her face grew red and she drew back into the hall.

Samuel laughed. "What's wrong?"

"I didn't know you needed such a big bed. I thought you would have built a smaller one for yourself."

He grabbed her hand and pulled her close. Looking around them as they stood at the bottom of the stairs, with the kitchen to one side and the bedroom behind them, he grinned. This was how he imagined his home would be. He only needed one more thing...

"I don't plan on living here alone."

"For sure you won't. Esther and Judith will be here with you."

"They won't live here forever. They'll get married and have their own homes before long."

"So who do you plan to share this house with?" She smiled, looking into his eyes.

"I think I know someone who would enjoy making this house into a home."

She lowered her gaze, suddenly shy.

"We've talked about it quite a bit, and you know we agree on so many things when it comes to having a family and running a household and farm."

Mary nodded.

"And I've seen the longing in your eyes."

She looked up. "Are you sure? After what happened..." She bit her lip and turned her head away.

Samuel put his hands on her shoulders. "What happened was in the past. Gone. Dead. Forgiven."

He swallowed. Forgiving the man who had attacked Mary was the hardest thing he had ever done. He smiled as she stepped closer, into his arms where she belonged.

"Mary," he whispered into her ear. "I love you so much. Will you be my wife? Will you help me make this house into our home? Will you trust me with our future?"

With her face buried in his chest, he felt her head nod, then she looked up at him.

"With all my heart."

Epilogue

"Isn't a fall wedding the best?" Judith tied Mary's white apron around her new blue dress. "I hope I can get married in the fall."

Esther tied her freshly cleaned shoe. "If you can find anyone who will marry you." She grinned at her sister.

Mary glanced at Ida Mae, fastening her own apron on the other side of the room. The four girls had decided to help each other get dressed for Mary and Samuel's wedding day in one of the upstairs bedrooms of the new house, but Mary had seen expressions flit across Ida Mae's face that made her think she would rather be alone. Her wedding had to make her sister relive the anticipation of her own planned wedding last year.

"Your dress is a beautiful shade of green, Ida Mae," she said. She was rewarded with a smile.

"*Denki.* And it goes well with your blue."

Esther patted her *kapp* to make sure it was in place. "Did you know that Thomas Weaver's favorite color is green?"

Ida Mae blushed bright pink. "I didn't know that."

Mary grinned as a smile turned up the corners of Ida Mae's mouth.

"Who are you going to visit first on your wedding trip?" Judith asked.

Mary ticked the planned visits off on her fingers. "First we'll stay with Bram and Ellie, and then Annie and Matthew." She looked at her audience. "We want to get those visits done before the new babies arrive." The girls grinned at each other. New nieces or nephews were such fun.

"And then you're going to Ohio, aren't you?" Ida Mae asked.

Mary nodded. *Mamm*, *Daed* and the rest of the family had arrived yesterday, and the reunion had been wonderful. But she was looking forward to traveling back to Ohio again. She couldn't imagine spending the first few weeks of her marriage among strangers, the way the *Englischers* did on their honeymoons. Visiting each other's family was the best way to form the family bonds that would last a lifetime. Her trip with Samuel would last for two months.

"We'll stay with the folks, and Aunt Susan and Uncle Henry. Then we'll go through Wayne County to visit the cousins there, and then back home before the winter weather comes."

Esther whispered something to Judith and the girls giggled.

"What is it?"

Judith giggled again. "We were just thinking how *wonderful-gut* it would be if you came home expecting a little one."

Mary felt her face heat. "Let us get married, first."

Even Ida Mae joined in the laughter that followed that remark.

Samuel had wanted to have the wedding at their new house, and Mary had agreed. The thought of starting their lives together in their own home was like the last piece of a quilt sewn in place. The church benches had been delivered yesterday, on Wednesday, and Samuel had reported that all was ready last night.

She and the girls, including Sadie, had spent the morning cooking the wedding dinner, along with most of the ladies from the church. Everyone had been in high spirits, and Mary could still hear Effie Hopplestadt's joyous voice above everyone else's. The aroma of the chicken and noodles in the oven wafted up the stairway.

"Mary, I think it's time to go downstairs." Judith stood at the window. "There is Preacher Jonas, and behind him is Bishop Kaufman's buggy." She pointed toward the road. "And look at the line of buggies that are coming! It's a good thing the day is fine, because some of the people are going to have to sit outside."

"You two go on down," Mary said. "I want to talk to Ida Mae for a minute."

Once the girls had left, Mary and Ida Mae looked at each other. It was a solemn moment. Mary was the first of their brothers and sisters to get married.

"So this is what it's like," Ida Mae said. "In an hour or so, you'll be Samuel's Mary for the rest of your life."

Mary blinked back tears. "I loved growing up with you. You're the best sister."

Ida Mae nodded, her own eyes wet and shiny. "You're right. I am the best sister."

At that, Mary giggled, then Ida Mae joined her, and

soon they were holding each other and laughing, tears streaming down their faces. Mary grabbed her handkerchief from her waistband and dabbed her eyes.

"*Ach*, I needed a laugh like that." She grinned at Ida Mae and they started laughing all over again.

Mary jumped when Esther knocked on the door.

"Are you two coming, or not? We're almost ready to start."

Ida Mae reached for Mary and gave her a quick hug. "In case I don't get an opportunity to say it later, blessings on your marriage."

Mary followed Ida Mae and Esther down the stairs. The big front room, with the walls pushed back to form a large open area, was filled with people, but Mary only saw one face. Samuel sat on the front row on the men's side, next to Bram and the ministers, smiling as he watched her walk into the room.

Mary took her place on the front row of the women's side with Ida Mae beside her. She clung to Ida Mae's hand, almost fearful that her happiness would send her floating to the ceiling.

"You're going to be all right," Ida Mae whispered.

Mary glanced at her soon-to-be husband, who was still watching her as Bishop Kaufman began singing the opening hymn. He grinned and gave her a wink.

Her face heated into a blush and she grinned back. Life with this man promised to be *wonderful-gut*.

* * * * *

If you enjoyed this Amish romance,
be sure to pick up these other Amish
historical romances from Jan Drexler:
THE PRODIGAL SON RETURNS
A MOTHER FOR HIS CHILDREN

Available now from Love Inspired Historical!
Find more great reads at www.LoveInspired.com

Dear Reader,

I hope you enjoyed this visit to Indiana's Amish Country with me!

Shipshewana and the surrounding area are home to the third largest Amish community in the country. Today's Shipshewana is a busy place, full of tourists and fun activities all through the year.

We love to visit our favorite businesses in the area: Das Essenhaus, Yoder's Department Store, E&S Sales, and many others. And if we're there on a Tuesday or Wednesday, we make the time to go to the Shipshewana Flea Market on the grounds of the Sale Barn.

The Sale Barn? Oh yes. It's the same place Samuel and Mary went in their story. The livestock auction is still held every week, year-round.

And while we're there, we enjoy breakfast at the Auction Restaurant. They serve the best fried mush I've ever eaten.

I love to hear from my readers! You can contact me through my website, www.JanDrexler.com, or visit me on Facebook!

Jan Drexler

MAIL-ORDER MARRIAGE PROMISE

Frontier Bachelors • by Regina Scott

When John Wallin's sister orders him a mail-order bride without his knowledge, can the bachelor find a way to move on from his past rejection and fulfill the marriage promise to lovely Dottie Tyrrell, who comes with a baby—and a secret?

PONY EXPRESS SPECIAL DELIVERY

Saddles and Spurs • by Rhonda Gibson

Maggie Fillmore's late husband had one final wish—that their unborn son would inherit their ranch. But when a greedy relative threatens to take the ranch, there's only one way Maggie can keep it: a marriage of convenience to the new Pony Express manager, Clayton Young.

RANCHER TO THE RESCUE

by Barbara Phinney

With their parents missing, Clare Walsh and her siblings could lose everything, including each other—unless she accepts rancher Noah Livingstone's proposal. And though they plan a union in name only, will Clare and Noah risk their hearts for a chance at a true-love connection?

THE OUTLAW'S SECOND CHANCE

by Angie Dicken

When Aubrey Huxley and Cort Stanton try to claim the same land in the Oklahoma Land Rush, they strike a deal: she can have the land for her horse ranch if he can work for her. But will she let him stay on when she learns he's a wanted man?

LIHCNM0817

Get 2 Free Books,
Plus 2 Free Gifts—
just for trying the Reader Service!

Love Inspired. HISTORICAL

SPECIAL EXCERPT FROM

Love Inspired HISTORICAL

*Maggie Fillmore's late husband had one final wish—
that their unborn son would inherit their ranch. But when a
greedy relative threatens to take the ranch, there's only one
way Maggie can keep it: a marriage of convenience to the
new Pony Express manager, Clayton Young.*

*Read on for a sneak preview of
PONY EXPRESS SPECIAL DELIVERY
by **Rhonda Gibson**,
available September 2017 from Love Inspired!*

"Have you come up with a name for the little tyke?"
Clayton Young asked.

Her gaze moved to the infant. He needed a name, but
Maggie didn't know what to call him.

Dinah looked to Maggie. "I like the name James."

Maggie looked down on her newborn's sweet face. "What
do you think of the name James, baby?" His eyes opened and
he yawned.

Her little sister, Dinah, clapped her hands. "He likes it."

Maggie looked up with a grin that quickly faded. Mr.
Young looked as if he'd swallowed a bug. "What's the matter, Mr. Young? Do you not like the name James?" She
didn't know why it mattered to her if he liked the name or
not, but it did.

"I like it just fine. It's just that my full name is Clayton
James Young."

Maggie didn't know what to think when the baby kicked
his legs and made what to every new mother sounded like a

LIHEXP0817

happy noise. "If you don't want me to name him…"

"No, it seems the little man likes his new name. If you want to call him James, that's all right with me." He stood and collected his and Dinah's plates. "Now, if you ladies will excuse me, I have a kitchen to clean up and a stew to get on the stove. Then I'm going into town to get the doctor so he can look over baby James." He nodded once and then left the room.

Maggie looked to Dinah, who stood by the door watching him leave. "Dinah, I'm curious. You seem to like Mr. Young."

Dinah nodded. "He's a nice man."

"What makes you say that?"

"He saved baby James and rocked me to sleep last night."

"He did?"

"Uh-huh. I was scared and Mr. Young picked me up and rocked me while I cried. I went to sleep and he put me in bed with you." Dinah smiled. "He told me everything was going to be all right. And it is."

Maggie rocked the baby. Not only had Mr. Young saved James, but he'd also soothed Dinah's fears. He'd made them all breakfast and was already planning a trip to town to bring back the doctor. What kind of man was Clayton James Young? Unfamiliar words whispered through her heart: the kind who took care of the people around him.

Don't miss
PONY EXPRESS SPECIAL DELIVERY *by Rhonda Gibson,*
available September 2017 wherever
Love Inspired® Historical books and ebooks are sold.

www.LoveInspired.com